DEADLY AMBUSH

Ben Raines walked through the small town of Tok, Alaska, taking in what was left of the sights.

The restaurants were filthy from years of cooking and very little cleaning. The walls were caked with grease. The motels were just as bad, their mattresses infested with lice and fleas, their carpets alive with various tiny hopping and crawling critters.

Ben ordered the carpets dragged outside and burned.

He was amused as he stood in front of a restaurant whose sign proclaimed the best Mexican, Italian, and American food in all of Alaska. He walked past a place that claimed to have in captivity the largest mosquito in all of Alaska, which was "Chained for the Public's Safety."

There were several thousand Rebels milling in and around Tok, taking in the sights. No one knew how the outlaws managed to get as close to Ben as they did.

But they did, and suddenly he was flat on his back in the street, shot in the chest. He was not moving.

14

COURAGE
IN THE
ASHES

WILLIAM W.
JOHNSTONE

PINNACLE BOOKS
Kensington Publishing Corp.
http://www.kensingtonbooks.com

PINNACLE BOOKS are published by

Kensington Publishing Corp.
850 Third Avenue
New York, NY 10022

All Kensington Titles, Imprints, and Distributed Lines are available
at special quantity discounts for bulk purchases for sales promo-
tions, premiums, fund-raising, and educational or institutional use.
Special book excerpts or customized printings can also be created
to fit specific needs. For details, write or phone the office of the
Kensington special sales manager: Kensington Publishing Corp.,
850 Third Avenue, New York, NY 10022, attn: Special Sales Depart-
ment, Phone: 1-800-221-2647.

Pinnacle and the P logo Reg. U.S. Pat. & TM Off.

ISBN-13: 978-0-7860-2021-0
ISBN-10: 0-7860-2021-8

First Pinnacle Books Printing: May 1999

10 9 8 7 6 5 4

Printed in the United States of America

Thunder is good, thunder is impressive; but it is the lightning that does the work.

Mark Twain

Courage is resistance to fear, mastery of fear—not absence of fear.

Mark Twain

Book One

1

The Rebels were getting restless and so was Ben
Raines. He just hid his impatience better.

Ben Raines and the Rebel army had wintered in
Central California. So effective had been their
previous campaign against the criminal element,
the street punks, and Night People in the state that
during these past three months not one shot had
been fired in anger.

The Rebels had rested, cleaned weapons,
mended gear, stored the supplies that came in on a
weekly basis from Base Camp One, and did the
other small things that every garrison since the
Roman Legions have done and bitched about.
Now, to a person, they were bored out of their
gourds.

The Rebels were not accustomed to this much
inactivity, and Ben knew if something wasn't done
to occupy their minds and bodies they were soon
going to be fighting among themselves; it had
happened before. When highly trained personnel

turn on each other in anger, it can get rough very quickly—and sometimes it can get deadly.

Ben called together all his unit commanders one raw February morning.

"In six weeks we're going to be heading into some of the toughest fighting we've ever faced," he told them. "I want the troops in better shape than they've ever been in. That goes for everybody, and I include myself in that. We're going to start PT, people—in the morning, and every morning and every afternoon until the day before we mount up and shove off. We've spent a long, lazy, loafing winter, and it's time to shape up. We need to know who needs to be placed on limited duty for a while. Suggestions?"

"We'll start PT in two days, Ben," Dr. Chase said. "First we take physicals—starting in the morning." He pointed a finger at Ben. "And you'll be the first in line."

"I wouldn't have it any other way," Ben said with a smile.

Chase stood up and looked around the large room in the old courthouse that Ben was using for his HQ. "And you boys and girls," he said, eyeballing all the unit commanders, "will be next in line after General Raines. Tomorrow morning. 0700 hours. Sharp."

The doctor turned to leave the room. Ben's words stopped him.

"Of course, Lamar, you'll take a physical, too. And if you don't pass it, you'll be sent back to Base Camp One with the rest of those who flunk."

Lamar glared at Ben, knowing that Ben had just

10

sandbagged him—again. "No one said a damn word about anybody being sent back to Base Camp One, Raines. I believe 'limited duty' was the phrase you used."

"Ahhh," Ben said. "Right you are, Lamar."

Chase, who was in his seventies, stomped out of the room.

Ben Raines and Lamar Chase, friends for as long as any Rebel could remember, had been playing one-upmanship for years.

It usually ended in a tie.

"We're moving toward Northstar March 15?" Ben's daughter, Tina asked.

"Right. And that date is not to be repeated again. It's just about two thousand miles from Seattle to the Alaskan border, and we're going to be facing hostiles all the way up. Flyovers confirm that a lot of people are living just across the border in Canada. The planes were fired upon. It's going to be a very interesting trip," he added dryly. "Dan, the first contingent of your Scouts will pull out a week ahead of us. Right now, let's start shaking the cobwebs out of our systems, people. Pass the word that playtime is over."

"Me ol' bones is a-achin' awreddy," General Ike McGowan said, standing up and looking like a bear.

"They'll be aching more three days from now," the mercenary, Colonel West, told him with a grin.

The Russian general, Striganov, whacked him on the back. "Come on, Ike, let's us middle-aged men show these kids a thing or two."

Laughing, the two men, who had once been

11

bitter enemies, left the room.

Ben's son, Buddy, who looked like he ate anvils for lunch, walked to his father's side. "You watch that knee, Father," he cautioned him. "You haven't been that many weeks out of surgery."

Ben smiled. "It's fine, son. Better than it's felt in years. I should have had surgery done on it a long time ago."

"You also tell lies from time to time," Tina told him.

"I get no respect from my kids," Ben said, smiling. "Me and Rodney Dangerfield."

"Who's Rodney Dangerfield?" a young Rebel aide asked.

The world was in the middle of the second decade since the planet had exploded in germ warfare and limited nuclear warfare. When the clouds of devastation were swept away, all that remained was a world filled with anarchy. Then along came Ben Raines.

Ben hadn't wanted to command an army of survivors. He ran from that job for months. He had tried to tell those who sought him that he was the wrong man. But they knew he was the right man.

Ben finally agreed, and when he did, he threw himself into the job, forming the Tri-States. The Tri-States represented everything that liberal politicians had been saying for years wouldn't work. It worked. And the newly formed dictatorship that governed the United States from the new capital of Richmond couldn't stand it. They destroyed Ben's Tri-States. But Ben wouldn't give up. He formed another army, fought the dictatorship, and beat it. Then the plague came and once more ravaged the earth. From out of the ashes of despair came one man and a small army of dedicated men and women: Ben Raines and his Rebels.*

They fought against anarchy, fear, darkness, devil-worshippers, cannibals, thugs, punks, street gangs, and all forms of lawlessness. Rebels lay buried from coast to coast, border to border—men and women who had willingly given their lives in pursuit of a dream of freedom and a life free of crime. Their names were inscribed on a marble wall back at Base Camp One, so they would always be remembered.

Down south, the Mexicans had banded together behind one man, General Payon, and were busy restoring their country—in a manner patterned after the rules and regulations laid down by one Ben Raines.

Canada, except for its westernmost province, was clean. And that westernmost area would soon be cleared, once the Rebels crossed over the border.

Alaska was the last frontier the Rebels faced in the Northern hemisphere.

During the winter, the entire Rebel army had been restructured from top to bottom. With the many new Rebels coming into the ranks, just out of training at several locations around the country, it had to be.

*OUT OF THE ASHES—ZEBRA BOOKS

Ben commanded First Battalion. Ike led Second Battalion. Third Battalion was Cecil's. West's mercenaries made up Fourth Battalion. Striganov commanded Fifth Battalion. Rebet took over Sixth Battalion. Danjou commanded Seventh Battalion. Thermopolis was in command of Eighth Battalion, which included Emil Hite and the bikers called the Wolfpack. Tina commanded Ninth Battalion. Dan Gray and his Scouts remained independent, able to roam at Ben's command. Ben's son, Buddy, led what Ben called the Rat Pack, a hundred or so highly trained and expert manhunters and woodspersons, who usually got the toughest jobs.

Each battalion contained 850 personnel—more or less. And each battalion had armor assigned to it, which made them much more mobile and independent.

But soldiers are soldiers, whether they are a ragtag bunch of reactionaries or an army as well-trained and highly motivated as Raines's Rebels. They're going to bitch when faced with physical training. And bitch they did.

Physicals over—and something like ninety-seven percent of them passed—the bitching stopped when Ben stepped onto the raised platform and faced the huge army. He walked to the microphone.

The men and women of the Rebels fell silent.

"You've done what many felt was the impossible," Ben's voice boomed over the training and staging area. "You've cleared the lower forty-eight states of crud and crap and scum. And you've done

14

it with your blood and sweat and courage. We've all seen friends fall; we've stood in silence over their graves. They did not die in vain. America is once more on the road to becoming a nation of law and order. Back in the fall, after Southern California became ours, I promised you a time of R & R. You've had it. Now it's time to get back to work. For you new people just joining us from Base Camp One and other training centers around the country, welcome to the Rebels. If I haven't met you all personally, I will. I want to shake your hands and look you in the eyes and know your faces. I've very proud of you all . . ."

Thermopolis, Ben's hippie-turned-warrior friend, stood with his wife, Rosebud, on the edge of the crowd. He smiled at Ben's words. "He'd have made a great evangelist. I can see it now: Brother Ben. Waving a Bible under the television lights and screwing the flock off-camera."

"Hush," Rosebud told him. "I want to hear this."

Therm sighed.

". . . We've got a tough campaign ahead of us," Ben continued. "And a tougher one still after that. We don't know what we'll be facing once we start the Northstar campaign. We don't know how many of the enemy we'll be facing. But we will be outnumbered. Get used to that. The Rebels are *always* outnumbered. The terrain will be rugged. Many times the weather will be working against us. Alaska is a place of contrasts, so we've all got to be in top condition before we strike. And we will be," he said without a smile. "Those that are not,

15

will not go. It's just as simple as that. All right, company commanders, let's get this circus on the move."

Rain or shine, cold and wet or miserable and tired, the Rebels worked out for the next month. They were already in good physical condition, but if the lax months had put any fat on them, it was soon gone; hard muscle took its place as the instructors pushed the troops with a vengeance.

When they weren't training, they were getting equipment ready for the long push north, boxing and packing supplies and the thousand other things required before an army moves out.

Bitching and cussing, General Ike McGowan, an ex-SEAL and one of Ben's closest friends, managed to drop fifteen pounds from his stocky frame. He still looked like a friendly bear. But in combat Ike was anything but friendly.

With a week to go before the Rebels began their push-off, Ben called a halt to the training and stood his people down. There was nothing more that could be done as far as readiness and preparedness were concerned.

"Don't push them any more," Dr. Chase warned Ben. "They can eat nails now. How's your knee?"

"Fine," Ben told him.

"You're probably lying; but I expected that." The doctor poured a cup of coffee and sat down, taking his place among the unit commanders gathered in the room.

Ben said, "All right, Dan. What have your Scouts reported?"

Colonel Dan Gray, a former British SAS officer,

stood up and took the pointer, moving to a large wall map. "We're going to hit some stiff resistance about fifty miles inside Canada." He pointed out the area. "Malcontents control a sector from Cache Creek all the way over to Golden. A lot of them are survivors from our assaults against Seattle and Vancouver. I would imagine they have smartened up and toughened up. We can expect a fight."

"How are they equipped?" General Striganov asked.

"Light weapons for the most part. Some mortars and heavy machine guns. My people could see no sign of tanks or heavy artillery."

"The Scouts halted their advance and back-tracked," Ben added. "They came back across the border."

"Must be a sizeable force," Cecil Jefferys said.

"Quite," Dan told him.

"We'll eyeball the area once we get it in visual," Ben said. "But we'll probably shell it and smash on through. I don't intend to lose Rebel life unnecessarily. Lamar, did the lab people come up with a good insect repellent?"

Summer in Alaska was bug season, which included not only mosquitoes, but black flies and a pest called no-see-ums, also known as punkies. They all either bit or stung.

"We couldn't improve much on Diethyl-meta-toluamide," Chase said. "Better known as DEET. It's very effective against mosquitoes; less effective against the other bugs. A slight breeze and low humidity is our best hope."

"Make sure there is plenty of mosquito net-

17

ting," Ben said to Beth, who was one of the people permanently assigned to him, part of a personal team which included Cooper, his driver, Corrie, his radio operator, Little Jersey, his bodyguard, and Linda Parsons, a trained nurse who was the team's medic. Smoot, his husky pup, rambled around the room, stopping every now and then for a friendly pat or a scratch behind the ears.

Ben said, "Let's double-check everything, people. Lamar, is everyone up to date on their shots?"

"Yes. I had records finishing up their checking on that yesterday."

"Corrie, order the planes up from Base Camp One."

"Yes, sir."

"Commanders, put your people on low alert."

That was acknowledged.

"No one leaves the staging area."

That was noted.

"Who spearheads, Ben?" the Russian asked.

Ben's reply was a smile, although he knew he would never be allowed to do that.

Dan Gray nixed it. "Not a chance, General. As usual, my Scouts will spearhead all the way."

"Then I'll be right behind you people," Ben said.

"There will be a buffer of tanks between you and the Scouts," Ike told him. "And a team between the tanks and you. That's the way it's got to be, Ben."

Ben shrugged his shoulders. "I had to try."

The Rebels all knew that Ben Raines would personally take the point if they didn't watch him.

So they always watched him closely, doing their best to form a net around him—a net that Ben always managed to find a hole through.

"We met no resistance all the way to the line," Ben's son, Buddy said. He and his Rat Pack had just returned from a recon mission to the Canadian border. "We found survivors in many areas—they seemed to have crawled out of the woodwork, so to speak—after the area was cleaned of the criminal element last year. But they showed no desire to join in our network of outposts."

Buddy had told the people that if they did not join with the Rebels, they would receive no help from them—in any way, shape, form, or fashion. Ben Raines's way was a hard one, but it had to be if the country was going to get back together. The nation would never be whole if everyone pulled in a different direction.

"Children?" Ben asked.

"No infants," his son said.

"Then to hell with them," Ben summed up the Rebel position.

2

The dawn of March fifteenth in central California was unusually cold. As was his custom, Ben had been up for several hours before the eastern skies began turning a gray shade of silver.

"Do you realize, General," Jersey said as she looked around the now-barren room, "that this is the longest we've stayed in one spot in months and months?"

"Does it make you long for a husband and motherhood?" Ben asked with a grin.

"*Hell*, no!" the diminutive Jersey said. "I guess I'm what I read about in those old magazines we find: a liberated woman. I like men, but on my terms."

"You can have me anytime you want, Jersey," Cooper said. "I'm yours, darlin'. Just name the terms."

Jersey picked up her M-16 and Cooper got a worried look on his face. Jersey grinned at him and he relaxed. "You ain't my type, Coop. I like the serious, scholarly type, like that guy over in Five Battalion who quotes poems. Real pretty ones."

"He used to teach English Literature at a college in upstate New York," Ben told her. "A PhD type. He's a nice fellow. I wondered where you'd been slipping off to at night."

Cooper started humming "Rockabye Baby." Jersey chased him out of the room, cussing him with every bootfall.

Ben looked around the room, checking to see if everything had been packed up. Linda joined him, and together they inspected each room of the home. Ben had found a family picture album during the first week of his stay and had placed it on the mantel of the fireplace in the den. They passed the now-cold hearth and Ben paused, picking up the photo album and looking at it in the light from the lantern. A man, a woman, and three kids stared out at him from the fading family portrait.

"I wonder what happened to them?" Linda asked, standing close to Ben.

"God only knows. They certainly look like they were a happy family." He closed the photo album and placed it back on the mantel. "You ready to go to work?"

"Where you lead, I follow," she said with a twinkle in her eyes.

Ben looked heavenward and smiled. He looked around him. "Where's Smoot?"

Linda said, "I swear, Ben, I think you care more

22

for that dog than you do me."

Ben's smile widened. "That's what a fiancé told me once. I told her she was probably right."

Linda poked him in the ribs, and together, laughing, they walked out of the house and into the gray misty light of early dawn.

Standing by the big nine-passenger wagon, Linda asked, "Is that story true, Ben? About the fiancé, I mean?"

"Yep. She didn't like dogs. I've always liked dogs. When the bombs and the germ-carrying pods hit, I was without one. But it didn't take me long to find one."

"A husky?"

"Uh-huh. I named him Juno. We had a good long life together. He was a very old dog when he was killed during the assault against Tri-States. But he tore the throat out of a goddamn government soldier before they killed him."

"You loved that old dog?" she asked quietly, noticing that all of Ben's personnel team had gathered around, listening.

"Sure," Ben's voice was low-pitched. "I've loved all my dogs."

"Do you think dogs go to heaven, General?" Corrie asked. She held Smoot on a leash.

"Personally? I think so. In Psalms it says, 'Man and beast thou savest, O Lord.' Ecclesiastes reads, 'For the fate of the sons of men and the fate of beasts is the same; as one dies, so dies the other. They all have the same breath, and man has no advantage over the beasts; for all is vanity. All go to one place; all are from the dust, and all turn to dust again. Who knows whether the spirit of man goes upward and the spirit of the beast goes down to earth.' In the New Testament, the Apostle Paul proclaims salvation for all creatures, including dogs. And learned theologians agreed that Paul indicated from that passage of his in Romans that he meant that animals are to be renewed." Ben looked up at the Methodist chaplain who had just walked up to join them, a cup of coffee in his hand. "Morning, Tom."

"General," the chaplain said. "I didn't know you were that familiar with the Bible."

"I find great comfort in reading the Bible, Tom. Especially the Old Testament. And you have to remember, I used to be a writer, and writers do a lot of research."

"Mind if I add something to your statements?"

"Not at all."

"Methodist John Wesley had no doubts about dogs and cats going to heaven. Wesley outlined what dogs and other animals would experience in Heaven. Personally, I believe that only human arrogance and ignorance stands in the way of people accepting that salvation extends to animals. I think a lot of people who are deliberately cruel to animals are going to be weeping and wailing come Judgement Day."

"I hope so, Tom," Ben said. "I certainly hope so. But in the meantime, when I see someone abusing an animal, I'll see that person gets to a grave much earlier than they anticipated."

Smiling and shaking his head, the chaplain walked away.

The chaplains from all faiths blessed and prayed for those in the column and returned to their vehicles. Ben looked at Corrie. "Give the orders, Corrie. Let's roll."

The column stretched out for miles. Almost ten thousand fighting men and women and hundreds of vehicles. Fighting machines of every description. Tanks from the huge 50-ton Abrams to the almost petite Dusters. APCs and Hummers and Jeeps and tanker trucks. And for the very first time in the history of the Rebel army scores of attack helicopters now drummed the sky overhead. Cobras and Apaches, old Huey gunships that had been found and carefully brought back to combat readiness slapped the sky overhead. Their pilots had just graduated from a long schooling. The Rebel ways of war were changing.

The Rebels had not previously used choppers because they had no one to fly them and no one to teach others how to fly them in combat. Only during the past two years had people with the right qualifications been found. A program was immediately launched, and now the Rebels had valuable air support as well as the finest ground support on the continent.

Some of the Hueys were equipped with 7.62 Gatling guns mounted on each side of the ship, as well as seven-shot 2.75 rocket launchers. The AH-

64s and AH-1 Cobras were equipped with cannon, rockets, and machine guns; some of the Apaches carried 30mm chain guns with 1,200 rounds available on demand.

The Rebels had always been a force to be reckoned with. Now they were awesome.

They made over a hundred miles the first day. The column was so long that the final vehicle was over two hours behind the point. They were moving at dawn the next day and rolled into southern Oregon by noon, staying on the old Interstate 5. They passed by the towns that lay silent and deserted on either side of the highway and they rolled past the cities they had destroyed during the Rebels' purge of the nation.

The Rebels were aware of eyes on them. More often than not the eyes were unfriendly. But those people who had decided to not join with the Rebel movement committed no hostile acts against them. They knew to do so would be suicide. The Rebels would have chopped them into bloody pieces in seconds.

"I don't understand them," Cooper said, as they passed a small group of men and women. The watchers did not wave, did not smile, did nothing except stare in silence. "We're offering them safety, food, medical care, schools . . . the whole bag. And they won't take it. Why?"

"Our way is too complicated for them, Coop," Ben said.

"But our laws aren't complicated! It's the simplest form of government that I've ever studied.

And you know I've been reading history and the study of civilization. It's fascinating."

"It's so simple it scares them, Coop," Ben said. "Before the Great War, people were used to government telling them what to do. We had so many laws that contradicted each other no one really knew what they could or couldn't do. The use of common sense had been removed from our daily lives and from the administration of justice. Now that we virtually have no form of law—outside of the Rebel system—many people just don't know what to do. Many of those folks we're seeing aren't bad people; they're just scared people. They've heard so many things about us they don't know what to believe. Many of those folks have lost all faith in *any* form of organized government. And with good reason, when you understand that our system prior to the Great War was terrible."

"Scouts report resistance up ahead, General," Corrie said, receiving the news through her headset. "Large force of heavily armed men have blocked the interstate and are refusing to let us pass."

"Get us up there, Coop. Let's see what we have."

Buddy met his father about a half a mile from the blockade. "They say they have formed their own government and claim this area as part of their territory," Ben's son told him. "We are not welcome here."

"Are you in radio contact with them?"

"Yes, sir."

"Give me the mike." Ben lifted the mike and said, "This is General Raines. You will kindly remove that blockade from the interstate and stand aside."

"You go to hell, Raines!" the reply came back.

"Are you insane?" Ben asked him. "My God, man, look around you. Look in the sky. Those are attack choppers hovering above you. One word from me and none of you will be alive ten seconds from now."

"We do not like your form of justice. We do not approve of your tactics."

"I don't give a damn what you like or dislike. I don't care if you form your own little society. You can live the way you choose, as long as you don't break what few laws we have on the books. Just clear the interstate of obstacles and let us pass, then you can go back worshipping a kumquat if that turns you on."

"You're a dictator!" the man's words screamed out of the speaker.

"I'm trying to restore this nation, you damn fool," Ben told him.

"Do you want me to clear the road?" Buddy asked.

"Not yet. Let's use words first. We can always use force." Ben lifted the mike. "I don't want to use force against you, mister. I'd like to meet with you. Let's talk this thing out. How about it?"

"I don't trust you, Ben Raines. Your way is godless and evil."

"Another one of those," Jersey said, disgust in

her voice.

"Do we meet, or not?" Ben questioned.

"I don't see that I have a choice," the man replied, bitter resignation in his words.

"Clear that blockade."

The makeshift barricade was pulled back, and the Scouts advanced cautiously. They secured the area and waved Ben forward.

The man Ben faced was about his own age, but with the hard, bright eyes of the religious zealot. He refused to shake hands with Ben.

"What's your problem?" Ben asked, taking an immediate dislike toward the man.

"You and your godless ways," the man told him bluntly.

"There are chaplains of all faiths back there in the column," Ben pointed out. "I don't see how you can accuse me of being godless."

"Have you been washed in the blood?"

"Do you mean baptized?"

"Yes."

"Of course. Years ago."

"You must be born again, Ben Raines. Baptized in the faith of the Holy Church of the Righteous of John Falls."

Ben blinked. "Who in the hell is John Falls?"

The little con artist, Emil Hite, approached, walking beside Thermopolis. "It's a scam, General," Emil said. "John Falls used to be a TV preacher back when. He had a hell of a following, too. They're all a bunch of fanatics. I think he came out of Georgia. Somewhere in the south.

Maybe Mississippi."

"Ahh," Ben said. "Now I know who you're talking about. I remember him. The boycotter and the book burner." He looked at Corrie. "Get the column moving, Corrie. I'm not going to waste much time with these people."

"You are a whoremonger and an infidel, Ben Raines," the spokesman for the group said. "We have followed your antics for years and find you wanting in the eyes of God."

"You speak for God, huh?"

"That is correct. We are God's chosen people."

"The last time I checked, it was the Jews who were the chosen people," Emil muttered. "Maybe I missed something."

The column began once more rolling north.

"You people do your thing, pal," Ben told the man. "Just don't start breaking the laws we've set up or we'll be back and step on you like a bug."

The man wheeled around and walked away, the rest of his group following.

"Why didn't you ask why they think you—we—are godless?" Linda asked.

"Because I don't care," Ben told her. "I don't care what they think of me, personally. As long as they obey the law, they can do and think as they please. But I have a hunch we'll have to deal with them at some point. At least we got past them without having to kill anybody. Let's go."

Back in the wagon, heading north, Linda said, "I remember that John Falls now. Little perch-mouthed hypocrite who set himself up as the 'conscience of the nation,' which is what I think he used to call himself."

"That's him," Ben said. "Whatever he didn't like—and he didn't like very much—he and his followers would boycott. Took me a while to place the name. I thought he was dead. He hates me; he used to boycott stores that carried my books."

"Why, for heaven's sake?" Jersey asked. "You never wrote anything nasty."

"I did in John Falls's opinion. He didn't like my stand on abortion being a woman's choice. I wanted to keep church and state separated— widely separated. John Falls once referred to me as a communist stooge." Ben laughed out loud. "That's how misguided the man was. Is. I can't even begin to imagine the mentality of anyone who would follow him. Narrow-minded assholes. To hell with him and his followers."

The countryside rolled by with an hypnotic sameness. The Rebels saw lots of smoke from chimneys off in the distance, but they did not investigate. Oregon was in their rearview mirrors before the advance team radioed back that there might be trouble up ahead.

"The road has been recently blocked, General," Corrie said. "Old cars and trucks and boards with spikes in them. We're going to have to detour."

Ben cursed under his breath, picked up a map, and studied it. The column had left the interstate—to avoid the ruins of the cities from Tacoma all the way up to Bellingham—and had angled east, picking up a good two-lane road that would

31

eventually lead them to Highway 97. They had planned to take that all the way into Canada.

"Let's see this blockade," Ben told Cooper. "It had to be put there for some reason. Order the Scouts to stand clear of it in case it's booby-trapped."

It was quite an elaborate blockade. Old junk cars and trucks completely blocked the road, both shoulders, and the ditches for what looked like half a mile.

Ben studied the area through binoculars then turned to Dan Gray. "But why?"

Dan shrugged his shoulders. "I can't think of a single reason. There isn't an inhabited town within a hundred miles of here. Our nearest outpost is to the east, in Odessa. I just spoke with them and they said the blockade wasn't there two weeks ago."

"Order tanks to start putting some rounds in that mess. Let's see if it's wired to blow."

A dozen HE 105 rounds were pumped into the tangle of rusted metal and spider-webbed glass slowly enough to give any booby traps time to explode after the initial impact of the rounds. Nothing happened.

"Push us a way through there," Ben ordered. "Be sure all the nails are swept up. Dan, as soon as a hole is punched through, send a team ahead to find out what this crap is all about, will you?"

It didn't take the Scouts long to find the source of the trouble. "Right up the road about five miles from the blockade," the team leader radioed back.

"About three to four hundred people, mostly men, have set up an outlaw camp in this old town. I don't know the name of it; no highway signs are left standing."

"Hold what you're got," Ben told him. "I'm on my way." He turned to his team. "I guess we're going to see some action before we reach Canada, boys and girls. Everybody ready to kick some ass?"

"Beats havin' to listen to Cooper's lousy jokes," Jersey said, and picked up her M-16.

3

"Holy crap!" the lookout whispered, looking at the seemingly endless line of vehicles coming toward his position. He grabbed up his CB mike. "Junior!" he hollered. "Damn it, Junior, come in!"

In the town, Junior managed to shove his pus-gut and big butt out of a chair and walk to the CB base, picking up the mike. "What you want, Luddy?" He cocked his head and listened. Was the damn ground moving?

"They's about a thousand tanks and other shit movin' towards us, Junior. Trucks full up with soldier boys . . . and girls. What you want me to do?"

"Luddy, have you been drinkin' again, boy?"

"Hell, no! Junior, them tanks has stopped up on a ridge and it 'pears to me they's about to shell the town."

"Git outta there, boy. Git your tail back here

where it's safe."

"*Safe!*" Luddy squalled. "Junior, din you hear me? They's a fuckin' *army* lookin' square at us. If that's Ben Raines out yonder, we bes' kiss our asses goodbye!"

"They're broadcasting on CB radio," Ben was told. "Channel nine."

Ben clicked on the CB radio in the wagon and keyed the mike. "This is General Ben Raines speaking to the inhabitants of the town. If you're friendly, we mean you no harm. If you are hostile, we'll blow you off the face of this earth. Give me a reply, please."

In Junior's home, a woman fell to her knees and began praying. It had been years since she had prayed, but she still remembered how.

"What the hell are you doin', woman?" Junior hollered.

"Prayin' for the Lord to take me easy," she told him. "'Cause Ben Raines don't like trash. And that's what we is—trash with a capital T."

"I ain't trash!" Junior bellowed. "You watch your mouth around me, woman."

"I had an aint in the Delta of Louisiana when Ben Raines set up down yonder. She told me that them that tried to resist him died, Junior. Real quick. I'd bear that in mind, Junior."

"I am waiting for a reply," Ben's voice came through the CB's speaker.

"Aw, uh, why, shore, we friendly." Junior grabbed the mike. "We jist good old country folk, is all. Y'all jist pass right on through our little town."

"The town is filthy and so are the people," Striganov said, lowering his binoculars. "It's an abomination. Even from this distance one can tell it is a cesspool."

"That wasn't a true southern accent on that man," Buddy said.

"You're right," his father agreed. "That's an affectation." He keyed the mike. "Everybody out in the street and no weapons. Do it now, please."

Slowly, the streets of the town began filling with people. Mostly men, but about twenty or so women with children. No one was carrying a weapon that could be seen.

"Let's go," Ben said, and got back into the wagon. "Tanks button up and spearhead. Let's give them a show of force."

"Lord God Almighty," a man in the town said.

"Pattons, Abrams, Walker Bulldogs and Dusters," a man said. "I seen 'em in 'Nam. Don't nobody rile Ben Raines. Don't nobody get smart-mouthed or out of line. Not if you want to live to see the sun come up tomorrow. Them's Rebels, people. And they mean as rattlesnakes if you mess with 'em. And for God's sake you wimmin get them kids cleaned up. If it's one thing the Rebels don't like it's nasty, underfed, and abused kids. If any of them snot-noses kick up a fuss, smack 'em in the mouth and get 'em out of sight."

The band of ne'er-do-wells and their women soon found themselves surrounded by about a thousand well-armed and very healthy-looking

Rebels. And they all knew who Ben was when he stepped out of the wagon. He wore no insignia, but there was something about the man, an aura that clung to him. Junior sized him up and didn't like what he saw.

Raines, he guessed, was about fifty, with a thick head of graying hair, unreadable eyes, and a hard, uncompromising face. He reckoned that some women would find the man handsome. Raines looked to be in top physical condition.

"Who is in charge here?" Ben asked.

Everybody looked at Junior and Junior wished the earth would open up and swallow him. "I reckon I is," he finally said.

"And your name is?"

"Junior."

"Junior what?"

"Junior Nelson. Would you be General Raines?"

"I am. Linda, get a team of medics and start checking out those children we saw the women whisking off as we drove in. If there is any sign of abuse—physical or sexual—I want to know about it immediately. Junior, do you people plan on staying in this town?"

"Ah, as far as I know, we does. For a time anyways."

"Did you put up that roadblock south of town?"

"Shore did. Got to keep the unwanted out, you know."

Ben stared hard at the man. Although Junior had committed no overt hostile act toward the Rebels, Ben sensed trouble. He had been fighting the Juniors of the nation for years and knew them for what they were: loud-mouthed, ignorant bullies, cruel and dangerous.

"You cain't take my baby!" a woman's cry reached the crowd.

"The hell I can't, lady," Linda's voice followed that. "If you won't take care of her, we know lots of people who will."

Buddy appeared, leading an elderly man and wife. The woman had a large bruise on the side of her face, and the man's left arm was in a sling. Ben cut his eyes back to Junior, who did his best to shrink in size. It didn't work.

"What's the problem, son?" Ben asked.

"This old couple were the sole inhabitants of the town," Buddy said. "They planted a garden each spring and canned their food, living off of that during the winter. They've been doing it for years. Then Junior and his gang appeared a couple of weeks ago. They ate up all the food the old couple had and beat them up. The man's arm is broken."

"See that they get medical attention." He looked at Junior. "Did you beat that old couple?"

"We come in here to protect them," Junior said. "They wouldn't give us no food for our services so we took some. The old man tried to stop us so I whupped up on him a little bit."

"That's very brave of you," Ben said sarcastically. "Why did you hit the woman?"

"She was hittin' me with a stick."

"Oh, my. I'm sure your life was in imminent

39

danger from such a vicious and unprovoked attack.''

"Huh?"

Ben hit him with the butt of his M-14. The stock caught Junior right in his big gut and doubled him over. The air whooshed out of the man. Ben brought the butt up and connected solidly with Junior's jaw. Junior folded to the ground and was still.

Linda walked through the crowd, carrying a little girl who looked about four. Linda's expression was tight and her eyes were angry.

"The child has bruises all over her body," Linda said. "She's been beaten and she's malnourished and frightened."

"What happened to her hair?"

"She had lice. So the mother shaved her head and was treating her scalp with raw gasoline."

Ben sighed. The ignorance of a certain class of people never failed to amaze, sadden, and sicken him. Back when the nation was more or less whole, he had watched the government pour billions of tax dollars into so-called impoverished areas over the span of three decades. At the end of that time, the majority of people in those areas were just as ignorant, just as stupid, just as cruel, just as mean-spirited, and just as resistant to change as they had been when the programs started. The elected officials of the government never seemed to have enough sense to realize that. So they started more programs. Fortunately, the Great War ended all that.

"Take the children and we'll have them flown to a relocation center for treatment and adoption," Ben said. "Take the elderly couple, too. They can live out their lives with dignity down at Base Camp One. Away from white trash such as this . . . rabble."

"What in the world are we going to do with this bunch?" Dan asked.

"I don't know," Ben admitted. "The world would be better off without them, that's for sure. But I can't shoot them."

"Oh, Lord!" a man hollered, falling to his knees on the littered old street. "He's done come in to murder us all. Strike this man dead, Lord. Flang a rattlesnake at him. Hurl down a bolt of lightnin'. Halp us, Lord."

Junior moaned and stirred on the street.

"We could take their weapons," a Rebel suggested. "But they'd just find more."

The trash who had suddenly found religion continued to plead for God to strike Ben dead.

"We've had hard times, General," a man said. "We been driftin' for years, lookin' for a peaceful place to settle in."

"Then you have seen the many Rebel outposts?" Ben questioned.

"Yeah," the man admitted.

"Why didn't you offer to settle near one?"

"We did. But they make a body work too hard. Got to keep your grass cut and plant gardens and keep your kids clean and send 'em to school and all that. That ain't for us. We's just not cut out for all that nonsense. We like to hunt and fish and trap and live free."

"And make your own rules," Ben added.

"'At's sure right, General. You right, there."

"And to hell with the rights and wishes of others.'"

"Well . . . if a man has a-plenty he ought to share his bounty with others less fortunate. Like us."

"Suppose that person doesn't wish to share what he has?"

"We got a right to eat, General."

"Get this son of a bitch away from me before I shoot him," Ben said.

The man quickly disappeared into the crowd.

Ben turned and walked back to his vehicle, his team walking with him. He leaned against a fender and slowly began to bring his anger under control.

After a few moments, he said, "Get Junior on his feet and bring him to me."

With his mouth swollen and minus a few teeth, Junior stood in front of Ben. The man made no effort to hide his hatred for Ben Raines.

"Junior," Ben said slowly, choosing his words carefully, "I don't like people like you and those who follow you. I never have. But I can't just line you up against a wall and shoot you. You have not raised a hand against me. I wish you would. But you're a coward, Junior. Most bullies are. We're going to leave you and your followers in this town, Junior. After we fingerprint you and take your pictures. There is a Rebel outpost east of here. I'm going to ask them to check on you folks from time to time. And I'm going to tell you what those patrols will find here, Junior. They're going to find a very clean and tidy town. They're going to find proper sanitation and running water. You can do it, Junior. But you're going to have to work. You're going to have to plant gardens, Junior. And tend them. Carefully. You're not going to brutalize anyone else. Ever again. You're going to be a model citizen. From this moment on. And if they don't find all those things being done, Junior, they're going to notify me. And no matter where I am, Junior, no matter if I am standing in the cathedral of Notre Dame, I'll come back here and I'll kill you, Junior. I'll put a .45 to your head and blow your fucking brains out. Do you understand all that, Junior?"

"You ain't got no right to do this to us."

"Oh, yes, I have, Junior. I've got ten thousand heavily armed men and women with me that says I have the right. I've got another thirty to forty thousand men and women in outposts from coast to coast and border to border that says I have the right. It's a brand new world that's dawning, Junior. And there is no place in it for people like the man who is standing in front of me now. So you'd better change, Junior."

Ben smiled at the man. "Now, Junior, I'm not a totally unreasonable man. If you and your people wish to leave this place, you may do so. You may find yourself a spot and live in squalor and ignorance for the rest of your unnatural lives."

Junior's eyes lit up. A smile creased his bruised mouth.

The light quickly faded and the smile was gone when Ben said, "But if you steal one thing from another human being, if you bully another human being, if you enslave another human being, if you abuse another child or commit another criminal act, I'll kill you, Junior. The government you grew up under tolerated people like you. But I won't. Is all that clear, Junior?"

"You don't leave a man much of a choice, Ben Raines," Junior said, a definite note of depression in his words.

"That's correct, Junior. The only choices I give you are right and wrong. It's up to you to choose. And you know the difference. So don't try to con me with a lot of psychiatric bullshit."

Junior smiled for the first time—a small smile. "I bet head-shrinkers don't care much for you either, do they, Ben Raines?"

"Let's just say the ones who work for the Rebels know better than to try to tell me that a person who is ten points shy of a so-called normal IQ doesn't know right from wrong, and that excuses whatever crime the person might be accused of."

Junior nodded his big head. "OK, Ben Raines. We'll play it your way."

"Ah, what do this mean, Junior?" Luddy asked.

"It means, Luddy, that you boys go round up all the garden tools you can find. You women go fetch all the books you can tote from that school over yonder. And it means, Luddy, that when the day's work is done, you got to wash your funky ass and shave your ugly face."

Ben laughed and patted the man on his arm. "You'll be a fine asset to the Rebel network, Junior."

Junior chuckled. "Well, Ben Raines," he looked around at all the tanks and machine guns and Rebel soldiers. "You do have a mighty convincin' way of gettin' a point acrost."

The little girl was the only child showing signs of physical abuse, so the Rebels, after much discussion, agreed to return the children to Junior's flock.

The elderly couple asked if they, too, could stay, since this had been their home for more than forty years. Ben looked at Junior.

"There won't nothin' happen to them," the big man replied. He smiled. "Give us a chance, Ben Raines. You see, for the first time in our lives, the existin' law—that's you—is really layin' down the law as to what we can and can't do. And backin' it up with more than words. Some folks need that, Ben Raines. And I know you'll do what you say, 'cause I've seen your graveyards. And you don't have to put up with the two best friends a criminal ever had: lawyers and liberals."

The Rebels rolled on, encountering no more

people, friendly or otherwise, until they were almost to the Canadian border. There they linked up with the Scouts, who had been sitting back and taking it easy after pulling back over the border.

Once in bivouac, Ben called a meeting of his commanders. He pointed to maps of British Columbia thumbtacked on the wall. "People, the Scouts tell me there is very large concentration of unfriendlies all across the south area of British Columbia. They stretch from Cache Creek in the western part of the province over to Golden, near the Alberta line. It's been mentioned that we might just knock a hole through their lines and deal with them on the return trip. Forget that. We deal with them now, get it done, and then move on.

"Ike, you and Tina take your battalions and move west. You'll clear out any bogies in Vancouver. Cecil, take your battalion and secure the Cache Creek area. Georgi, you take Merritt, Logan Lake, and end up in Kamloops. I'll take my people, along with Therm and his Eight Battalion and head straight up 97, ending at Salmon Arm. Rebet, you drive hard north to Revelstoke. Danjou, you and West swing back east and then cut north here at 95 and take it all the way to Golden. That's it, people. We start moving into position in the morning and cut our wolves loose in seventy-two hours. Good luck."

The commanders left the room to gather their units and start the drive into position for jump-off. It was the last week in March. It had been four months since any Rebel had fired a shot in anger—

46

the longest any of them had gone in years. It had been a disconcerting feeling.

Ben looked around the nearly deserted dining room of the old motel complex. It finally came to him who had been missing. "Where's Emil?" he asked Therm.

The hippie grinned. "He found some early blooming berries alongside the road yesterday evening. He picked two buckets full and ate them all. He has been, shall we say, indisposed for about eighteen hours."

"Has he been to see the medics?"

"Yes. They said it was the worst case of diarrhea any of them could remember. Emil thinks he's going to die. He's called for all the chaplains."

Ben chuckled. "What kind of berries were they?"

"I honestly don't know. The doctors checked him out for poisoning; but those tests came out negative. He just has the squirts, that's all."

Linda picked up her kit. "I'd better go see him. Diarrhea can be a lot more dangerous than people suspect."

"Oh, relax," Ben said. "Emil's so full of shit he can afford to lose some of it."

"Look who's talking," Linda popped back as she headed out the door.

Ben endured the laughter from his team with a smile. He was just glad Lamar Chase hadn't stuck around to hear it. He'd have never heard the end of it.

*   *   *

Ben and his team were gathered around the big Chevy on the morning of the push-off, drinking coffee and talking in low tones. A light mist was falling.

"Check all units, Corrie," Ben said.

A few moments later, she said, "All units reporting in and all in position."

"Mount up, people. Corrie, radio everyone to mount up. Scouts out. Tanks one mile behind them."

Seconds later, the rumble of tanks filled the misty air. They belched and snorted and clanked into position.

"Let's go, folks," Ben said. "The friendly natives of British Columbia are waiting to entertain us."

They rolled through Osoyoos and found it a ghost town. The stores along the business district had obviously been looted and very nearly destroyed years back. The light mist that was falling gave everything a surreal look in the grayness of early dawn.

"Scouts say to check out the body just up ahead," Corrie said. "The tanks are pulling over to it."

Ben rolled down the window and looked at the body of a man gently swaying at the end of a noose tied to a lamppost. A sign was secured to his chest, secured by a knife blade driven into the dead man's chest. The sign was printed in crude block letters: BEN RAINES SYMPATHIZER.

"Do we cut him down and bury him?" Cooper asked.

"Have the support people coming up behind us do that," Ben said.

Corrie gave the orders.

"Move on," Ben said, waving his hand at the tank commander who had opened the hatch and was watching him.

Ben took one more look at the hanging man. "Why do I get the impression that somebody up here really doesn't like me very much?"

4

Dan Gray and his Scouts and Buddy and his Rat
Pack had split their people and were taking the
smaller and less-traveled highways, flushing out
hostiles and clearing their sectors with brutal
efficiency. They stayed in contact with the others,
not wanting to get too far ahead and find
themselves trapped with only light weapons and
no armor.

Second and Nine Battalion found themselves
bogged down for a time, fighting hard-entrenched
outlaws around the Vancouver area. They were
gaining ground a foot at a time.

Cecil had his hands full in the town of Hope,
which had been taken over by outlaws and slavers.
Georgi Striganov was stalled just south of the
town of Princeton. Rebet, West, and Danjou had
managed to cross the border and were immediately
caught up in hard firefights.

"Tell them to call in air strikes," Ben told

Corrie, after she had given him the news. "Choppers and fighters in the air." He looked around him. So far, none of his people had fired a shot. "I thought I was taking the area with the most hostiles," he bitched. "Instead I find it's a cakewalk. Damn!" He shook his head in disgust.

Ben and Therm's people had pushed up to the town of Oliver and stopped, not wanting to drive too far north of the others.

The town was a burned-out, looted ruin that had been picked over a hundred times during the hard years since the Great War. The Rebels could find nothing to salvage.

"Scouts report a very large force in the town of Penticton," Corrie told Ben, after acknowledging the radio signal from the advance team of Scouts. "That's about twenty miles north of our location."

"How large is very large?" Ben asked.

"Approximately five hundred men. No sign of women or children."

"Mount up," Ben gave the orders. "Tanks spearhead. Let's go."

At the edge of the small city—population about twenty two thousand before the Great War—Ben met with the Scouts.

"We told them to surrender," the Scout team leader said. "They told us to go to hell and come in and get them."

"Well, let's not keep them waiting," Ben said. "Corrie, give the orders to start shelling."

Tanks, mortars, and SP artillery lined up and

within a minute were dropping rounds into the town.

"Friendlies are coming in from the east," Corrie told him. "About a hundred of them. Lightly armed."

Ben moved back from the booming of artillery so he could meet with the citizens.

"Everybody you pushed out of the United States landed on us," the citizen told Ben. "And that's not a criticism, General Raines—just the way it turned out."

"I understand," Ben replied, studying the man. He appeared a solid type, but Ben had learned the hard way not to trust anyone until they had proven themselves. The cannibalistic Night People had learned to mix in well with normal types if they wanted to stay alive against the advancing Rebel army. These people, considering the circumstances, were reasonably clean and free of the distinctive body odor of the creepies.

"We've got some wounded with us," the citizen told Ben. "And we're out of rations."

Ben began to relax some. No creepie would ask for rations and they certainly wouldn't ask to be taken to an aid station. Any blood sample would give them away the first time a slide was put under a microscope.

"That's a mean group in that town, General," the Canadian told Ben. "Gene Booker was one of our most vicious criminals before the war. He's spent the last decade robbing and raping and killing from one end of this province to the other."

"Yeah. I remember that Canada didn't have the death penalty," Ben said. "Peace and love and all that shit."

"Not all of us agreed with our government's decisions, General," the citizen said quietly, his voice just audible over the booming of the big guns.

"I won't put up with criminals," Ben told the man. "If my people fight and bleed and die for this land, our rules apply."

"As you wish, General. But you may find some peaceful resistance to your rules."

"They can peacefully resist all they want to. But when they do, they'll find themselves on their own, without benefit of Rebel protection, medical aid, or assistance of any kind."

A woman in the group smiled. "He said, 'some,' General. That doesn't include us."

Ben nodded his head. "Order the shelling stopped and the tanks to advance, Corrie," Ben told her. "Let's take the town and see what we have."

The Rebels took the town building by building, with the Canadians fighting right alongside them. And they were, to a person, tough, no-nonsense fighters, their skills honed razor-sharp by years of guerrilla fighting against outlaws, punks, and creepies, all just to stay alive in their own country.

The leader of the group was Jon Andersen, a former official in the government of British Columbia. After several blocks of the town of Penticton had been taken, Ben found himself in a building with Jon and a few of Jon's followers. Ben took a sip of water from his canteen and offered the canteen to Jon. The man drank deeply, then capped the canteen and handed it back.

"We wondered when you people would get up here," he said to Ben. "The Russian, Striganov, set up outposts over in Alberta and Saskatchewan and pretty well cleared those areas. Then he left and joined forces with you. He turned out to be a good man after all."

"Yes, he did," Ben agreed. "But we had some pretty good fights before he converted."

A hard burst of machine-gun fire knocked paneling and plaster from the wall behind them. The slugs drove through the shattered windows of the brick home.

Ben heard the clanking of a tank. Then the booming of a 105 ended the yammering of the machine gun. The tank clanked up, reversed its turret, and drove right through the home. The screaming of those being crushed under the treads lasted only a moment.

After the screaming had ceased, Jon looked at Ben. "You fight a mean, nasty war, Ben Raines."

"I fight to win, Jon. That's the only way to fight a war. Come on."

Ben's team and those with Jon ran from the house. They hit the ground when an enemy machine gun found their range and opened up. Ben rolled, came up on his knees behind what was left of a 105-round-shattered tree, and leveled his old Thunder Lizard. The M-14 yowled and bucked on full auto, and the .308 rounds silenced the machine gun.

Ben ran forward, chunked a Fire-Frag grenade into the bullet-pocked house, and hit the dirt. The grenade blew, and the area fell silent for a moment. Ben, his team right behind him, slammed into the house, knocking the door—which was hanging by one hinge—to the littered floor.

A wounded outlaw, cussing and screaming at Ben, leveled a pistol at him. Cooper, Beth, Jersey, Corrie, and Ben all fired at once. The rounds tore into the man. The pistol clattered to the bloody floor.

The Rebels and the Canadians moved on to the next block.

Kneeling behind a row of rusted and ruined old trucks, cars, and station wagons resting on their rims, Ben said, "Get me reports from all battalions, Corrie. Let's see what the others are doing."

"Gunships are converging on what is left of the Vancouver harbor," she told him after bumping all units. "Ike has called for the gunships to concentrate on destroying all ships and boats in the harbor while his and Tina's people blow the bridges connecting the city to the mainland. When that is done, Ike will redirect his artillery and destroy the city."

"Good. Cecil?"

"He's busted through Hope and is barreling toward the retreating outlaws. He says his people routed them; they're running in a panic. Georgi has almost taken his objective and Rebet, West, and Danjou say they will break through no later than noon."

"All right. Good. Let's get this town taken and on the road. I think Cec is turning this into a race," Ben added with a smile.

With the tanks spearheading and the outlaws now knowing they could not win against a better-equipped and much more highly motivated force, the city was in Rebel hands by noon. Jon Andersen and his people stayed out of the way and watched, wondering what Ben Raines was going to do with the prisoners, including Gene Booker, the murderer, rapist, mugger, thief and slave-trader.

But Ben passed that buck to Jon.

"You mentioned that you and your people wanted to live in this town; you wanted this town to be an outpost," Ben told him. "Fine. You're in charge."

"And if I decide to spare his life?" Jon asked.

"We'll make the next town an outpost. Or the next, or the next."

"And us?" Jon waved his hand, indicating the others in his group.

"You're on your own."

Gene Booker laughed at the expression on Jon Andersen's face.

Jon ignored that and stared at Ben, leaning up against his Chevy, rolling a cigarette. "Maybe our two nations, maybe the world, needs a man as hard as you, Ben Raines. Whether that's right or wrong, we've got you, don't we?"

"That's right, Jon." Ben lit his smoke and stared

at the Canadian.

"Shit," Booker said. "I'm a free man already. That pussy don't have the nerve to pop a cap on me."

"Do they get a trial?" Jon asked.

Someone in the Rebels ranks laughed at that.

"The rule of thumb is this, Jon: we offer adversaries surrender terms. If they refuse, they're dead."

"Come on, Andersen!" Booker taunted Jon. "Come on, come on. Hell, Jon, you might as well take off your pants now and let me fuck your ass. You know I'm gonna do it sooner or later."

"You're filth," Jon told him. "Filth. Maybe you don't deserve to live. Maybe we were wrong."

"Aw, Jon, me boy," Booker said. "You know you can't kill me. I was an abused child. I was born into poverty. The other kids made fun of me."

"So were a lot of us," a Rebel spoke from the ranks. "Save that shit for somebody else. Not that you're going to have the time to find anyone that stupid."

Jon cut his eyes to Ben. "What Booker says is true. I know that for a fact."

"So what?"

"Your system of justice does not take that into consideration?"

"No. We don't kill children or certifiable idiots. Those are the only two exceptions."

Gene looked around him. His gaze stopped on Thermopolis. "A hippie? Here? Now?"

Therm shrugged his muscular shoulders. "Like

Popeye: I yam what I yam."

"Jon," Gene Booker said in all seriousness. "I was struck on the head by a constable when I was a boy. It affected me. You know it did. You remember what the court-appointed psychiatrists all said about me."

Ben laughed and toed out the butt of his cigarette. "Damn, Booker, you sure know all the right words, don't you. I bet you were a real jailhouse lawyer."

"Fuck you, Raines!" Booker said. "You're the savage here, not me."

"There are those who will certainly agree with that, Booker," Ben admitted. "But fortunately, we've got them outnumbered and outgunned."

Booker's eyes touched upon the collar of a chaplain. "You're a Catholic priest, right?"

"Either that or an Episcopalian, Presbyterian, or an over-zealous Methodist," the priest said with a smile.

"And you're not going to interfere in this!"

"Oh, my, no," the priest said. "But I will give you a very proper Catholic burial."

"You got to hear my confession!"

"Oh, no. I just ate lunch. You see, son, the Catholic Church has changed since the Great War. I don't have the inclination to tell you and you certainly don't have the time to hear all about the rebirth of Catholicism and all the changes it's gone through. I will say this: we no longer believe that an individual can live a life of crime and on his or her deathbed confess to all and be granted entrance to Heaven. In plainer terms, suffice it to say that this priest thinks that right now, Gene Booker, you are in a world of shit, boy."

Booker stared bug-eyed at the chaplain. "I ain't believin' this!" he hollered. "I want to see your Monsignor!"

"Oh, I am a Monsignor," the priest told him.

"Shit!" Booker said.

"Get it done," Ben told Andersen.

Booker started cussing the man. He cussed the man, his wife, his kids, his mother and father, and everyone else that he could think of that might be remotely related to the man.

Jon ended the cussing with a single shot, sending the bullet into the man's brain.

He looked at Ben as he holstered his pistol. "The others?"

"We'll deal with them. Put your people to work clearing the airfield outside of town. We'll be bringing supplies in for you very shortly. Welcome to the Rebels, Jon Andersen."

The Rebels began once more rolling north, but not too far north, for Ike and Tina were going to have a good two or three days work clearing out the suburbs around Vancouver, and other battalions did not wish to get too far north of them in case of a counterattack.

Cecil halted his advance at a tiny town called Spuzzum. Georgi called a halt on the north side of Coquihalla Pass and set up camp for the night.

Ben stopped his advance at Summerland. Rebet called it a day at Castlegar, and West and Danjou made camp just south of Mount Fisher.

Before turning off the lantern that evening and crawling into the double sleeping bag placed on the inflatable air mattress, Linda asked, "How far to Alaska, Ben?"

Ben chuckled. "Oh, about two thousand miles. It'll go faster than you think once we're past Prince George."

"Alaska going to be rough?"

"I don't really know. It'll be a fight, for sure. And there is no way we're going to touch base with those towns past road's end."

"I don't understand. And don't tell me I should have paid more attention in geography class."

Ben laughed. "No, I won't. I will admit I was pretty dumb about Alaska until I started studying maps. You might say that anything west of a line running south to north from Cook Inlet to Prudhoe Bay will be an area that we won't investigate. There are no roads."

"Where is Nome and how do you get to it."

"It's on the Seward Peninsula and you have to fly there. Unless you want to take a dog sled. It's the trail's end, or it used to be, for the thousand-mile Iditarod Sled Dog Race. That used to start in Anchorage and end in Nome."

"So we won't be going there?"

"No. There are a lot of places in Alaska we won't be visiting."

"The Trans-Alaska Pipeline?"

"Oh, we'll see it."

"No. I meant, what about it?"

"It was my understanding that the entire operation was shut down right at the start of the Great War. If that is true, I don't intend to reopen it."

"If that is true, Ben, how are the people living there getting fuel to heat their homes and run their vehicles?"

"I think it's open to a limited degree. This is guesswork, Linda. We'll know for sure once we get there. And when we get there, we've got to strike hard and fast and have it over with by fall. Then we've got to get the hell gone south."

"The Eskimos, the Indians up there?"

"The crud and crap may have killed them all. But I'd think they just moved west into uninhabited areas and went right on doing what they've been doing for thousands of years: surviving. They did quite well before the white man came along and fucked up their lives, and they can go right on living as they damn well please after we've left."

"You don't intend to impose Rebel law on them?"

"No. I don't have the right to order a culture change. Our worlds are not going to clash, Linda. The bear and the whale and the seal have returned; the tribes will never grow so large as to wipe them out. The white man did all that."

She turned out the lamp, crawled in beside Ben, and giggled.

"What the hell's so funny?" Ben asked.

"Pretend we're Eskimos and rub noses with me."

"Is that all you want me to do?"

"I'm sure you'll think of something else."

She was right.

5

The Rebels waited until Ike and Tina's troops had neutralized Vancouver and left the city—and any outlaws who might still be alive in it—burning and isolated, before they pushed off on another leg toward Northstar.

Moments before they were due to shove off, Corrie received a communiqué. Communications had intercepted a message from an outlaw group in Prince George. She taped the message and took it to Ben.

Ben listened to the communiqué and nodded his head. "They're smartening up. They know they can't defend the cities and towns against us, so they've decided to pack it up and head for Alaska. If—and it's a big if—we can believe the communiqué. Corrie, go to scramble and get me all unit commanders on the horn."

"I tend to accept the communiqué as legitimate, Ben," Georgi Striganov radioed his response. "But with these reservations. One: these outlaws up here are the most intelligent we are to face in this last campaign. They are survivors from many battles against us. They know our tactics well. Two: they will surely set up ambush points along the highway, and there is only one highway we can take to Northstar. Three: they have done this knowing we will suspect an ambush and that it will slow us down, giving them time to set up and be waiting for us when we reach our objective."

"I agree with Georgi's assessment," Cecil said.

The others agreed with the Russian, and so did Ben.

"OK," Ben said. "We're agreed on that. Now then, we know they don't have any form of SAMs. They have ground-only rocket launchers, heavy machine guns, and mortars—I'm talking about the outlaws here in BC. I don't know what we'll be facing in Northstar. I recommend we use our choppers to range out and act as forward recon."

They all agreed with that, and Ben ordered the helicopter gunships up.

"Let's hit it, people," Ben signed off.

At Summerland, a town that once boasted a population of nearly ten thousand, Ben was met by a sad-looking group of about two hundred citizens, all of them wandering aimlessly about.

"Former slaves," Ben said, before he even talked to any of them. "Pull over there, Coop," he pointed. "Let's see what we can do for them."

"The outlaws left yesterday," a man told him, his face bearing the bruises of a dozen recent beatings. "They took our younger men and women with them . . ."

Ben guessed the average age of this group to be around fifty years old.

". . . It's been hell up here for a long time, General. We fought and fought well for several years, all the time on the run. But we just didn't have the firepower to hold out. The outlaws overran us a long time ago."

"I understand," Ben said, and he did. Canadian gun laws were much tougher than those in the United States—back when such rules were enforced. But like the U.S. Government, the Canadian powers-that-be never seemed to realize that criminals don't pay any attention to rules and regulations and laws. The only group of people who are punished by restrictive gun laws are the law-abiding citizens.

"Get some of these vehicles left behind running so these people can join Jon Andersen's group south of us," Ben ordered. "Have the medics check these folks out and then issue them arms and equipment. This will beef up Jon's group and give us one hell of an outpost."

"Not all of these people wish to participate in your outpost network, General," the spokesman for the survivors said.

"Then point them out and send them on their way," Ben told him. "There is no middle ground here."

"We have a right to our opinions," a woman told Ben. "And we chose not to join your organization." The man beside her nodded his head in agreement, as did about a dozen others standing near.

"That is certainly your privilege, madam," Ben replied. "So goodbye."

He turned to walk away.

"Wait a minute!" the man beside the woman yelled.

Ben turned around.

"What about us?" the man demanded.

"What about you?" Ben countered.

"We need food and clothing and medical attention."

"I would say you have a problem." Ben's words were as icy as the arctic in the dead of winter.

"You'll just leave us, to fend for ourselves?"

"That's what you want, isn't it?"

"Well . . . yes. I suppose it is. But the Christian thing for you to do is to help us first."

"The Lord helps those who help themselves. Good luck to you all."

"You're a son of a bitch, Ben Raines!" the woman shouted.

"Actually, my mother was a very nice lady. A Christian lady. She would work tirelessly to help those who needed it; but she didn't believe in something for nothing. She was compassionate but tough. I once saw her pick up a shotgun and threaten to blow the head off of a hunter who was trespassing on our farmland. She was a lady of very firm beliefs. She also believed in applying the belt to the butts of her children when any of us deserved it. And we usually did—on a daily basis."

"I'm sure you led the list of getting spanked," Therm said with a smile.

"I believe I did set a family record for lickings

one summer," Ben admitted.

"God will damn you to hell for deserting us!" the woman yelled.

"I doubt it. Let's go, people!" Ben yelled. "We've got miles ahead of us." He turned to the spokesman of the group who was heading south to join Andersen's people. "Can you leave them behind?"

The man sighed and nodded his head. "Yes. If that is the only way the majority of us can survive. But I have to say this: I believe, General Raines, that you are the hardest man I have ever encountered."

Therm smiled, knowing what Ben was going to say, and he wasn't disappointed.

"Hard times, brother," Ben said. "Hard times."

Peachland was still burning when the Rebels pulled up and stopped at the outskirts of the small town.

"Gunships report the retreating outlaws have blown the bridges at Kelowna and just north of Vernon," Corrie told him.

"Damn!" Ben said, lifting and studying a map. "We'll have to take this secondary road on the west side of the lake. It's going to slow us down to a crawl. Tell those gunships to engage the enemy and do some damage, Corrie."

"They have prisoners, Ben," Lamar Chase said quietly.

"I am fully aware of that, Lamar." Ben walked away, to stand alone, as leaders of great armies have done since the beginnings of large-scale warfare.

Ben and Therm's battalions moved at almost a snail's pace on the badly rutted, and, in spots, nearly impassable secondary road. Many times the long column was forced to stop while engineers repaired the road. With nightfall approaching, they shut it down at Wilson Landing. The other battalions were also reporting bridges being blown and many barricades on the highways.

One bright spot: the gunships reported that they had scored a lot of hits on the retreating outlaws.

A forward recon team pulled back in after being relieved of the lonely and dangerous duty. They reported to Ben.

"Those gunships did a number on the outlaws' asses, General," a team leader reported, unable to hide the grin on his face. "They lost a lot of men. Tomorrow you can see for yourself the damage they did."

"And we lost no gunships in the process," Ben said, having already received and reviewed a preliminary report.

"No, sir. Not a one. Several have bullet holes in them, but none were downed."

"Thank you," Ben said with a smile. "Go get yourself some food and rest." After the Scout had left, Ben checked with Corrie on the other battalions. All were secure for the night. He poured a mug of coffee and stepped outside. Jersey slipped out right behind him, to stand several meters away, alert for trouble.

On this night, Ben did not expect trouble in the

form of a night attack from the outlaws. Although they could come at any time, he knew that sneak attacks were more likely later, when they were deep in northern British Columbia, where the timber and brush growing lush and thick on both sides of the road and the rolling hills and mountains would offer plenty of good cover for an ambush. That was when the gunships would prove invaluable.

"Cold out here," he muttered, his breath steaming in the fading light.

Thermopolis walked up to join him. He, too, held a mug of coffee.

"Got your people all settled in?" Ben asked.

"Yes. Even Emil, thank God. Ever since we crossed over into Canada he's been like a city kid exploring a country drainage ditch."

"Interesting analogy," Ben said. "But I know what you mean."

The men stood shoulder to shoulder for a moment, not speaking.

Ben finally broke the silence, but when he spoke, it was in a whisper. "It's too goddamn quiet, Therm."

"I know. I was thinking a few minutes ago— just before I walked up—that they wouldn't be dumb enough to try an attack just yet. That they'd probably wait until we were all stretched out on some lonesome road."

"I was thinking the same thing."

Jersey was listening and said, "I'll tell Corrie to bring everyone to high alert. You guys get your asses down and out of sight, damnit!"

Therm smiled. "Not much respect for her elders there, but she has a good point."

"Maybe it's a false feeling on our part. But just in case it isn't, good luck."

"Same to you."

Therm walked away into the gathering gloom, and Ben stepped back into the house he was using that night.

"Get everyone ready to cut all lights on my command," Ben said, glancing at his watch. It would take Thermopolis about three minutes to get back to his battalion area. If an attack was imminent, it would come soon, for those watching would know the Rebels had just eaten and were relaxing.

"Fools," Ben muttered.

"Beg pardon, Ben?" Linda looked at him.

"We're seventeen hundred strong here, with manned tanks and APCs all around our perimeter. They're fools to try anything."

"They're desperate people, General," Cooper said, squatting by a window, his M-16 ready.

"I don't understand them," Linda admitted. "You did flyovers, dropping leaflets urging them to surrender. You told them that you'd help them turn their lives around, Ben. You offered them amnesty. Yet not one outlaw has offered to surrender. I don't understand it."

"That's the reason I was so hard on those people back in Summerland. Outlaws seldom change their ways. And these people are in their second decade of lawlessness. I got through to Junior back in the States. I scared him. And I think it will hold.

72

Some of those outlaws out here in the night right now would probably make good citizens if I could talk to them. But they're not going to give me that chance. So to hell with them." He checked his watch then looked over at Corrie. "Give the order to ready the flares," Ben said.

She gave the orders and nodded at Ben.

"Everything go dark in ten, Corrie. Count it down."

She counted to the mark, gave the orders, and the camp was plunged into darkness.

Ben watched the luminous second hand on his watch. "Flares up."

The flares went up just as an outlaw tripped a perimeter banger wire, and that section was immediately torn apart by gunfire. The outlaw and those with him were torn into bloody chunks by the heavy machine-gun fire. Others, confident of their ability to move through the night, but not really knowing how the Rebels secured their camps, walked into Claymore-mined areas and were mangled by the deadly antipersonnel mines.

But half a hundred outlaws had managed to penetrate the camp's security. One made the mistake of throwing himself through a window of Ben's quarters. Ben turned and gave him a burst from his Thunder Lizard. The .308 rounds lifted the man up on his tiptoes and knocked him back through the window he had just jumped through. He left a smear of blood on the dusty windowsill.

"Light up the sky, Corrie." Ben yelled to be heard over the rattle of gunfire. "Keep the flares going."

73

The Rebels would not move from their assigned positions; they would do that only after signaling by radio contact. So anything else that moved in the flare-filled night was fair game, and the Rebels took full advantage of their hard training.

The fire-fight was brief and bloody and deadly . . . for the outlaws. The Rebels wore body armor and helmets that would stop nearly all standard pistol rounds and many rifle rounds. Ben Raines equipped his people with the best of everything and had his lab people constantly working to come up with new and better equipment.

"Cease firing," Ben ordered.

The camp fell silent almost immediately. Then, gradually, the moaning of the many wounded began filling the cold air.

"Patrols out," Ben ordered. "Secure us but do not pursue the enemy. Everyone else stay in their holes. Get me a report from Eight Battalion."

"Everything is smooth over there, General," Corrie told him.

"All right, let's see what we've got outside."

The Rebels began dragging the outlaw wounded to Chase's medics, not always being very gentle about it. They knew that most of them were going to be shot or hanged anyway.

Ben walked up to one outlaw, who had suffered only a minor wound, and pulled out his .45. He jacked the hammer back and put the muzzle against the man's head. "You might live through a trial that will be conducted by Jon Andersen's people, or you can die right now. The choice is yours to make. State your decision."

The outlaw was so scared he was trembling from his ankles to his shoulders. He knew he was facing a man who would kill him in a heartbeat. "I'll take a trial," he managed to stammer the words.

"If I decide to give you one," Ben told him. "I want all the information you have in that slimy brain of yours. You can do it voluntarily and live, or I'll pump you so full of drugs you'll be a vegetable when you come out of it. Either way, I'll get the information. Do you understand that?"

"Yes, sir! I'll tell you anything you want to know. Anything at all."

"Get him out of here," Ben ordered. "Interrogate him dry."

Some of the newer Rebels in Ben's battalion exchanged glances. They'd been told what a hardass Ben Raines was, and some had not believed it. They believed it now.

"The big hotshot Ben Raines," an outlaw sneered at Ben from his position on the cold ground.

Ben looked down at him. The man had been gut-shot and probably was not long for this world. "You got something on your mind, punk?"

"Yeah. Seein' you dead, you law-and-order son of a bitch!" The man jerked up his arm, a tiny .22 caliber derringer in his hand.

Ben shot him between the eyes.

One young outlaw, not much more than a teenager, started weeping as he lay on the ground. Ben walked over to him, stared down at him, and noted that his wounds were not much more than scratches.

"Get up on your feet, damn you!" Ben told him.

The boy crawled to his boots. Tears streaked his face and snot hung from his nose.

"Blow your nose," Ben told him. "You're disgusting."

The young man honked into a dirty handkerchief. At least he didn't blow his snot onto the ground, a habit that Ben had always felt was repulsive, unsanitary, and reserved solely for people who lacked consideration for the health of others.

"What's your name?" Ben asked.

"Jerry Harris, sir."

"How old are you?"

"Eighteen, I think, sir."

"How long have you been with this pack of trash?"

"Nearabouts six months, sir."

"Why?"

"I . . . beg your pardon, sir?"

"Why did you join with this shit group?"

The question seemed to confuse the young man. Finally, he said, "There ain't no law, sir. Or there wasn't 'til you come along. There ain't no jobs, no future, no past, no nothing."

"That's horseshit!" Ben snapped at him. "The future is anything you want to make it. You're just a lazy, no-count punk, and that's all you'll ever be."

"I ain't neither!" the young man flared, his eyes flashing.

"Then prove it!" Ben roared at him.

"How? You want me to get a job? Where, for

76

God's sake? Show me a factory, I'll go to work. Show me a store that's open for business. I'll clerk in it. You . . ."

Ben slapped him. The open-handed blow snapped the boy's head to one side and bloodied his lips. "Don't hand me excuses, boy. That's cop-out bullshit. That sounds like some of the crap the so-called peace and love generation used to hand out—years before you were born. Tell me, what did you do before joining up with these outlaws?"

"I . . . uh . . . stayed with my folks. We grew gardens and hunted and stuff like that."

"Where are your folks now?"

"Dead, sir."

"How?"

He shrugged his shoulders. "They didn't make the winter, sir. After Daddy died, Mama just give up."

"Are you feeding me a line of bullshit or are you telling me the truth?"

"I ain't about to lie to you, General Raines."

"How do you know my name?"

"I seen pictures of you. There are carvins of you in the deep timber. Them that live in the woods worship you. General, after my folks died, I figured . . . well, what the hell? The whole world is upside down. Everything is all screwed up. What did my parents live for and what did they die for? You show me something to live for, General. Show me."

Ben spotted Thermopolis standing at the edge of the clearing. "You think you can show him, Therm?"

The hippie-turned-warrior smiled. "Oh, I think so. Come on, Jerry. Life is worth a lot more than you think."

"You're gonna have to convince me."

"Oh, I think I can. It's easy when you take into consideration that if I can't, Ben Raines is going to shoot you."

6

The outlaws that attacked the camp of the Rebels took a terrible loss of life. All the prisoners agreed that the group suffered probably a fifty percent loss. Whether or not they were telling the truth was something else to be taken into consideration.

Ben turned the prisoners over to Jon Andersen's group and they were tried. Most of them were hanged. A few were horsewhipped and set free.

Thermopolis persuaded Ben to let Jerry Harris come along with the Rebels. "He says he's never killed anyone and I believe him," Therm said. "And don't try to con me, Ben; you like the kid or you would have turned him over for trial."

"I will agree that there might be more than a spark of decency in the boy," Ben said.

"Becoming liberal in your advancing age, Raines?" Doctor Chase asked with a chuckle.

"Very funny," Ben replied. "Mount up and let's get gone from here. We're wasting time."

"He doesn't like me," Jerry said, once Ben had walked away.

"You've got to prove yourself with Ben," Lamar told the young man. "You went bad and that's two strikes against you from the get-go. Ben is law and order, boy. One hundred percent, all the way down the line. With the emphasis placed on order."

"I don't understand," Jerry said.

"Ben Raines is the law, boy. His philosophy, his concepts, his interpretations. The administration of justice will never be as it was in the northern hemisphere. Two hundred years from now, when all of us are dust, the ideals that Ben Raines put forth will still be the base upon which the existing government functions. You're a part of history in the making, son, so don't screw it up."

All the Rebel battalions moved out, from Squamish in the west to Cranbrook in the eastern part of the state, all pushing north. The failed attack against Ben's camp and the terrible casualties the outlaws suffered must have spread like a forest fire among the outlaws, for there were no more mass attacks against any Rebel battalion.

The army of Rebels advanced slowly but steadily, sometimes making no more than twenty-five miles a day due to the bad roads and blown bridges and overpasses. They passed the point where the gunships had done their work, and it was a death-site of bloated and stinking bodies and jumbled rows of burned-out cars and trucks. The gunships had done in ten minutes what it would have taken Rebel ground troops all day to do, even with artillery. The Rebels picked through the rubble, salvaging weapons and ammo and other equipment. The Rebels never left anything behind that might someday be put to use.

The Rebels pushed on toward Northstar.

They found survivors along the way. Some ran away from the Rebels. Others straightened out the steel in their backbones and agreed to become a part of the movement.

And far to the north of Ben's army, the outlaw leaders who had once terrorized southern British Columbia met and tried to lay out plans to halt the advancing army.

"We're never going to halt them," Dickie Momford said. "All we're goin' to do is maybe slow them down some. But we'll never stop them."

"I don't like that kind of talk," Jack Hayes said.

"I don't give a damn what you like," Dickie told him. "Step out of your dream world, Jack, and face reality. Huge armies have tried to stop Raines, armies with tanks and artillery and everything we don't have. Raines and his Rebels stepped on them like they was bugs and kept on comin'."

"He's right," Gil Brister said. "This is it for us, boys."

Art LeBarre looked at him through the smoke of the campfire. "What do you mean, Gil?"

"He means," an outlaw who called himself Turner said, "that this is our last shot. We either surrender, or we die. Them's the onliest choices we got."

"Mighty slim chances," Harris Orr said. He heated his coffee and spooned in a dollop of honey to cut the harshness of the brew. "Damned if we do and damned if we don't, the way I see it.''

"This ain't his country," Pat Brown bitched. "What's he doin' up here, anyways?"

Turner chuckled. "This ain't *nobody's* country, Pat. Jist like it was two hundred years ago. It's up for grabs, and Raines is gonna grab it.''

"Well, what the hell's he gonna do with it?" Peters asked.

"Kill us, for one thing," Momford said. "And I ain't lookin' forward to that day a-tall.''

"Them ol' boys that passed through a while back," Jack Hayes said. "Villar and that dark-lookin' man. Hot Fart or whatever he called hisself . . .''

"Khansim," Art said. "The A-rab. The Hot Wind. What about them?''

"We could throw in with them. If we showed Raines enough force, he might be willin' to make a deal.''

Turner smiled and shook his head. "Raines don't make no deals with criminals. You boys ain't been studyin' this man like I have over the years. Remember, boys, I come up from the U-nited States years back, runnin' from Raines and his Rebels. Boys, this man took about five thousand Rebels into New York City and whupped about fifty thousand of them nasty, stinkin' Night People, then destroyed the city. He took his Rebels and cut a path acrost America from border to border. That son of a bitch Raines has been shot a dozen times, he's fell off mountains, he's been captured, tortured, sentenced to death no tellin' how many times, and he still keeps on comin'. He kilt Sam Hartline with his bare hands. He's destroyed whole armies, right down to the last person. You can't stop him; we can't stop him; can't *nobody* stop him.''

''Then what can we do?'' Peters asked.

''Die,'' Turner said softly.

This was not his country, and Ben recognized that. So with the exception of Vancouver, few towns and cities were put to the torch by the Rebels as they relentlessly marched north. They took their time, stopping often to help patch together the ruined lives of those citizens they encountered. Most were glad to see the Rebels. But there was always the exception.

Ben ran into that at a little town just south of Salmon Arm.

''We don't want your help,'' the man said. ''So just leave.''

''Suits me,'' Ben said, and turned to leave.

''You have sick people in this town,'' Lamar told him. ''They need medical attention.''

''Not on your terms,'' he was informed. ''We are pacifists. We do not believe in violence and we will not fight.''

''That's very noble,'' the doctor said. ''But what will you do if the outlaws return?''

''God will see us through.''

Ben leaned against the Chevy and rolled a smoke. Therm joined him.

''So how will you handle this?'' Therm asked.

''Leave. To hell with them.''

"Just walk off and leave them to die, Ben?"

"It's their choice, Therm."

"I believe they are sincere people."

"Oh, so do I. But that doesn't change a thing. I won't force them to face reality. I wouldn't stop a man from entering a cage to face an angry grizzly with only a switch in his hand; but I'd damn sure call him a fool."

Lamar joined the men. "These people are in desperate need of medical attention, Ben."

"That's their problem, Lamar."

"They are not our enemies, Ben."

"And they are not our friends. There is no such thing as neutral in this war, Lamar. I won't recognize it. Mount up, we're moving out."

"Was he right or wrong?" Jerry Harris asked Therm, as the Rebels put the small town in their rearview mirrors.

"He's Ben Raines," Thermopolis replied.

"That's not much of an answer."

"It's the best I can do. The boss can be right, or the boss can be wrong. But he's still the boss."

At Cache Creek Ike and Tina linked up with the others battalions they were to travel with and halted there. Ben and Thermopolis halted their advance at Salmon Arm. Rebet pulled up at Revelstoke. Danjou and West reached their objective at Golden and halted. The areas behind the Rebel battalions had been swept clean.

Ben studied his maps, laid out his plans, and got on the horn to all unit commanders. "We'll all rest for twenty-four hours and go over equipment and wait for resupplies. When that's done, Rebet, you and West and Danjou cross over into Alberta and push north to Jasper, then cut back across the continental range and head up to Prince George on Highway 16. I'll take Highway 5 north. Ike, you and Cecil and Tina and Georgi drive north on 97. We'll all link up at Prince George and make further plans there. Scouts out. Good luck."

Buddy had linked up with his father's battalion, waiting for Dan's people, who had traveled north, following a road that dead-ended at Mica Creek. Dan's Scouts backtracked and checked in, reporting finding a few survivors along the way and no outlaws.

Upon his return, Dan linked up with Ben, and at dawn all battalions pushed off.

The Rebels hit small pockets of resistance made up of die-hard outlaws and thugs who had refused to head north with the major outlaw gangs who had operated in the area for years and had enough sense to get out of Ben Raines' way. The pockets of punks, thugs, and crud were crushed with hardly a delay in the Rebels' progress.

One outlaw's dying words summed up the campaign thus far: "Hell, we didn't even slow 'em up."

Ben's group cleared a one-hundred-mile path and stopped at Clearwater after his forward recon people reported about a hundred survivors living in the small town, all of them requiring medical attention and all of them asking to be a part of the Rebel outpost system.

"Jack Hayes is the man you've got to look out for," a citizen told Ben during his interviewing of the survivors. "Word I get is that he's gathered up all the bigger gangs that operated in this area and they all headed north. One really big bunch of men moved through here not too many months back. They took Highway 97 north. They didn't bother a soul on their way through. They were heading for Alaska, I was told."

"Did you see them?" Ben asked.

"No. It was reported to me. Me and my bunch were holed up in the deep timber in the Wells Gray Park, just north of here. But he said somebody named Villar was the boss of the army."

Dan's smile resembled a death's head as he locked eyes with Ben. The Englishman had a very personal reason for catching up with Lan Villar. Villar had been working with the IRA years back and kidnapped some school children in London. One of the kids was Dan's youngest sister. She was repeatedly raped and died horribly. Dan tracked Villar halfway around the globe in an attempt to kill him. Only the Great War saved Villar's butt.

Now Dan was once more closing in.

"How many men?" Ben asked the citizen.

The man shrugged his shoulders. "Between five hundred and a thousand. But they were well-armed, well-dressed, and looked very professional, so it was reported to me. They had artillery they were pulling behind trucks."

Ben nodded his head and smiled. Dan understood the smile; the citizen knew only that he was very thankful Ben Raines was an ally, not an enemy. After the man had gone to seek medical attention, Ben, Therm, Dan, and Buddy met in private.

"For the most part," Ben said, "I believe we can end the reign of terror in the northern hemisphere with this campaign. We've pushed the crud into a box and they have no way out. Not unless they can get to a port and get ships ready to sail. I don't believe they'll do that. Khamsin and Villar left South America and Europe because they couldn't compete with the forces of evil that had surfaced on those continents. We'll crush them in Alaska, and then see what they were running from in Europe."

"I've talked with Hans Strobel at length," Dan said. Hans had been one of Lan Villar's platoon leaders. Captured, he was found to be very disillusioned with the terrorist, had switched sides, and was now a respected member of the Rebels, commanding a team of Gray's Scouts. "Hans says that if anyone can crush those forces now operating in Europe it's us. But he's warned repeatedly that it won't be easy."

"I know. And I've wavered in my thinking about going in light," Ben said. "We have enough outposts throughout the nation to contain the criminal element left, and Sister Voleta's forces. They'll have their hands full, but I think they can do it, with the help of the Rebels we'll leave behind. Cecil has finally admitted that it would be best if he stayed stateside to run things. He knows this is his last campaign before being tied to a desk. We'll take seven battalions overseas. But for right now, let's concentrate on Northstar."

"All battalions are reporting only very light resistance, and little of that," Dan said. "I just came from communications. Danjou says so far it's been a milk run for his people."

"It won't be when we hit Alaska," Ben said. "I'm confident that we'll be successful, but we're in for some fierce fighting before it's over."

Corrie entered the room. "Ike reports that Williams Lake has been secured. He's going to hold up there until you pull even, General. He says that his recon people have reported there are many survivors in the town of Quesnel; but among them are a number of outlaws who have requested amnesty."

Ben looked at a map. "That's about a hundred miles north of Williams Lake. We'll be linking up with Danjou, West, and Rebet sometime late tomorrow or early the next day. Tell Ike to go ahead and push on to Quesnel, then link up with us at Prince George. Tell him to handle the amnesty situation as he sees fit."

"Yes, sir."

The others in the room knew that those outlaws seeking amnesty had better play it straight and truthful with Ike; the former Navy SEAL was not known for extending many tender, loving mercies toward thugs and crud. To those who knew Ike well, he was a big loveable teddy bear. Cross him and he could quickly turn into a savage, rampaging grizzly.

"I want Villar," Dan said softly.

"We'll do our best to see that you get him," Ben assured the man.

"I want to beat that bastard to death with my bare fists," the former SAS commando said. "And I want it to last a long, long time."

Rarely did Dan Gray show this much emotion about anything. Even Ben was surprised at the hate that shone in the Englishman's eyes.

"I don't know that it will make my sis rest any easier in the grave," Dan said. "But it will certainly give me a great deal of satisfaction." He rose from his chair and left the room. He spoke to Dr. Chase at the door and stepped outside.

"All through with the survivors here, Ben," Lamar said, pouring a cup of coffee and then taking a chair at the table. "We've got us another outpost." He paused, then said, "Dan looked rather grim."

"We were discussing Lan Villar," Ben told him.

"Revenge is a strange emotion," Chase said. "I hope that Dan will be satisfied once he kills Villar. Most people I've talked with about it say that once it's over it's seldom as fulfilling as one had anticipated."

"It wasn't that way at all for me," Therm said. "I came away with the feeling that the man I'd sought and found and destroyed would never again do horrible things to another innocent person."

"You, Therm?" Chase looked at him. "I thought you were a man of peace."

"I am, for the most part. But I'm not so naive as to believe that turning the other cheek always works. There are some in this world who would just knock the shit out of you again as soon as you got up and offered them the other cheek."

"You've changed since joining the Rebels, haven't you, Therm?" Buddy asked.

"To a degree. I will never admit that Ben's way is necessarily the right way. But it's the best way toward accomplishing the end that we all desire. After it's over—if it's ever over—we're just going to have to sit down and hash out the little details of living day to day and getting along with our fellow human beings."

Ben stood up and stretched. "You three can sit here and engage in deep philosophical discussions if you like. I'm going to bed."

Thermopolis, Buddy, and Chase were gearing up for a marathon bull session when Ben walked into his quarters and closed the door. Linda smiled at him from the double sleeping bag, invitation in her eyes. Beats the hell out of talking any day.

7

Ben and his battalions made camp near the junction of Canadian Highways 5 and 16 late the next afternoon. They had not seen a living soul— friendly or unfriendly—during the nearly 150-mile run. Rebet, Danjou, and West were bivouacked just east of them, over the province line between Jasper and Mount Robson Park.

Corrie got West on the horn and handed the mike to Ben. "See any action, West?"

"Damn little, Ben. It was a milk run all the way. We could have slept through this one."

"It might be a good idea to get all the sleep we can, while we can," Ben told him. "All the outlaws are waiting for us in Alaska. See you in the morning."

"Providing we can get over this mountain range," West said with a laugh.

They were going to drive just south of the highest point in the Canadian Rockies, some 3,950 meters high.

The Rebels linked up and pulled out at midmorning. It was 275 miles from the junction to Prince George. The long column passed through tiny towns, stopping often to investigate. They found no one alive until they reached the tiny hamlet of McBride. Scouts had reported back that they were decidedly friendly.

A group of about a hundred happy-faced men and women greeted the Rebels, waving tiny Canadian and American flags and cheering as the Rebel column seemed to go on forever.

"Put over, Coop," Ben said. "Let's meet the people."

The small kids were scrambling all over the tanks, as kids will do anywhere. A man stepped forward out of the crowd, walking with a cane, one hand extended in welcome, a huge smile on his face. He was heavily armed, as were all the adults in the crowd.

Ben started laughing, and, to the amazement of all the Rebels, threw his arms around the man and hugged him. The men hugged each other and jumped up and down like classmates after a football victory.

"You old son of a bitch!" Ben yelled. "I thought they killed you back in the Tri-States!"

Clint Voltan.

"I took some lead, Ben. A few survivors dragged me off into the brush and we laid low until the area cleared. I was unconscious most of the time." He thumped the side of his leg with his cane and grinned. "Artificial, Ben. But it gets me around.

Anyway, when I came to my senses, I was in Canada and only had one leg. A doctor sawed it off with a carpenter's saw on the way up. I was a little pissed at first, but then they told me gangrene had set in." He grinned and shrugged his shoulders. "So what the hell? I get around pretty good."

"You're looking fat and sassy, Clint. Damn but it's good to see you." Then Ben put it all together and smiled. *"You're* the reason we haven't seen any outlaws along this stretch of road, right?"

"Me and my bunch, yeah. And you won't see any in Prince George either. Oh, they were there, but they hauled ass when they heard you and your Rebs was on the way. We've got the best radio equipment in this part of the province, I reckon. You're going to have your hands full in Alaska, Ben."

"Why didn't you let me know you were alive, Clint?"

"Well, what would have been the point? I'm not much good with this bum leg, and I had my hands full up here just like you did down in the States."

"Nora . . . ?"

He shook his head. "She didn't make it out, Ben. I've remarried and I'm happy. Really happy now that I know you boys and girls are in the area."

"Want this town to become one of our outposts, Clint?"

"You just try to keep it out of the system, Ben!"

Cecil and Ike came over from Prince George with

some of the older Rebels, and it was old home week for a few hours as the survivors from the Tri-States swapped stories and enjoyed each other's company.

"I got to say it again, boys," Clint said. "You guys are going to be busy in Alaska."

"How many from this area went up there, Clint?" Ike asked.

"I'd guess several thousand at the low end. Two thousand from the Washington-Oregon region. Say a thousand from Alberta. You're looking at at least ten thousand well-armed and well-trained men and women. I'd personally put the figure at maybe twelve to fifteen thousand. They're organized. They plant gardens and home-can food. They've got people all over the lower forty-eight during the growing season bringing back food. They have electricity and all the conveniences that you guys have. Lots of sections up there where they can raise chickens and hogs and cattle. And they do. They're ready for you, boys."

"What do you know about their weapons?" Ben asked.

"They've got artillery and mortars and heavy machine guns. Those are the reports I got from spotters along the way." He looked at Ben. "You look relieved. How so?"

"The numbers. I was anticipating a much larger force of men."

"They've got you outnumbered, Ben."

"Big deal. The Rebels are always outnumbered."

94

* * *

Ike, Cecil, Tina, and Danjou would take Highway 16 over to Prince Rupert on the Pacific coast. Ben would take the remaining battalions and head north. The battalions would link up just across the line in the Yukon, at Watson Lake, on the Alaska Highway.

Clint had been accurate when he said they would meet no outlaws in Prince George. The outlaws had looted and stripped the town and pulled out. Survivors were trickling back in when Raines's Rebels arrived in the small city.

"They're five or six hard days ahead of you, General," the woman who seemed to be in charge of the two hundred or so survivors told him. "And they're heavily armed. You will have your work cut out for you when you hit Alaska." She stared at him for a moment. "We have prisoners."

"And . . . ?"

"How do you want us to deal with them?"

"It's your country," Ben told her. "You captured them, you deal with them, bearing in mind that you're going to have to live here. I'm assuming you plan to do that."

"Oh, yes," the woman said. "This is our home. The prisoners, they're murderers, rapists, slavers . . . scum of the worst kind." She stood looking at him.

"Are you asking me to do your dirty work for you, ma'am?" Ben posed the question softly.

She sighed audibly. "It appears that way,

doesn't it?''

"Yes. You've got to make up your own minds about what type of justice you hand down up here," Ben told her. "But look at it realistically. You and your group didn't turn to a life of viciousness. You all tried to live decent lives in the face of more tragedy than any of you had ever faced before. You took the hard and right road. Those prisoners of yours took the road of lawlessness. Nobody made them do it. Nobody forced them. They had as much control over their destinies as you did. The majority of them are human crud and crap. They always will be. But what type of justice you choose to hand them is going to be totally up to you people.''

She forced a smile. "We'd like to be a part of your outpost system, General.''

"Fine with me. Just be sure you understand the rules.''

"We understand them, General Raines. We've spoken with Voltan many, many times. He has *zero* crime in his sector.''

"And do you understand how he managed that while being surrounded by the most vicious gangs of punks in British Columbia?''

"Yes. One has to make the laws simple enough for all to understand and then do what you say you're going to do . . . with no exceptions.''

"Yes. But it's a very difficult thing to do. There can be no deals. No plea bargaining. No exceptions to the rule. Your children have to grow up understanding that breaking the law is wrong and the punishment will be equal for all. They have to be taught that, both in the home and in the schools. And you're going to meet some stiff resistance to that. Anyone who takes a human life during the commission of a crime is put to death. No exceptions. None. Ever. Get with Voltan and go over Rebel application of law. You'll lose some followers when you set up your society our way; but the ones who remain will be the strongest, the steadiest, and the most reliable."

"And the ones who choose not to live under Rebel rule, General?"

"They can go to hell, ma'am. We're trying to rebuild nations, not hold a Sunday school class. And I don't apologize for our methods. Not at all. I've lost too many good, brave men and women to give a shit about the so-called rights of whiners, prima donnas, and lazy, good-for-nothing people who want something without paying the price for it. And sometimes that price is in blood. Good luck to you, ma'am."

Ben headed north on Highway 97, toward the town of Mackenzie, while Ike took the other battalions and headed west on Highway 16. Ben encountered no resistance on the push to Mackenzie. There he found a small group of survivors who had been holding out until the Rebels arrived.

"The outlaws who didn't head north are waiting for you at Dawson Creek, General," he was told. "And they're a mean, scummy bunch."

"Women and children with them?"

"Women. No kids. The women abandon them as soon as they give birth. We've got a half a dozen of their babies here. That should tell you what types you're dealing with."

"It does indeed," Ben said. He turned to Corrie. "Bump the gunships. Tell them to load up full and get up here." He turned back to the survivor. "Is there anything at Dawson Creek worth saving?"

"Not anymore. Slaves that have escaped from there say the outlaws have pretty well trashed the town."

Ben smiled. "Well, we'll just trash the outlaws then."

Ben looked up from his vantage point outside the small city of Dawson Creek. It was an hour past dawn. The gunships would be coming in from the east in just a few moments, coming in with the sun behind their backs, and they would be spread out in a group attack position.

The outlaws in the city had been taunting Ben and his people, using CB bands. They cursed Ben and they cursed the Rebels, using the vilest of language.

"To hell with the gunships!" a young Rebel from Thermopolis' battalion said. "Let's go in and kick their asses personal and up close."

"Settle down!" Therm shouted. "That's what they want us to do. That road leading into town is probably mined and the buildings closer to us are wired to go. Just settle down."

Ben smiled as Chase said, "Turning into a hell of a good commander, Ben. I never would have believed it."

"You just don't like men with long hair, Lamar."

"That is not true, Raines!"

"Yes, it is. Now hush up, here come the gunships."

"Hush up?"

"Yes. Be quiet."

As the sounds of the big blades chopping the air grew louder, the taunting and cursing from the outlaws in the town died into silence.

Ben picked up his CD mike and said, "This is General Raines. I much prefer rousting you assholes this way. Have fun, punks."

The Cobras, Apaches, and Hueys opened up, filling the air with rockets and lead. As soon as the lead choppers finished, the second wave began. When all but four choppers had veered to land beside the long column of Rebel vehicles—the four gunships still airborne were well out of artillery range—Ben gave the orders for tanks to begin shelling.

Ninety millimeter, 105's, and 76mm cannon opened up and did not stop for three long, earth-pounding minutes. They fired high explosive, napalm, and willie peter.

"APCs in," Ben said.

The armored personnel carriers were already

loaded up, each carrying ten infantry troops, a driver and a Rebel manning the 20mm Vulcan Gatling gun. Before the rear ramps were dropped, the gunners sprayed the area with 20mm fire, then gave the Rebels cover fire as they got into position.

But the outlaws had lost their zeal for the fight. Two squadrons of gunships and three minutes of intense artillery fire had set the town blazing and the outlaws running for their lives.

Ben had anticipated that. "Take them out," he told Corrie.

Corrie relayed the orders to the pilots, and the gunships swooped low, strafing the running outlaws, making pass after pass, until the field was littered with silent, bloody bodies.

"Bring them in, Corrie." Ben turned to Therm. "As soon as the fires die down, we'll go see what we've got, Therm. Salvage teams get ready to go in," he ordered. The Rebels would take every weapon, every round of ammo, and anything else they might possibly find a use for.

The Rebels in the town began securing the area. They were Gray's Scouts and Buddy's Rat Pack, and they did not take prisoners.

That was why the Rebels were the most feared Army on the face of the earth, and they were known worldwide. Ben Raines gave you two choices: surrender or die. And he seldom backed down from those options. Occasionally, as in Jerry Harris' case, he would see something there to salvage, or as in the case of Junior, make a point for others to understand. But those times were rare indeed.

It did not take the Rebels long to sweep and secure the town.

"Come on, Therm," Ben said, climbing into the back of an APC, and his team went with him. "Let's see what's left of the place."

"Not much," Therm muttered, after banging his head getting out of the cramped APC. Emil Hite had ridden with them, and the little con artist stubbed his toe and rolled down the ramp of the APC. Luckily for all close to him, his M-16 did not fire.

"The very essence of grace under pressure," Thermopolis observed, a smile on his lips, as Emil got to his boots with as much dignity as possible.

Georgi, Rebet, and West had angled off on Highway 29 to check out the towns of Hudson's Hope and Fort St. John. Ben and his battalions would link up with them there the next day.

"Son of a bitch!" a badly wounded outlaw cursed Ben as he lay dying on the littered ground. He looked to be in his late twenties or early thirties.

"It was your choice," Ben told him, his words cold. "You just made the wrong choice."

"They'll kill you in Alaska, hotshot," the outlaw gasped. "They know you're comin' and they're waitin' for you. You bastard!"

"That's how you want to go out," a chaplain asked the dying man. "With a curse on your lips?"

"You go fuck yourself!" the outlaw told the

man. He stared hard at the chaplain. "With a nose like you're wearin', you gotta be a damn Jew."

"That's right, son," the man said. "But I've ministered to the needs of all faiths over the years. Is there anything you want to tell me? Besides committing an impossible act upon my person, that is."

If the outlaw did have anything worth saying, it died on his lips. The Jewish chaplain shook his head. "So much hate in them. Why, General?"

"It isn't hate, Nat. It's ignorance. And it's nobody's fault but their own. They have—had— brains. They could have read, studied, learned, but they chose not to. They chose to remain ignorant and bigoted and narrow-minded. It was all up to them. The blame cannot be placed on any*thing* else, or any*body* else."

"You really believe that, don't you, General?"

"I not only believe it, I know it's true. And I think you do too, or you wouldn't be here. And don't give me any garbage about your love for all humanity and about your being a nonviolent type, Nat; I've seen you pick up an M-16 too many times and use it when the going got rough."

The chaplain smiled, and then laughed, as he stood in the middle of destruction and death. "No secrets from you, huh, General?"

"Not many, Nat," Ben said. "Not many."

The Jewish chaplain spotted the Baptist chaplain kneeling beside a dying outlaw and walked over to join him, his motives being, Ben guessed, that between the two of them they might be able to get the outlaw bastard located closer to the fringes of hell, instead of near the hotter and more unpleasant interior.

"We'll have it wrapped up here in about an hour, General," a platoon leader told Ben. "Burn the bodies of the dead?"

Ben nodded. "Yes. Any prisoners?"

"There won't be in about twenty minutes," the lieutenant said flatly.

8

Ben received word that Ike and his battalions were kicking ass and taking names all the way from New Hazelton to Prince Rupert. There had been a holdout of survivors in Terrace, and Ike had ordered an airlift of badly needed supplies flown into that small city's airfield. Another Rebel outpost was intact.

Ben headed north on 97, leaving the smoking ruins of Dawson Creek behind him, and linked up with his other battalions at Fort St. John. It was a seventy-five-mile run, and, since there was a good airfield outside Fort St. John, Ben decided to bivouac there and wait for the planes to resupply them. Before the Great War, Fort St. John had been a thriving city of nearly fifteen thousand. Now there were about four hundred people who straggled in from the brush after the outlaws pulled out for Alaska.

A tough and hardy bunch, they had not left their homes and businesses out of fear of the outlaws and assorted human scum, but simply because the outlaws were so numerous it would have been foolish to try to stand and fight.

"You and your people did the right thing," Ben told the leader of the group. "If you had not taken to the brush, you would have all been long dead." Ben brought the group's leaders up to date on what had taken place in the southern part of the province and of the outposts they had established along the way.

"That's for us," the spokesperson for all the survivors told Ben. "I was an advocate of Canada joining the United States long before the Great War fell on us."

"We'll get you set up," Ben assured the woman. And another bright spot of order and reason was in place amid the darkness of anarchy that surrounded them.

After dinner, Ben spread maps out on a long table in the meeting room of what had once been a social lodge of some sort and began studying the route that lay ahead of them.

"It's right at nine hundred and fifty miles from here to the Yukon border, and only one way to get there." He thumped the map. "Highway 97. Flybys have reports that many bridges are blown, so that means our engineers will be busy with Bailey bridges and our people will have to be constantly on the alert for ambushes. We're going to have eyes-in-the-skies ahead of us at all times. But even with all that going for us, we can't ever afford to let down our guard. Probably ninety percent of our route is paved, so with the exception of having to ford rivers where the bridges have been blown, we'll make good time. Ike's route, however, on the Cassiar Highway, has a lot of sections of gravel on it. He'll be slowed up. His route is about 650 miles to the border, as compared to our 950, so we should arrive there at about the same time.

"The outlaws will probably hit us on this run, people, and it's a sure bet they'll do it more than once, so heads up at all times. There are no major towns of any size on this run. Fort Nelson is the only place that has, according to these old maps, a runway large enough to land our supply planes. We'll have to be resupplied there. Flybys show the airfield to be intact. So that leads me to think the outlaws also have planes they're using. Please keep in mind at all times that this bunch of outlaws we'll be facing is the smartest of the lot. They're survivors; they've stayed alive for years and for sure they have defense lines that we're going to be hard-pressed to crack. So I don't want anybody to get arrogant about this campaign just because it's been relatively easy up to this point.

"Dan, start your Scouts out in the morning. The main column will be a day behind them. The choppers will go up two hours before we push off. Questions?"

There were none.

"Let's do it," Ben said.

The Rebels covered a hundred miles the first day. That was the most they would cover that quickly until reaching the Yukon. The outlaws did not want to cut themselves off from an escape route they might have to use very fast, so most of the blown bridges were between Fort St. John and the Yukon border.

The Rebels bivouacked near the ruins of what had once been the tiny town of Pink Mountain. A Rebel search party found the bones of what appeared to be several hundred people. They had been shot—according to the doctors—and buried in a mass grave: men, women, children, and tiny infants.

After the pit had been fully uncovered—or as much as Ben would allow—Chase knelt down and inspected one skeleton. He shook his head and cursed.

"What's the matter?" Dan asked. "Other than the obvious, of course."

"This woman was pregnant," the doctor said, standing up. "Baby looks to be—this is just a guess—about seven months old. Sorry, goddamn bastards!"

"Cover it up," Ben ordered. "We'll have a service for these poor people. That's about the only thing we can do for them."

"We can avenge them," Dr. Chase said hotly.

"We don't know who did it," Ben spoke softly. "Perhaps we've already killed those responsible."

Striganov stepped out of the pit, a lady's locket in his hand, the lid open. "No, we haven't," he said. He held out a piece of very thin paper, onion skin, Ben guessed.

Georgi Striganov read: "'Jack Hayes and Art

LeBarre and gangs will kill us in the morning. God have mercy on our souls. Praise General Ben Raines and hasten his arrival.' It appears to have been nearly the entire town in this pit."

"Yes. Looks that way," Ben said softly. "Cover it back up and get the chaplains." He walked back to his tent and stepped inside, closing the flap.

"Perhaps I should not have read the note," the Russian remarked.

Emil shook his head. "No, General Striganov. You did exactly the right thing. The reading of that note just may have saved a hundred or more Rebel lives and shortened this campaign by weeks, maybe months."

"Sometimes, Emil," Therm said, looking at the small man, "you make a lot of sense. You're right. Ben will show no mercy from this point on. He will be relentless in his pursuit and destruction of the outlaw gangs."

Dan picked up a shovel. Colonel he was, but he would order no man to do work that he was perfectly capable of doing and near enough to do. "Let's get to it, lads and lassies," he said, going to work. "Let's finish while we have the light."

Ben was silent as they pulled out at dawn the next morning, and none of his team, including Linda, offered to break into his thoughts.

Finally, after about an hour, Ben said, "That was a nice service the chaplains held for the victims of that massacre. I hope it makes them rest easier in that . . . motherfucking pit!"

Everyone then knew that Ben was not in a real peachy mood.

"Don't you wish that?" Ben asked Coop.

"Yes, sir! I sure do."

"Fine."

Smoot peeked out from under Jersey's arm, uncertain whether to hop into the front seat and snuggle next to Ben or stay right where she was.

She elected to stay right where she was.

"Smart pup," Jersey muttered, scratching Smoot behind the ears.

"Did you say something, Jersey?" Ben asked.

"Not a thing, General."

They rode on in silence for another few miles. Ben said, "Corrie, bump Base Camp One and have them get busy printing surrender leaflets. I want them up here ASAP. The wording will be as follows: A message from General Ben Raines, commanding officer of the Rebel Army, to all outlaws residing in the state of Alaska. The day of the criminal is over. This will be your only chance to surrender. Once the campaign against you begins, all surrender and amnesty terms will be withdrawn. The Rebel Army will take no prisoners. Anyone who initiates any form of hostile act against a member of the Rebel Army will be shot on sight. Lay down your weapons and surrender peacefully. This will be your only chance to do so. Got all that, Corrie?"

"Yes, sir."

"Bump all commanders and inform them of that decision."

"Right, sir."

Ben turned his head to gaze out the window. "I hate punks," he said.

When the long column reached Fort Nelson, the leaflets were waiting for Ben. Ben read over the leaflets and nodded his head in approval.

"Beth, make a note that the pilots will start dropping the leaflets three days before we cross over the Alaskan border. I want everyone up there to have the opportunity to read it and decide their fate."

"Yes, sir."

"Get all battalion commanders, company commanders, and platoon leaders over here."

"Right now, sir."

"The old man is hot, huh?" a rebel asked Beth as she rounded up all the personnel.

"Steaming. I've been with him for a long time, and I've never seen him this angry. His eyes make you want to back up."

"This is going to be one hell of a campaign."

"Brother, you damn sure got that right," Beth told him.

The commanders, from battalion to platoon, gathered in a classroom of an old high school in Fort Nelson. Ben passed around the leaflets for all to read.

"That's the way it's going to be, people. No exceptions except for children. I'm going to give the outlaws seventy-two hours to reach a decision, and then we start burying them. That is a figure of speech only; I have no intention of wasting time

111

burying the bastards. They can rot where they fall until we have time to douse them with gasoline and burn them. I figure three days to Watson Lake; we link up with the other battalions there. We'll take Highway 1 to Whitehorse, Whitehorse into Alaska. The planes will take off from Whitehorse, dropping the leaflets. Also at Whitehorse our communications people will start bombarding the airwaves with surrender messages. Those will cease the instant we cross into Alaska.

"Ike and his people will take Alaska 2 and proceed toward Fairbanks. I will lead the assault against Anchorage. That's it, people. Ike's battalions will be here in the morning. We shove off the next day."

So far, it had been a cakewalk for the Rebels. For nearly two thousand miles they had seen little combat. To a person they knew all that was about to change. The mood of the Rebels changed abruptly. Most horseplay ceased and the men and women became serious. Letters were written and chaplains suddenly got very busy. Equipment was checked—for the umpteenth time, but this time much more carefully. The Rebels all knew the crud holed up in Alaska had had years to prepare for this invasion and it was going to be a tough one.

The battalion commanders spent hours going over maps of the state. Recon pilots brought back pictures and graphs from their heat-seekers, detailing where the heaviest concentrations of warm, breathing bodies were located.

The columns rolled slowly into Whitehorse and found survivors waiting for them.

The men, women, and children who had been forced to live in the brush to survive stood in the streets and watched in silence, relief on their faces as the miles-long column rolled into and through the small city.

The Rebels had been on the road for nearly six weeks.

"Almost a thousand people here now, General," Ben was informed. "And more coming in. We've been forced to live in small groups, living off the land and keeping a very low profile."

"I understand. All that is over, now. What can you tell me about the outlaws up in Alaska?"

"The scum of the earth," a woman said. "And worse even more now that Jack Hayes and Art LeBarre and their gangs of trash have joined them. Everyone here can tell you horror stories about the gangs now up in Alaska."

"Yes," another survivor said. "We've read your surrender leaflets. They won't surrender, General. They can't. They know that even if you gave them amnesty, we'd kill them the instant we spotted them. There is that much hate and loathing and contempt for them among us. They've made our lives a living hell for years. It's indescribable."

"I was taken prisoner several years ago," another woman said. "I was raped repeatedly and watched my youngest daughter raped and sodomized until she died. She was ten. I swear before God Almighty I will kill any who surrender to you. Or you'll have to kill me."

"Get your lives back in order," Ben told the crowd. "We'll have planes coming in daily from our Base Camp One, bringing in supplies and food and medicines for you people. The reign of terror is just about over in the northern hemisphere."

Jack Hayes, Art LeBarre, and dozens of other gang leaders who had fled to Alaska to escape the wrath of Ben Raines and his Rebel army read the leaflets that had dropped from bellies of high-flying airplanes all over the eastern half of Alaska.

"This crap don't mean jack-shit to me," a burly gang leader called Foley said. "Outside of Alaska, my life ain't worth a plugged nickel . . . and a nickel ain't been worth nothin' in years. This goddamn Ben Raines is just gonna have to come in here and dig me out. To hell with him." He wadded up the surrender paper and threw it on the floor.

The others meeting in the lodge just east of the Denali National Park were unanimous in that, some a bit more philosophical than Foley.

"We've had a good run, boys," Dixson said. "We've had our share of pussy and tight asses. Now we got to pay the piper. And the man tootin' the horn is Ben Raines." He chuckled, but it contained a grimness. "I remember when Raines first surfaced after the Great War. Ever'body said he wouldn't last. Ever'body was wrong. We best start diggin' in, boys. There's gonna be hell to pay in a few days."

"You act like we're beat 'fore we start?" Outlaw Bonny Jefferson said.

"Oh, we are," Dixson said. "It'll take Raines some time to do it, but we're dead in the dirt, boys."

"That's your ass!" Smithers said.

Dixson smiled. "Yours, too, pal."

9

Ben took his contingent of Rebels and moved toward Alaska on Highway 1. They would stop at Beaver Creek—some three hundred miles away—and wait until Ike's people made their half circle, from Whitehorse to Dawson, crossing over into Alaska and linking up with Ben at Tok, Alaska. The commanders would then meet for one final briefing before they again split their forces for the initial campaign.

Neither force encountered any more blown bridges on this last leg toward Northstar. Neither did they see any signs of life, friendly or hostile.

What they saw was a lot of beautiful country; a beautiful and pristine land, as it must have been when God made it.

"I got a question, General," Cooper said.

"Let's hear it."

"What about Juneau and Sitka and Ketchikan?"

"Juneau's the old capital, Coop," Ben told him. "There are a lot of towns down in that area that are

117

inaccessible by car. I don't know what we're going to do about them. Flyovers show that there are people in that area—all over that area. But not that many of them. We don't know whether they are friendly or hostile. They won't respond to radio calls. Maybe they just want to be left alone. We don't know. We'll just have to deal with that problem on the way out."

They were traveling the Alaska Highway, about a hundred miles from Beaver Creek, when a forward recon team bumped Corrie.

"Scouts have prisoners, sir," Corrie informed Ben. "About fifty outlaws surrendered and are asking for amnesty."

"We'll honor their requests. Where are they?"

"Just up ahead at a little place called Destruction Bay."

"We'll bivouac there for the night. I want to interrogate these outlaws."

Ben sat behind a table and stared at the leaders of the surrendered band. They were a beaten and woebegone-looking bunch, beaten without the Rebels having to fire a shot at any of them.

"When we leave this area," Ben told them, "you people are free to go. But I warn you now, you will not be armed and if any citizens that you men terrorized over the years finds you, they'll kill you on the spot."

"We know," one outlaw said. "They'll not find us. Speakin' just for me, I'm headin' into the deep timber and keepin' my head down for a couple of years. You'll never see me again, General. I promise you that. And I thank you for lettin' us live."

"What are we facing in Alaska?"

"About fifteen thousand men and women," another said. "They got machine guns, mortars, and some light artillery."

"Any Night People in the cities?"

"No, sir. We killed them all. Or most of them. If they's any left, we don't know where they are."

"Prisoners?"

"Lots of slaves. As soon as you cross over, gang leaders like Foley and Dixson and a dozen others will tell you that if you attack them, they'll kill the slaves. But they're going to kill them anyways, General. That's the plan. They ain't gonna tote them slaves along; it would slow them down too much."

Ben stood up and pointed to a map. "What is west of Highways 3 and the Dalton Highway?"

"Eskimos and Indians. We left them alone and they done the same to us."

"Juneau and Sitka and Ketchikan?"

"They're in the hands of some sort of peacenik groups. Environmentalists, I guess you'd call them. They come in real fast, right after the Great War. They don't bother nobody 'less you bother them. Then they'll fight like hell. Outlaws and warlords has tried to take them a dozen times over the years. Ain't nobody managed to run 'em out yet and I don't figure anybody ever will. Unless it's you people."

Ben shook his head. The environmentalists

were safe from the advancing Rebels. Lovers of the Earth and the animals were welcomed by the Rebels. He dismissed the surrendered outlaws and returned to the studying of maps. After an hour, he rubbed his eyes and left the maps for a later time. He walked outside to stand by the shores of Kluane Lake. It was late afternoon, and the mercury hovered between cool and downright cold.

Ben's team stood away from him, but close enough to form a protective blanket around him. Ben picked up a flat stone and skipped it across the waters, then squatted down to gaze across the rippled waters of the lake. He was testing the knee that had been operated on back during the winter months in California. Before the operation, he would have experienced pain within seconds of squatting down. Now he smiled. The knee was pain-free.

He stood up quickly. Again, the knee was free of pain. He turned to face his team, spinning on the balls of his feet. Again there was no pain.

He smiled at his team. "Let's go kick the shit out of some outlaws, people."

Ben and his battalions traveled the final one hundred miles to the Alaskan border and stood down just one mile from the land of "The Last Frontier." He turned to Corrie.

"What's the word on Ike?"

"Standing ready to go, General."

"All the leaflets been dropped?"

"Yes, sir. Thousands of them. Ike reports no

further outlaws have offered to meet our surrender terms in his sector."

"Then they must be awfully anxious to die," Ben said. He took a final puff of his cigarette and carefully ground out the butt under the heel of his boot. "All right, Corrie, give the orders to take Northstar."

Scouts moved out across the border. They would range several miles ahead of the main columns. When they reported back in, the largest known standing army in the world, under the command of one man, moved across the border and entered the last bastion of organized lawlessness in the northern hemisphere. There was still Sister Voleta to deal with; but Ben wasn't worried about that witch. He would step on her like a bug on the return trip East.

Once firmly inside the Alaskan borders, Ben halted and waited for word from the Scouts. They had orders to take a few prisoners alive and bring them back to Ben. Ben knew that would not take long.

Corrie said, "Both our Scouts and Ike's Scouts are in a firefight, sir. Our people say they'll be bringing some live talkies back in a few minutes."

Ben smiled. "Confident, aren't they?"

"They had a good teacher," Jersey said, looking at Ben.

The four prisoners were scared and with good reason. They were standing in front of Ben Raines, the most powerful man—in terms of military might—in the known world. Any bravado they might have had in them had vanished when they looked into the muzzles of Rebel rifles. Now it was up to this one man whether they lived or died.

"You men talk to me," Ben told them. "And you tell me the truth when I ask you a question. If you live or die depends on your truthfulness. What is between here and Northway Junction?"

"If we tell you a lie, how're you gonna do anything to us once we're gone one direction and you another?" an outlaw challenged.

"Because you're going with us," Ben said with a smile. "And if you've told us a lie about an ambush or troop strength, I'll shoot you. Is that understood?"

"Couldn't be any plainer," another outlaw said. "They's people waitin' for your boys and girls at Northway Junction. The plan is to fall back to Northway, then to Nabesna Village, and finally to use three-wheelers overland to Tetlin on the lake. They'll booby-trap there and bug out 'crost country to Highway 1. That's the plan."

"Prisoners? Slaves?"

"No, sir," another said. "What slaves there was along this stretch has done been killed."

"Did you hold slaves?" Ben asked softly.

"No, sir. We was soldiers. Only the gang leaders and such has the right to own slaves."

"Is that the way it is all over Alaska?"

"I . . . can't rightly say, General. Some gang leaders and warlords has different rules. Since the Great War, we pretty much stay in our own territory. It ain't safe to go wanderin' around much."

"No honor among thieves?" Ben asked, his smile hard.

"Yes, sir," the fourth prisoner said. "I reckon it's something like that."

Ben waved them away. When they were gone, he turned to Georgi Striganov, Dan Gray, and the other commanders of his battalions. "It's about sixty miles to Northway Junction. We'll advance and play their game for a time. When we get to the cut-off point, we'll hold on the main highway and let the choppers go to work."

Ben paused, studying a map. "I want recon flights, fixed-wing and helicopter, over this area south of us, all the way down to the Gulf of Alaska. If there are friendlies down there, I want them to know who we are. If they are hostile, get rid of them."

"Right, sir," Dan said, and left to get the planes and choppers up.

"Corrie, let's find out what's going on with Ike."

Within seconds, Ike came on the horn. "The town of Boundary is ours, Ben. It wasn't much of a fight. We've got about a 2,100-foot runway here in fair shape. Earth and gravel."

"Prisoners?"

"They didn't like our terms of surrender. We're scooping out a hole now."

"That's ten-four. We're moving out." Ben looked at an old travel guide of Alaska. "There's a five-thousand-foot runway at Northway. We'll leave a contingent there and use that as a base for aircraft reconing south. Let's roll, people. The scenic beauties of Alaska await us."

"I wonder if anyone can make me some mukluks?" Cooper said.

"Hell, Cooper," Beth said. "You didn't even know what they were until you read about them a few minutes ago."

"I'll give you a knot on the head if you don't keep this damn wagon between the ditches," Jersey said.

"Drive," Ben said, climbing into the wagon and putting an end to the friendly bickering. He looked around. Smoot was beside Linda. He winked at Linda and she smiled.

Moments later, after listening intently to a message coming through her earphones, Corrie said, "Base Camp One just confirmed that we are now high-tech in weapons, sir. The first plane-loads of rockets for the helicopters is on their way. Anything the attack helicopters could do before the Great War, they can do again. With the exception of nuclear warheads."

For two years, since instructors had been found for the attack helicopters, Ben's war machine at Base Camp One had been working around the clock, refurbishing the 'copters' deadly arsenal. Eventually, pilots would be trained to fly the big jet transports. But so far, only a few men and women could fly the big jets.

General Georgi Striganov now had a dozen of the awesome Mi-24 Hind D and E attack heli-copters, with several more dozen grounded for lack of trained pilots. It was taking time, but soon the

Rebels would be adequately equipped to head for Europe. Ben figured a maximum of six months and they could put out to sea.

Providing they could find qualified personnel to "drive the goddamn boats," as Ben often put it.

"Bump Ike," Ben said, after a dozen miles had rolled by. "We want to coordinate this right down to the second."

"Thirty miles from target," Corrie said.

Ben looked at his watch. "We're right on line. Tell Georgi to get his attack choppers warming up and ready to go. We're not going to leave very much behind us, folks. I don't like it, but that's the way it has to be." Ben was thoughtful for a moment, then he said, "To hell with it. Bring the column to a halt. Order the Hinds in. I'll be damned if I'll lose Rebels when it doesn't have to be. Order Ike to halt and hold what he's got."

"General Striganov agrees, sir. His Hinds are ready."

"Tell them to get airborne."

Within minutes, the big Hinds, which have been called flying tanks, were slapping the air with their huge fifty-five-foot main blades. Their arsenal was not just impressive, it was awesome. Each Hind carried, on its twin-launch rails, Swatter and Sagger missiles, two thirty-two-round rocket launchers for 57mm rockets, a 23mm twin-barrel cannon, Grail antiaircraft missiles (converted for ground targets), 240mm, 210mm, and 160mm rockets, and two 250-pound bombs.

Georgi rode up on a motorcycle he'd borrowed from one of the outlaw bikers now aligned with the Rebels and grinned at Ben. "They'll save many Rebel lives, I believe."

"Yes," Ben agreed.

"They're beautiful, in a deadly sort of way," Beth remarked, standing by the side of the big nine-passenger wagon.

"They won't even reach cruising speed," the Russian said. "That's 185 miles an hour. They'll be over the target in a few minutes. I have given them orders for the first six to attack the town, the second six to pursue the outlaws on their three-wheelers and finish them."

Ben nodded. "Corrie, advise Ike to have his Apaches ready to assault Tok in the morning. If need be," he added.

"Yes, sir."

Huge columns of smoke began rising from the towns as a dozen 250-pound bombs were dropped on Northway and Northway Junction. Thirty miles away, those in the column could not hear the rattle of chain guns and the slashing of rockets, but they knew the towns were finished.

Striganov had returned to his command.

"That's it, General," Corrie said. "The towns are clear."

"Move out," Ben ordered.

By the time Ben's column had reached the smoking, burning ruins of the towns the Hinds were returning, having chased the outlaws into the brush and finished them.

There was nothing left of the small villages except broken and charred bodies of the outlaws who had been caught by the deadly fire of the gunships before they could spring their ambush. Ben left them for the carrions.

"Move on up toward Tetlin Junction," he ordered. "We'll bivouac about twenty miles from the town." He lifted a map. "Says here there isn't much to the place. But you can bet it's big enough to hold a few outlaws."

Linda had been strangely silent. As they moved out, she said, "Surely by now they know they can't beat us. They have—according to what we've learned—very good communications equipment. So word has to have spread throughout the country. Would you still accept their surrender, Ben?"

"No," Ben said. "I would not. I've offered them surrender terms. They refused. To hell with them."

"Is that your final word, Ben?" she asked softly, as she petted Smoot.

"That is my final word."

"I wonder if they realize that?" she asked.

"They know my reputation."

"I wonder what they're thinking?"

10

The Athabascan Indians had been long gone from Tok—pronounced like coke—and had left the town to the outlaws. It had once held a population of about twelve hundred. But for years now it had been the headquarters of an outlaw who called himself Moose. Moose looked at his band of crud, punks, and trash and shook his head. They numbered about three hundred, and although they were heavily armed and well-armed, Moose knew with a sinking feeling that one platoon of Raines's Rebels could wipe out their asses and not even work up a sweat doing it.

He had been stunned speechless when four of the men from Northway and Northway Junction had staggered into his town, all wild-eyed and scared shitless, telling tales of attack helicopters as big as tanks. Moose knew those had to be the Russian Hind helicopters. And if Raines had those, it stood to reason he also had the Apache, Cobra, and Huey gunships.

For years, limited to infantry-style warfare, Ben Raines had been kicking ass all over the United States. But now he had gone high tech. The son of a bitch!

And Moose knew the goddamn law-and-order bastard wasn't about to accept any surrender now. He'd laid out his terms and given them a few days to either accept or reject. Now it was too late. Raines didn't believe in jacking around with outlaws.

Moose longed for the old days—really, not that many years back—when even a piss-poor lawyer could snort and beller and moan and sob and get a murderer off with only a few years in the bucket.

The good old days.

No more.

In the outposts that Raines had established in the lower forty-eight, what lawyers there were (those who would even admit to being an attorney) walked light and didn't rock the boat around Rebels. Ben Raines didn't like lawyers, and that meant that the Rebels didn't like lawyers.

"Shit!" Moose said.

"Do we make a fight of it, Moose?" one of his lieutenants asked.

"Are you out of your damn mind?" Moose said, looking at the man. "Hell, no, we don't stand and fight."

"What are we gonna do, Moose?" his woman, Big Jean asked.

"Carry our asses out of here, that's what. Get all the rest of our shit packed. We're pullin' out now!"

"Where?" she asked.

Moose sighed. Tell the truth, he didn't know. Most, so he'd heard on the short wave, were heading into the cities. But the cities were going to be death traps. Raines would just surround them and pound them into burning rubble with cannon fire.

"There ain't no stoppin' that man," Moose muttered. "It's over for us."

Big Jean started crying. Moose popped her on the side of the head with a big hamlike hand and knocked her up against a wall in the lobby of the hotel. "Shut up, bitch! We don't have the time for no female hysterics. Go pack our rags and let's get gone. Gordy, get me Jake on the horn."

Jake was the outlaw leader in a town about seventy miles south of Tok.

"Jake. Moose here. You heard about Raines and his people? Yeah. That's right. Listen to me, Jake. There ain't no way one gang alone is gonna stop that man. We got to group up and make some plans. You with me? OK. That's good. Get on the horn and talk to Buster down in Glenallen. You'll do that. Fine. Tell him to talk it up with guys he can trust. I'll be seein' you in about two-three hours."

Moose looked around the old hotel's lobby, which was filled to overflowing with his men. Some wore looks of undisguised fear at the merciless advancing of Raines Rebels; others were openly defiant. The words 'a fight to the death' jumped into the brain of Moose. *There ain't no turnin' back for none of us. We either win, or we die.*

131

Moose looked at the message from Ben Raines, lying on the old front desk of the hotel. His eyes picked out lines: THIS WILL BE YOUR ONLY CHANCE TO SURRENDER. THE DAY OF THE CRIMINAL IS OVER. THE REBEL ARMY WILL TAKE NO PRISONERS.

"Let's go, people," Moose said. "Get cracking. We got to clear out of here. Raines is on the way."

"It says here," Beth said, reading from a tattered copy of an Alaskan travel guide, "that this hotel offers clean, comfortable rooms starting at twenty-five dollars a night."

"I bet we can beat that price," Coop said. "We'll just have to dicker a little bit with the desk clerk."

"Coming up on the town," Corrie said, after receiving a message from the Scouts. "Scouts say it's deserted."

"Keep Smoot on a leash," Ben said. "There are lots of huskies running loose. Probably reverted back to the wild to stay alive. They'll be running in packs; we've all seen them. Pull up over there, Coop. By that hotel."

Scouts were moving from building to building, checking each one carefully for booby traps. Ben and his team waited by the wagon until the all clear was given.

"We found where they'd planned to booby-trap the place," Dan said. "But from the looks of things, they pulled out in such a hurry they didn't take the time to activate the explosives. They're certainly on the run."

"But to where?" Georgi Striganov asked, lifting a map. "If they get west of Highway 3, we'll have lost them. It would take years to comb out that area."

Ben shook his head. "They'd die out there. Most wouldn't survive the first winter. They'll make a stand of it somewhere along the way. They have to."

Smoot did not fight the leash, choosing to sit close to Beth. The husky mascot seemed to realize that this was dangerous country and there were too many half-wild dogs running around looking for something to eat. And that Smoot would fit the menu.

"Ike coming in," Ben was informed. "'Bout two miles out of town."

"We didn't see anything," Ike told Ben. The commanders sat in the dining room of the old Westmark Hotel. "We met that small bit of resistance once we got inside the border, and after that, nothing."

"General," Dan said, walking up to the table.

Ben looked up. Dan had a very grim expression on his face. "What's wrong, Dan?"

"Another mass grave just outside of town. It's years old. Doctor Chase says it looks like the people were forced to stand in the pit and were then machine-gunned. Men, women, kids, dogs, and cats."

Ben slowly nodded his head. "Have the chaplains conduct a service."

"We have a few survivors, General. They've been living, or existing is a better word, just north

133

of the town, across the Tanana River."

Ben interviewed the survivors. They were alive, but that was about the best one could say for them.

"We started out several hundred strong, General," one man told him. "But as the years wore on our numbers dropped. Due mostly to bad diet and the cold."

"Do you know anything about those in that mass grave outside of town?"

"Yes, sir. Moose and his gang hit the town about five years ago. We just weren't ready for them. We fought, but not nearly well enough. My wife, daughter, and the family pet were executed. I played dead and slipped out after dark. Joined some others in the brush."

"What we've heard all along is true," Ben said, speaking to no one in particular. "The outlaws up here are the most vicious of them all."

The survivor laughed, but the sound held little humor. "General, that's an understatement. These gangs roaming Alaska are the scum of the earth. The worst of the worst. Survivors of your purge in the lower forty-eight. They torture for the fun of it. They rape men and boys just to hear them scream. They'll pass women around like trading baseball cards. They'll pull the teeth out of men and women and boys and girls to insure they can't bite during forced oral sex. They set animals on fire for sport, betting on how long they can stay alive while burning. It's horrible."

"How many pockets of survivors are there?"

"In this area, you're looking at it. I don't know about west of the Alaskan Railroad. We didn't dare use radios to find other people. The outlaws have the best communications equipment. General, they made games out of hunting us down. They made captured men rape other male prisoners. They forced men and women and children to engage in the most disgusting and perverted of sexual acts." He could not continue.

The man started crying, openly and unashamedly. A medic gently led him away. The commanders sat in the dining room in silence for a moment.

Linda walked in, her face tight with rage. Ben looked up as she walked to the table.

"Don't ever ask me to assist any wounded outlaws, Ben." She had long ago stopped addressing him as "General." As intimate as they were, that would have been ridiculous.

"I won't," Ben's words were softly spoken. He waited, knowing there was more.

"A five-year-old girl just died on the operating table, Ben. She'd been raped and sodomized. Torn apart. The infection was too severe for us to save her."

Ben nodded his head. He'd seen it before; but it never failed to shock him. He poured Linda a glass of brandy and held it out for her. She cursed and slapped it out of his hand. Smoot went under the table and lay between Ben's boots. Several of the commanders gathered around wished they could do the same thing. Emil climbed out a rear window of the dining room, Thermopolis right behind him.

Ben sat and waited for Linda to unload on him.

He did not have a long wait. She cussed men who would do such horrible and inhuman things to another human being. She told Ben what she would like to see done to such people. Dan stood in the doorway for a moment, listening in awe, then beat a hasty retreat. Linda told Ben that if she ever got her hands on any outlaw, she would hack off his privates with a dull knife and cauterize the wound with a blow torch.

Ike grimaced and crossed his legs.

Dr. Chase entered the dining room and stood listening. When Linda paused for breath, he said, "And what she said goes double for me, Ben. I've been listening to horror stories for an hour. They're nearly unbelievable in their savagery. Don't expect my people to work on any outlaw."

"I won't ask any of you to do that, Lamar," Ben assured the man.

"Good." He whirled around and left the room, Linda right behind him.

Buddy had been listening just outside the door. When the doctor and RN had left, he walked to the table and sat down. "I talked with several of the survivors, Father. Lan Villar and his followers have taken over the Kenai National Wildlife Refuge. They know that you will not destroy it to get at them."

Ben grunted. Smart move on their part, he thought. "Go on, son."

"Lan has his HQ in the town of Kenai. It was about seventy five hundred population before the Great War. There is an eight thousand foot runway there. Natural gas and oil refineries are

136

located there. Lan Villar has about five thousand men in his army."

"Well, he managed to pick up a few, didn't he?" Ben said, pouring a fresh cup of coffee.

"More will surely join him as we advance," Ben's son said.

"Probably," Ben said, a strange smile on his lips.

"Something amusing?" Cecil asked.

"Maybe. Do you know where his HQ is located in the town, son?"

"As a matter of fact, I do. It's in the post office building, on Cavier Street."

"Interesting," Ben said. "Very interesting."

No one pressed him on his plans. Ben would work them out carefully in his mind and then lay them out for the others to see.

The commanders firmed up plans for the campaign—which so far had been a milk run—and then broke up the meeting, each returning to their unit. Ben walked the town, taking in what was left of the sights.

The restaurants were filthy from years of cooking and very little cleaning. The walls were caked with grease. Ben couldn't imagine anyone even remotely entertaining the thought of eating amid such filth.

The motels were just as bad, their mattresses infested with lice and fleas, their carpets alive with various tiny hopping and crawling critters.

Ben ordered the carpets and mattresses dragged outside and burned.

He was amused as he stood in front of a

restaurant whose sign proclaimed the best Mexican, American, and Italian food in all of Alaska.

Another cafe had a sign boasting the best sourdough pancakes in all of Alaska. He walked past a place that claimed to have in captivity the largest mosquito in all of Alaska, "Chained for the Public's Safety."

There were several thousand Rebels milling in and around Tok, talking and taking in the sights. No one knew how the outlaws managed to get close to Ben.

But they did, and suddenly he was flat on his back in the street, shot in the chest. He was not moving.

11

The firefight that followed the shooting of General Raines was very short and very savage. Platoons of Rebels threw themselves around the area where Ben lay, putting up a human barricade around him while the medics worked frantically. The outlaws that had shot Ben were put down hard. One was taken alive. He was very eager to talk. Then the Rebels hanged him from a flagpole at an old RV village.

Ike and Cecil followed the medics to the field hospital. A grim-faced Dr. Chase met them outside.

"I won't lie to you, boys," he told them. "It's bad. The bullet entered between armpit and flak-jacket. He must have been waving at someone when the sniper fired. The bullet shattered a rib and went wandering off somewhere. We can't find the bullet and Ben cannot—repeat, *cannot*—be moved. We won't know how much damage was done until we get inside. He's being opened up right now."

"What are the odds of him coming out of this?" Ike asked.

Lamar opened his mouth to speak. He closed his mouth and shook his head. He finally said, "Call the chaplains. Excuse me, I've got to get to the OR."

Cecil groaned and put a hand to his chest.

"What the hell's the matter with you?" Chase yelled.

"Must be indigestion," Cecil said, then he could not suppress the groan of pain that escaped his lips.

"Indigestion, hell. You haven't been taking your blood pressure medicine, have you, you big ox? Get him on the ground, Ike!" Chase said. "Medics!" he roared. "Get the hell out here."

"Blood pressure is off the wall," a medic said. "He's having a heart attack." He waved for a stretcher while Lamar was barking out orders.

Lamar turned to Ike seconds after Cecil was carried inside the field hospital. "You're in command, Ike. You've got to take over One Battalion and run the show. Cecil's out of it for the duration, I'm afraid."

"You knew he had a bum ticker, Lamar?"

"He wanted one more campaign, Ike. He was going to stay behind when Ben took the others to Europe."

"Lamar, I don't mean to put pressure on you, but I got to say this: if Ben . . ." he stumbled, unable to say the word. "If Ben . . . doesn't make

140

it, there'll be a bloodbath up here. No one will be able to contain these troops. They'll turn this land into bloody, smoking scorched earth, and nothing or no one will be able to stop them."

"You better try to do it, fatso," Chase told the chubby former SEAL. "Because once we doctors do what we can for Ben, the rest is going to be left up to God."

He walked into the field hospital. The crusty old doctor didn't want Ike to see the tears spilling out of his eyes.

"I am having a most difficult time holding my troops in check," General Georgi Striganov said, a mug of coffee in one big hand. He was sitting in the dining room of a motel. His troops included his own Russian personnel, that of his fellow Russian Rebet, and the French Canadian, Danjou.

"Likewise," the mercenary, West, admitted.

The other commanders, including Thermopolis, nodded in agreement. Thermopolis said, "My bikers are ready to kill anything that moves. I don't know how much longer I can hold them in check."

"What's the word on Dad?" Tina asked.

"The same as it was five minutes ago, kid," Ike told her. He had just returned from the hospital. "The doctors are having to look for the bullet with their fingers." He shuddered at the thought. "Buddy, you take over my Second Battalion."

Buddy stared at him. "I would prefer to continue operating on my own, Ike. I . . ."

"Goddamnit, did you hear me?" Ike roared. "Do

141

you want me to make that a direct order, *Captain* Raines?"

"No, sir," Buddy said softly. "I shall assume command immediately."

"Thank you. Dan, you take over Third Battalion and appoint someone to take over your Scouts."

"Right, sir."

"Buddy, put your XO in charge of your Rat Pack."

"Yes, sir."

"Tina, you and West will stay here with your battalions and support groups. I want this area secured and secured hard."

"Right, sir," they both said.

"Cecil was lucky. His heart attack was not a bad one. But it was a warning, Dr. Chase told me. He's to be flown back to Base Camp in the morning. He's out of this game for the duration. He will take over as permanent base commander down south . . ." He looked up as a Rebel ran into the room.

"General Raines just died! They're trying to get his heart started now."

It was all shades of blue, with a misty light that seemed to sparkle around Ben. He was in a tunnel, he guessed. A long tunnel. He could barely make out the entrance, or exit, at the other end.

He began walking toward the opening. But he was walking uphill, it seemed. It was hard going, and he was forced to stop for a rest.

There was someone standing in the opening. Ben smiled. His old high school sweetheart. He hadn't thought of her in years.

"Hello, Becky," he said.

"Ben," she said. "Turn around. Go back. It isn't time."

"Feels like it to me, Becky. I'm dead, aren't I?"

"Not for long, Ben. I'll see you when it's your time."

She vanished.

Salina took her place. A small boy stood by her side. Ben knew who that was. His son.

"This can't be hell, Salina. God wouldn't put a child in hell."

"You're looking good, Ben," she said.

"Good? I'm dead, baby!"

"No. You're just in limbo, Ben. It's not your time yet. See you, Ben."

She faded and Rani took her place. Jordy was with her. "Hi, Ben," Jordy called.

"Hi, Jordy."

"You go on back now, Ben," Rani said. "Go on. It's not your time." She vanished.

Jerre stood near the opening.

"Jerre," Ben said.

"It's good to see you, Ben. But it won't be for long. You haven't been called yet. The Force is not ready for you."

"The Force?"

"I can't explain that. Only death explains life's mysteries. And you've got a lot to do before that time comes. I told you years ago that you had places to go and great things to do. You haven't done them all yet. Ben? You've got a good woman now. She loves you. Love her in return while you both still have each other."

"How do you know about her?"

Jerre smiled.

"What do you mean: 'While we both still have each other?'"

"I'll see you, Ben." She faded from sight.

Ben awakened to intense pain and the murmur of voices.

"All right," he recognized Dr. Fieldman's voice. "It's beating on its own now. I think he's clear."

"Damn bullet was hiding under his lower gut," Doctor Lancaster said. "How the hell did it get down there?"

Ben opened his eyes and looked into the eyes of Linda Parsons. "You big bastard," she told him. "Don't you ever scare me like that again."

"Yes, dear," Ben muttered under the mask that covered his mouth and nose.

Cecil was wheeled into Ben's room the next morning. The men, close friends for years, grinned at each other. Cecil patted Ben's hand. Ben was unable to move either arm for the needles sticking into them.

"Ol' Hoss," Ben said, his words softly spoken but with firmness behind them. "You'll be back before you know it."

Cecil shook his head. "No, Ben. I shouldn't have come on this campaign. Lamar tried to talk me out of it back in California. But . . . hell, you know how it is about combat and men.''

"I know."

"I have good news, ol' buddy. You'll be back on your feet in no time. The bullet was lodged near your heart. They found the slight tear. It fell during all the doctors' fumbling around and bounced off your heart, stopping it momentarily. You're not that badly hurt."

"I was in a tunnel, Cec. While I was dead. I saw and spoke with Salina and my son. With Rani and Jordy. With Jerre. With my old high school sweetheart, Becky. I was dead, Cec. There is life after death."

"I've never doubted it, Ben." He gripped Ben's arm. "I've got to go, Ben. The force be with you," he said with a grin.

Ben's eyes turned serious. "Why did you say that?"

"It's from that old movie, Ben. You know? What's the matter?"

"Jerre told me about the Force. I think she wanted to tell me more but didn't have the time, or she wasn't permitted to do so."

"Jerre?" Dr. Chase said, entering the room. "What about Jerre?"

Ben told him what he had experienced in death.

Lamar nodded his head. "I read a book about the Force, years ago. A horror story." He looked at Ben. "Hell, I just remembered something: you wrote it!"

"Yes. I remember it. *Darkly, The Thunder*. I recall now that I felt so strange while I was doing that manuscript. It was an . . . eerie sensation. Like I was trodding on very shaky ground . . . unexplored ground."*

Chase looked at Ben for a moment. "A great many people who died on the operating table and had their hearts started again have spoken of being in a tunnel with a light at the end of it. I don't know what it represents, other than a sign there is life after death. In any case, we're all glad to have you back, Ben. You'd better get ready for your flight, Cecil."

The men said their goodbyes and Cecil was wheeled out of Ben's room. "I'm going to give you a few minutes with Ike, Ben. And I mean a *few* minutes."

"All right, Lamar. You're the boss."

Ike walked in, all smiles.

"Sit down, Ike. We haven't got much time. I'm pretty tired. Bring me up to date."

"I've taken over your battalion, Ben. I've put Buddy in charge of Second Battalion. Dan has taken command of Third Battalion. Four and Nine Battalions will remain here at Tok. The rest of us will push off and continue the Northstar campaign."

"That sounds good to me, Ike. Tell me how you plan the assault."

"Second, Third, and Fifth Battalions, under the command of Georgi Striganov, will take Fairbanks. I'll take One, Six, Seven, and Eight Battalions into Anchorage."

"Fine. As soon as Fairbanks and Anchorage are

*DARKLY THE THUNDER—ZEBRA BOOKS

taken, wait for Dan before you start the assault against the Kenai Peninsula. I promised Dan first crack at Lan Villar."

"Good enough. When does Chase say you'll be back on top?"

"He won't say. Weeks, I'm sure. Did you find out how those outlaws got past our security?"

"Yes. They were hiding under the floor of a building. They were a suicide team."

"They damn near accomplished their mission. Tell the people back at Base Camp One to start work on body armor that gives more protection at the armpits. That's a very uncomfortable place to get shot," Ben said with a smile.

Chase entered the room. "That's it, Ike," the chief of medicine said. "Out."

Ike did not argue. He stood up, patted Ben on the arm, and left the room.

Chase waited while a nurse took temperature, BP, and so forth, marked his chart, and left the room. "You're out of this fight, Ben. Resign yourself to that fact. For now, get some rest. You won't have any more visitors this day. I've posted guards outside this room to insure that. Night, night, General."

The men and women of Second Battalion looked at Buddy from formation. They had fought under Ike's command since inception, and a new CO, while not unsettling to any of them, was at least a very strange feeling. They had no doubts about Buddy's ability to lead. He'd proven that he was a

147

very capable leader. If there had been any doubts about that, Ike would not have chosen him.

But the older Rebels all knew that the shifting around of Sergeant-Major Adamson to the Second Battalion was intended as a stabilizing force for the young Buddy, someone to lean on if questions arose. Nobody argued with a Command Sergeant-Major. Not even Ben Raines.

Third Battalion stared at Colonel Dan Gray as he faced them a day before jump-off time. Dan Gray was almost as much of a living legend as Ben Raines, Cecil Jefferys, and Ike McGowan.

"There will be very few changes made," Dan assured them. "I do not intend to take General Jefferys's place. That would be impossible. No one could do that. We'll just continue doing our jobs and get this Northstar affair wrapped up neatly. Stand down until 0500 tomorrow morning."

Ben looked at his son. "If Ike didn't think you could do the job, boy, he wouldn't have put you in command. So relax."

"It's a strange feeling commanding so many people, Father. I don't know whether I like the feeling of having so many lives riding on my words."

"Which is why Striganov is overall commander of the three battalions for this assault. Get used to command, son. I won't be around forever. This incident shows how vulnerable I am—we all are. It's all going to fall on your shoulders someday."

"Mine and Tina's," the young man corrected.

"That's true. But Tina and West will be married someday. When they do, I expect them to drop out of combat and settle down. Both of them want a family. They both have said as much. Ask questions, son. If you're in doubt, ask questions. Don't be afraid to do so. The Rebels won't lose any respect for you if you do. They'll lose respect for you if you don't."

"I'll do my best, Father."

"I know you will. Now get out of here and get back to your command. Good luck, son."

Ben watched his son exit the room. Time to start turning part of it over to younger hands and hearts, he thought. Buddy's got to learn command. He cut his eyes as Chase walked in and looked at his chart.

"Your recuperative powers never cease to amaze me, Raines," the old doctor said. "BP has stabilized, temp is fine. You refuse pain medication. But if you think you're going to be back on your combat boots in a few weeks, you're wrong. We cut you wide open and spread your ribs and moved your innards around, Ben."

"I don't think that at all, Lamar. I won't be leading this campaign and I know it."

Chase took a chair by the side of the bed. "Don't push Buddy too hard, Ben. Let him have a taste of high command and see if it's to his liking. And it might not be."

"Yes. I know that. Whatever the outcome, I'm going to leave Dan at battalion level. I may shift Buddy to CO of the Scouts if he's too uncomfortable in battalion command. We'll see. Is there any chance I can be wheeled out in the morning to see the troops leave?"

"No."

Ben smiled. "You're a cranky old fart, you know that?"

Chase grinned. "Maybe. But as long as you're in that bed, in this hospital, you take orders from me. Now get some rest."

"If you'd take these needles out of my arms, I'd salute you."

"Not a chance. That's supper you're having right now. Pretend it's roast beef and gravy. Enjoy."

12

With a little help from Dr. Chase and a tiny pill, Ben slept right through the departure of the Rebels.

Far to the south and west, Lan Villar was mapping out plans.

"We know from radio interceptions that Raines was hurt bad enough to lay him out for this campaign," Lan told his commanders. "That's the hardest bastard to kill I ever saw in my life. We know he put his punk kid in charge of one battalion and shifted around some of his commanders. They left this morning to fight two fronts. One in Fairbanks, the other in Anchorage. That means they're saving us for last." He shook his head. "I never thought the son of a bitch would come up here. I thought we'd be safe this far north."

"We're never gonna be safe again," Parr said. The young man was not the same one who had come out of Florida with a large force of men to fight Ben Raines. He had learned the bitter hard truth about Ben Raines and his Rebels and it had torn his confidence to shreds.

Khamsin, the so-called Hot Wind from Libya, looked at the young man. Like Parr, Khamsin had been humiliated by the Rebels. He had watched his once-mighty army reduced to rabble. He had prayed to Allah for help in fighting Raines. Raines had kicked Allah out of the way and reduced the Hot Wind to a mild breeze.

Ashley smiled at Parr's words. It had been a long run for Ashley and his men. Now they were digging in for their final fight against the Rebels. And Ashley had no doubts as to what the outcome would be. He hated Ben Raines, but he was also envious of the man. Ben Raines was like that old-time Texas Ranger who said that you can't stop a man who knows he's right and just keeps on coming.

"Might as well stick a goddamn gun in our mouths and pull the trigger," Parr said.

Lan Villar didn't have anything to say about that. But in his mind he knew the truth in the young man's words. His only wish was that Dan Gray would not get his hands on him. He knew he would die awfully hard if the Englishman ever took him alive. And if there was a way, Dan Gray would do just that.

"You're awfully quiet, Lan," Ashley said.

Lan cut his eyes to stare at the man for a moment before replying. "You believe in life after death, Ashley?"

"Why . . . certainly."

"And you think you'll reside for eternity . . . where? Heaven or hell?"

Ashley smiled. "I don't believe in those places, Lan. Do you?"

The terrorist shook his head. "I don't know." He sat down on the corner of an old desk. "Tell me this: if offered to you, would any of you surrender to Ben Raines?"

None of them raised a hand.

"Now this is interesting," Lan said. "You, Parr, you've been pissing and moaning about dying ever since Raines tore our butts up down in the States. Why wouldn't you take surrender terms?"

The young man looked at the older man. "I ain't kowtowin' to Ben Raines and his damn Rebels. You think I'm gonna put my ass on a truck patch and grow vegetables and the like just because Ben Raines says I got to? I don't like rules and all that crap. I'll go out fightin'."

"Ashley?" Lan asked.

"I will go to my grave with words of astonishment on my tongue, knowing that Ben Raines has achieved the impossible: a nation, for all intents and purposes, free of crime. For when his Rebels finally storm and breach our last rampart and we die under the sword, he will have achieved that goal."

"You should have been a goddamn preacher," Parr muttered. "Storm the ramparts!"

"Cretin," Ashley said.

Khamsin shook his head and Lan laughed out loud.

Buddy, Georgi, and Dan hit no resistance until they reached the small town of Dot Lake, about fifty miles from Tok. The firefight lasted less than fifteen minutes before the outlaws were crushed, some of them quite literally so under the treads of main battle tanks. The Rebels surged forward toward Fairbanks. They took no prisoners.

The leader of the outlaw gang in the small town manged to get off one frantic message before a tank drove right through the wood-frame building and crushed him. The message chilled to the bone those outlaws listening all over Alaska.

"They's hundreds and hundreds of 'em!" he screamed into the microphone. "Fuckin' helicopters in the sky and Rebels ever' damn where and . . ."

He died under the treads of a battle tank.

The tank poked its lethal snout out the other side of the house and kept on clanking, its treads leaving a bloody trail behind it.

"Take your battalion and spearhead, Buddy," Striganov told the young man. "We can expect trouble at Delta Junction."

When Buddy came to the outskirts of the town, he pulled up short and stared at the grisly scene before him. A human chain had been stretched across the highway. The men and women and kids had been shot and then tied to wires stretched across the highway. The road was slick with their blood.

A crudely printed sign was hanging from the neck of one child: REBELS, ADVANCE ANY FURTHER AND THIS IS WHAT WE'LL DO WITH THE OTHER PRISONERS WE HOLD.

Buddy knew then that Scouts had seen this and reported back to General Striganov. The Russian was putting him to the test. Buddy met the eyes of his XO.

"The other prisoners are already dead," Buddy said. "That is their plan and it's been confirmed in a lot of towns. Have those bodies checked for booby traps and cut them down. We'll take the town and then bury those poor people."

"Yes, sir."

"They ain't buyin' it," an outlaw said from the edge of town, watching the action through long lenses and reporting back by radio.

A gang member dropped to his knees in the filthy house and began praying. "Why didn't I surrender when I had the chance?" he moaned. "I don't want them Rebels to put me up agin a wall and shoot me. I'm gonna surrender now. I'm gonna be good from now on. To hell with you people, I'm gonna . . ."

Die. The leader of this cell of crud and crap shot the man in the back of the head with a .45, splattering his brains all over the floor.

The slaves of the outlaws lay on the floor of another building, all dead. The outlaw leader heard the still-faint sounds of advancing tanks and a trickle of fear-sweat slid down his back. He clenched his fists in rage and fright. "Goddamn you, Ben Raines!" he screamed, just as the building he was standing in exploded in fire and chunks of concrete blocks and splintered wood. The outlaw was torn apart by the incoming 105mm M456 high-explosive rounds from an M60A3 main battle tank.

"Oh, God, help me!" A man who had spent the past decade and a half robbing and raping and murdering screamed in agony as tank treads smashed his legs into the roadbed. He tried to crawl away. A Rebel ended his yowling with an M-16 round to his head.

Half a hundred outlaws began running for their lives, some of them jumping into cars and four-wheel drive trucks and racing out of town. Fear-balls stuck in their throats as they tore up a slight grade, and from the crest they watched as two M24-Hinds rose into the air and unleashed their awesome firepower.

The two lead vehicles were lifted off their tires and exploded into a thousand pieces of white-hot metal as rockets incinerated those inside.

Twenty-three millimeter cannon, fired from twin barrels, began hammering the roadway, their rockets exploding fuel tanks and frying those inside the vehicles.

The Hinds circled and strafed the remaining vehicles until nothing was left but death, fire and ashes. The huge Hinds rose further into the air and hammered back to their refueling depots, their jobs done for this afternoon.

"Over here, sir!" a Rebel yelled to Buddy.

Buddy walked over and looked into one of the few buildings still intact in the town. The former slaves lay in still, silent, bloody rows, where they had been cut down by automatic weapons' fire.

"My God, there are children in there," Buddy whispered.

"Yes, sir," a Rebel spoke through tight lips. "We have prisoners, sir."

"You better not have them ten minutes from now," Buddy told her.

She smiled. The new battalion commander was working out just fine. She'd pass the word. Buddy Raines was just as hard-nosed and tough as his father. Some said he was better-looking than the General. She didn't think so. But then, she'd always liked older men.

Buddy waved to a platoon leader. "Yes, sir?"

"Get a burial team and get those bodies out of that building, Lieutenant. Prepare them for burial."

"Right, sir."

Striganov and Dan drove up and dismounted, walking over to the house. The Russian and the Englishman looked inside the building and grimaced at the sight.

Just as they were walking toward Buddy, the sounds of shots came to them.

"A pocket of trouble, son?" Georgi asked.

"Not anymore, sir," the young Raines replied. "That was a firing squad."

*　　*　　*

Ike and his battalions hit no trouble until they reached Glenallen. There, a stubborn group of outlaws had chosen to stand and fight rather than follow Moose's suggestion to get the hell gone from that area.

"You're all stupid," Moose had told them. "Dumb. Raines is gonna roll right over you and mash you flat."

"He's got a bunch of women in his army," the leader of the gang said. "Hell, women can't fight. Ever'body knows that. Women ain't good for nothin' 'cept to fuck."

"You're a fool!" Moose told him, then left that area as quickly as he could.

"Listen to this," Therm said, walking up to Ike. Thermopolis held a small transistor radio in his hand. "They've got the radio station going. All talk, you might say," he added dryly. He turned up the volume.

"All you cunts in the Rebel Army listen up," the voice came through the tiny speaker. "You show your ass in this town and you're gonna get a dick shoved up it."

A female tank commander popped her head out of the open hatch of a main battle tank. "What the hell did he say?" she asked.

Ike leaned against his Hummer and smiled, a plan formed up in his mind. "Turn the volume up, Therm."

"Any man who would fight alongside some

158

pussy is a pussy," the voice sprang out of the speaker.

"Is that right?" a Rebel said sarcastically.

"The Rebel Army ain't got nothin' but a bunch of fags and cunts in it." The voice continued spewing garbage.

"All the men stand down for this one," Ike told his communications specialist. "Advise the ladies that this town is theirs."

"Yes, *sir!*" she said, and gave the orders. She quickly gave the orders and handed her backpack radio to a startled Thermopolis. "Here," she told him. "You handle it for a few minutes." She unslung her M-16 and walked off.

"I don't know how to work this goddamn thing," Therm said, looking at the complicated piece of equipment. "I never could figure out how to program my own VCR."

"Well, don't look at me," Ike said, glancing at the radio. "I know how to turn it on and that's just about it."

The voice continued to spew profanities out of the speaker, telling in very crude detail what he and his men would do to any female Rebel who dared enter this man's town.

Thermopolis looked around as his wife, Rosebud, and several of her friends from the old commune started walking up the road, to the crest of a small rise. "Where are you going?" he called.

"To teach some men some facts about women," she called over her shoulder. "Just work the damn radio."

"Hell, I don't know how!" he called.

"You'll figure it out. I have a great deal of faith in you." She kept walking, her M-16 at combat-ready.

The tank commander buttoned down her hatch, and the MBT clanked forward, the muzzle of the 105mm level.

Rosebud assumed a prone position on the crest of the rise and put a full clip of .223's into a frame house on the edge of town. Fly, Swallow, Wren, and Zelotes followed suit and put approximately 120 fast rounds into the frame house. Men started bailing out of the side and back doors.

The MBT clanked up and put one round into the bullet-pocked house. The house exploded. Wood and glass erupted into the air. A half a dozen other tanks lumbered up. Each was commanded by women Rebels.

"Fall in, ladies," a tank commander told the swelling group of women on the crest of the rise. "Let's go teach some rednecks about women."

"Holy shit!" an outlaw breathed, looking at the sight through binoculars. "I'm gone, man. Like right now." He jumped up and took a .308 slug from a sniper rifle right through his guts. He lay on the street and screamed until a sniper named Doris put a round through his head.

The MBTs rumbled forward. Several platoons of women walked behind them. Other tanks followed the women.

"Never piss off the weaker sex," Ike told Therm.

"Are we going in after them?" Therm asked.

"Hell, no! Besides, you really think they need any help?"

"I suppose not," he admitted.

One MBT smashed into a house and drove clear through it, charging out the other side. The men who were in the home now were a permanent part of the foundation, for they had been mashed into bloody globs under the treads of the 63-ton fighting machine.

Several outlaws jumped into the cab of a pickup truck and tried to make a run for it. The commander of an MBT swung the turret, leveled the 105, and the pickup truck vanished in a ball of exploding flames.

M73 and M85 machine guns began yammering and howling. The 7.62 and .50-caliber slugs kocked holes in the buildings of the town, sending outlaws scrambling into the open. The tight-lipped and extremely pissed-off gunners chopped them into raw chunks.

Some outlaws cleared the town, running for their lives, only to race headlong into the very hostile and accurate rifle fire of Rosebud and her friends, who lay on the crest of the hill, carefully picking their targets.

The driver of a LAV-25 smashed into and through a shed, coming snout to face with a big pus-gutted outlaw. The commander lowered her Hughes M242 Bushmaster 25mm chain gun and smiled at the outlaw as the chain gun came level with his face. Using her outside speaker, she said,

"Are you the asshole who said women were good for nothing except sucking dicks?"

"Uh . . ." the outlaw replied.

"I'll take that as affirmative," she said. She inched the assault vehicle forward, pinning the man against a tree. She dropped the chain gun several inches. "Suck it," she told him.

The outlaw-murderer-rapist then proceeded to give the muzzle of the Bushmaster an outstanding blow-job.

"I think we should move in now," Thermopolis told Ike.

"You move in," Ike replied. "I ain't movin' a lick 'til those ladies get the mad out of their systems."

"I suppose you're right."

"Cain't you take a joke?" an outlaw screamed, running down the road, a Duster right on his tail. He had lost his rifle and was fleeing for his life.

"I'm about to take out a joke," the crew chief muttered. She accelerated and ran over him, leaving a glob of crud on the blacktop.

The town of Glenallen had never been more than a very small hamlet, with a population of about five hundred before the Great War. When the Rebels radioed back that the town was secure, only a few buildings were left standing and no outlaws were alive. A few had escaped, running into the brush and timber. But their attitude toward women—especially women Rebels—had changed.

"Now we can go in," Thermopolis said.

"I'll follow you," Ike told him.

"You're the General," Therm said. "You lead."

Ike got into his Hummer and buttoned it up tight.

"Coward," Therm told him.

"Smart," Ike countered.

The column moved forward, stopping in the middle of the ruined town. Ike grinned and saluted a woman tank commander. She smiled and returned the salute.

"Mission accomplished, General McGowan," she called.

"Damn sure is," Ike muttered. He started to ask how the muzzle of her 25mm Bushmaster got all wet. He decided he really didn't want to know.

13

"Give me a report, Jersey," Ben said from his hospital bed.

"First section is approximately 150 miles outside of Anchorage and second section is standing down for the night about fifty miles outside of Delta Junction. No Rebel casualties reported."

"Any firefights?"

"Small ones. Nothing major. A bunch of outlaw trash and rednecks insulted the women Rebels' ability to fight in a small town called Glenallen. Ike told the women to take the town. They took it."

Ben smiled. "I just bet they did. Anything new from the lower forty-eight?"

"Intelligence reports that Sister Voleta is firmly established in Michigan, her movement growing slowly but steadily."

"We'll deal with her on the way back east," Ben said. "Thank you, Jersey."

She left his room. Corrie was outside the door, holding Smoot on a leash. Ben wanted the dog in with him but Doctor Chase had nixed that for the time being.

"How is he?" Beth asked.

"Getting restless," Jersey said. "I bet you he'll be up and going before Northstar is over."

"No bet there," Cooper said. "But Chase will have the final say on that."

"Get that damn dog out of my hospital!" Chase roared.

"You leave my dog alone!" Ben hollered.

Moose looked at the gathering of gang leaders. "Another gang just went under the heel of the Rebels," he told them. "I tried to warn them nuts at Glenallen that they was too small a force to stand and fight the Rebels. They wouldn't listen and now they're dead. People, we got to get smarter than Ben Raines if we're gonna make it out of this alive. That's all there is to it, and there ain't no other way."

"How do we do that?" Foley asked. "There ain't none of us ever gonna win no prizes for smarts."

"Maybe that's the way to go," an outlaw leader said. "Play on Raines' sympathies."

"Raines don't have no sympathy for outlaws, Smithers. None a-tall. He don't buy none of that headshrinker crap about the poor underprivileged folks turning criminal 'cause they got a hard-on towards society . . . or some such shit as that. And

166

we all know he's right."

"My daddy used to whip me something fierce," Bonny Jefferson said. "He made me what I am today."

Hoots and catcalls and rough laughter greeted Bonny's words. Jake said, "There ain't nobody made you what you is except yourself, Bonny. So don't go layin' your past on someone else's doorstep. I've read Raines' work, back when I was in prison down in Kansas. He wrote a hell of an action-adventure book and a good western. I wanted to kill the son of a bitch then—'course I still do—but in my heart I knew he was right." He sighed. "But I ain't about to go changin' my ways this late in the game. Has anybody got a plan?"

"All that equipment at them military bases," Dixson said. "All them tanks and heavy artillery and stuff and folks just let 'em rust out."

"Couldn't nobody run the goddamn things," a lifelong resident and criminal of Alaska said. "Too complicated. Too late now. All the guns been stripped off the hulls."

"What do we have to fight Raines with?" Buster asked. "We got to tally this up."

The men were meeting in a town just north of Anchorage. Alaska's largest city was filled to overflowing with almost any type of undesirable one might care to name. Almost ten thousand of them. And they were dug in and ready for a fight.

"We can make a damn good stand of it," Foley said. "But we got to face this fact: the Rebs will overwhelm us eventually. If we could have got those assholes up in Fairbanks to join us, we might have had a chance of actually holding Raines off and maybe striking a deal with him."

"Ben Raines don't make deals with the likes of us," Jake said. "So put that out of your mind. He's found the mass graves and he'll find more as they advance, all the rooms full of dead slaves, and he's heard all the stories the survivors has told about us. He won't make no deals with us."

"Jake's right," Moose said. "We're all lookin' at the end, boys."

The gang members sat in silence, letting that soak in. One finally stood up from the table and walked to a dirty window, staring out. "I'll not piss and moan about it," he said. "Ben Raines don't offer no quarter, by God, I ain't gonna expect or give none. I'll fight 'til they kill me."

"I'll go along with that," Dixson said.

"All right, here it is," Moose said. "I don't like it, but it's the best I can come up with. Raines is gonna have planes and choppers all over the goddamn place, so splittin' up and takin' to the timber ain't worth a damn. He's settin' up them outposts and armin' the survivors. If we did try to hide, they'd kill us the instant we surfaced. So . . . I guess I got to eat my previous words and say we join up with them down in Anchorage. Any objections?"

"Strength in numbers," Foley said.

"And when Anchorage falls?" Bonny said.

"We head down onto the peninsula and join up with that terrorist bunch that come through."

"And after that?" Buster asked.

"We're dead," Moose said. "So it don't really matter, does it?"

"We'll hit trouble tomorrow at Delta Junction," Georgi said to his commanders. "Fort Greely was located just outside of there, so the outlaws in the town will be heavily armed. Scouts report that a very elaborate system of roadblocks are now in place. A survivor—a former slave of the crud and crap—says they plan to inflict as many casualties on us as possible, then fall back to Fairbanks and link up with the scum who control that city. Tomorrow morning, the campaign ceases to be a milk run."

"How many are we facing?" Buddy asked.

"About a thousand men. With heavy machine guns, mortars, rocket launchers."

Dan lifted a dog-eared copy of a tourist guide and studied it for a moment. He smiled, but the humor did not reach his eyes. "Says here that an annual barbecue is held on the first Sunday in August in Delta Junction. We're going to be a little bit early for that. Perhaps we can host our own barbecue?"

The Russian smiled at him. "An excellent suggestion, Colonel. Tell the artillery to commence firing as soon as they're ready."

One hundred and fives and 155's began shelling

the town within the hour, hurling 42.9-pound and 102.5-pound high explosive antipersonnel grenades into the town, dropping them in with deadly accuracy. Cursing the Rebels in general and Ben Raines in particular, the outlaws who had operated out of the town with savage impunity for years began their retreat toward Fairbanks. They left behind them the bodies of more than five hundred who had been killed during the first moments of the artillery barrage, which caught them totally unprepared. They had been operating under the assumption that the Rebels wanted to save the towns. They learned very quickly that the Rebels did not give a damn for the physical makeup of the towns. The Rebels were interested in disposing of outlaws in the most efficient manner available to them.

Under cover of darkness, the Rebels moved closer, staying behind the main battle tanks. Dawn found three battalions of Rebels sitting at the back door of the burning and shattered town.

Georgi, Dan, and Buddy studied the ruined town through long lenses.

"Take it," Georgi ordered.

Scouts were the first ones in. They reported back that there was no sign of life in what was left of the town at the end of the Alaska Highway. From this point, the Rebels would be traveling on the Richardson Highway toward Fairbanks, one hundred miles away.

Buddy picked through the smoking rubble, inspecting a dozen or more bodies. He walked back to Georgi and Dan.

"They shot their wounded in the back of the head," he told the older men. "And I want a doctor to look at the sores on these bodies."

A Rebel doctor took skin samples and scrapings and drew blood. "Get into gloves and handle these bodies carefully, stack them in the rubble, and burn what is left of the town," he ordered. "Anyone with an open cut stay the hell out of town. These people were suffering from advanced syphilis. I'll get word back to Dr. Chase."

"So it's a sure bet those in Fairbanks will also be infected," Ben said after Lamar broke the news to him.

"Some of them, yes. I just spoke with Ike. His people have not yet encountered any such problems down south."

"I want to get out of bed."

"You'll keep your ass in bed until I tell you to get out of bed. And if you argue with me I'll knock you down with drugs and you can stay in never-never land for a couple of weeks."

"You wouldn't!"

"You'd like to maybe place a wager on that?"

The Rebels continued their relentless advances on two fronts. They could all sense that the North American campaign was rapidly drawing to a close and Europe was right around the corner. They knew that the taking of two of the largest cities in Alaska was not going to be easy, but they

171

also knew it would be nothing like their taking and destroying of New York City or Los Angeles.

On the Kenai Peninsula, Lan Villar monitored radio transmissions and shook his head in disgust and despair. "How in the hell did Ben Raines ever get so powerful?" he questioned. "He started out with a Mississippi Redneck, a Navy doctor, and a nigger, and ended up with the largest army in the entire damn world! He fought the Russian, then the damn Russian joined him. He fought the mercenary, then the damn mercenary joined up with him. How in the hell did he ever put together so many people of like mind?"

"I had several divisions," Khamsin said. "Thousands of the finest fighting men in all the world. Now I have perhaps one company left of my original force. I had ships. Now Raines' people have them on the east coast and are refitting them. The bastards and bitches will use *my* ships to transport *them* to Europe. And here we sit, waiting to die. I held out my hand to Allah and he allowed Ben Raines to shit in it!"

Ashley chuckled. "People like you swell my ass, Khamsin—to use an old Louisiana expression. You're a barbarian and nothing more. You've spilled blood all over the world and claim it to be in the name of Allah. At least Ben Raines doesn't claim that what he's doing is in the name of God."

"You're disgusting, Ashley!" the Hot Wind told the man. "I should cut your tongue out for defiling the name of Allah. You are not worthy to speak his name."

"You couldn't cut a piece of baloney, Khamsin. You're a paper tiger. You have no army, no following, nothing. You're here only because we," he jerked a thumb toward Lan, "allowed you to tag along. Nobody gives a rat's ass for your so-called religious mumblings. This isn't a holy war and it never has been. We—and that certainly includes you—are nothing more than dregs of society trying to stay alive against a force whose time has come. So fuck you and fuck the camel you rode in on."

Lan laughed at the expression on the Libyan's face. Khamsin stalked out the room, his dark face even darker with rage.

"You sure didn't make any brownie points with those remarks," Parr said.

"At this stage of the game," Ashley said with a shrug of his shoulders, "what possible difference does it make?"

The events in Alaska were being monitored as closely as possible by many in the United States. Ben had deliberately ordered all but the most secret of transmissions to be broadcast on unscrambled frequencies. He wanted the outlaw element to hear what was taking place. He had his communications people broadcast a daily progress report back to Base Camp One and to the many outposts throughout the lower forty-eight.

All over what had once been the United States of America, men and women were giving up their

173

careers in crime and picking out little parcels of land to farm and raise cattle and hogs and chickens and live as quietly and as decently as possible. It was either that or get put up against a wall and shot by the many Rebel patrols that crisscrossed the country.

Men and women who for the past decade and a half had looted and raped and murdered and in general raised hell in their sectors were keeping a very low profile. Except in a very few areas, the Rebels were firmly in control. Their laws were few, but break one and the penalty was harsh.

In the lower forty-eight, for many, life was returning to normal very quickly. Outlaws simply had no place left to run. Once caught, there was no throwing oneself on the mercy of the courts, no plea bargaining, in most cases no long legal maneuvering. Hardened criminals got a bullet or a rope. Drug dealers were executed practically on the spot. An arrangement of common sense had taken the place of a complicated unworkable judicial system.

There were many who did not like it. There were more who did. Those who did not like the system did not have to live under the rules of the new order. Anyone was free to choose his or her own lifestyle as long as no existing laws were broken. But those who did not subscribe to the Rebel way received no help from the Rebels, no help of any kind. And the Rebels had a habit of moving into areas who opposed their way and looking things over very carefully. If children were found to be

abused, uneducated, mistreated, neglected, malnourished, the Rebels took them to raise as their
own.

Legal under the old system? No. Morally right?
Probably. The Rebels had a saying: "If you don't
like it, take it up with Ben Raines."

Georgi pushed hard up to Fairbanks, pausing
only once to inspect a small town just south of the
city. North Pole, Alaska was located just fourteen
miles south of Fairbanks and was in pretty good
shape, considering the fact that outlaws had called
it home for more than a decade.

Georgi set up his CP in the old mall and walked
to communications. "Get my helicopter squadron
commanders, please," he requested. "Do a flyover
of Fort Wainwright," he ordered. "Then report
back to me once that is accomplished."

The old Army fort had been picked over, looted,
and much of it destroyed, the chopper pilots
radioed back.

"Return to base," Georgi told them. "And report to me immediately upon touchdown."

When the pilots had reported in, the Russian
offered them coffee, seated them, and pointed to a
map. "I want you all to start ferrying troops to
these three locations." He thumped the map with
the tip of a pointer. "Livengood and Chatanika to
the north, on Highways 2 and 6, and Nenana to the
south, on Highway 3. As soon as we start our
assault against Fairbanks, there will be those who

will run." He smiled a warrior's smile. "We don't want them to be able to run very far."

Georgi took a sip of coffee, grimaced (he'd forgotten to honey it), looked around for the jug, found it and sweetened his coffee. Several of his pilots laughed at his expression and Georgi laughed with them. "You all can carry eight, but let's take into account food and supplies for a week and cut that back to six with supplies. That's seventy-two personnel per trip. I want a full company in each location. Get together and work out the arithmetic. Just get the troops in position ASAP. Then start ferrying in spare parts, mechanics, fuel and ammo and rockets for your machines. I want two Hinds in place with each company. That's it, people. Take off and good luck."

Far to the south, Ike was briefing his people. "I'm not going to risk our attack helicopters until we know for sure whether the crud in that city have SAMs. So the artillery will pound the hell out of the place and then we'll take it like we used to: house to house. There's only one way in and that's straight in. I'm not going to fly troops down to block off any escape on Highway 1. That would be too great an opportunity for Villar and his crap and crud to come up from behind and put them in a box. So for a fact, we'll have a lot of work cut out for us on the peninsula dealing with those who cut and run from the city.

"Now, then, we've got to pound our way in to here," he hit the map with a pointer, "Muldoon Road, then spread out south and start working in to the west. Me and my bunch will go in on Highway 1, pushing straight toward downtown. Therm, drop down and take Debarr Road. Rebet, Lights Boulevard. Danjou, Tudor Road." He looked at his watch. "Artillery starts in one hour. We go in at dawn."

14

All afternoon the big attack choppers ferried troops, while to the south and west of Fairbanks artillerymen laid out rounds ranging in weight from 42 pounds to 200 pounds. The 155's would throw the M692 antipersonnel shells. Each shell contained 36 antipersonnel mines. The eight-inch guns, the 203mm monsters, would hurl the 200-pound M404 HE rounds. Each round contained 104 M43A1 grenades.

When they all started firing, it sounded like hell had unleashed its demons.

To those in the city, hell *had* unleashed its demons.

The artillery was set up from just south of Highway 2 over to near Fort Wainwright, and they started dropping their rounds in just to the west of the Steese Expressway, working them in toward the heart of the city.

Fairbanks had once been a city where a person could walk shoulder to shoulder with miners, Indians, Eskimos, mushers, pioneers and merchants. It was a transportation hub serving the North Slope oil fields and Arctic villages. All that was before the Great War; after that, the outlaws moved in and took over.

Fairbanks once had a rich cultural life, with writers, painters, weavers, sculptors, poets, musicians, and actors. The outlaws killed them or made slaves out of them.

One outlaw had made his CP in the old Log Cabin Visitor Information Center on 1st Ave. It used to be a pretty place, with its sod roof, huge stone fireplace, and varnished logs. It took a direct hit from a 155, and the place blew apart, killing all inside.

Fairbanks, at one time, was a very interesting city, where modern hotels and shopping malls stood beside log cabins and historic wood-frame buildings. When General Georgi Striganov ordered in WP rounds, the city started burning and the outlaws went into a panic.

None of them really understood what they had chosen to go up against. They might have thought Raines' Rebels were no better equipped than themselves, with small arms and machine guns and a few mortars. They did not expect artillery that could stand back eighteen thousand yards and hurl two-hundred-pound rounds in on them. The outlaws had guessed wrong, and they died for it.

They also misjudged Ben Raines' cold contempt for anyone who elected to follow a life of crime, who chose to trample upon the rights of law-abiding citizens—a contempt that bordered on raw hatred.

Georgi ordered the shelling stopped. "Tanks in," he ordered. "Troops behind them. Move out."

The Rebels crashed across the Chena River and across the Steese Expressway and barreled into the city, crushing anyone who dared stand in their way. None of the several thousand outlaws offered to surrender. They knew better than to try that. The Rebels had warned them that they would take no prisoners.

Buddy stepped into the lobby of a hotel on First Street and lifted his Thompson, clearing the lobby of crud and crap. With a squad behind him, he began clearing the floors of human flotsam, using a .45 caliber sweeper.

Dan led a team into an apartment complex that smelled like hogs had been using it for years and began cleaning it out—with grenades. When the interior of the building was burning to his satisfaction, he and his Rebels moved up the street.

Georgi, not one to stand back and let others do the fighting, ducked into what had once been a restaurant and, with his AK-47, began serving up hot lead to those gang members who had chosen to fight from that location. Georgi tossed in a grenade for dessert and stepped back out into the street.

The Fire-Frag mini-Claymore blew and spread brains and blood all over the filthy restaurant. "Nasty bastards," the Russian muttered, and looked around him to see what other mischief he could get into. It didn't take him long to discover he had outdistanced his personal team and was pinned down in what had once been a dress shop.

Georgi made himself comfortable behind a counter and got ready for a good fight. An outlaw ran screaming through the back door, and Georgi dusted him with his AK. The outlaw had been carrying a twenty-round drum-fed machine shotgun, and two other drums dangled from his shoulder. Georgi laid aside his AK and checked out the 12-gauge magnum shoulder buster.

"Interesting," he said. "What a mess a person could make with this monster." He got his chance before he could pull his next breath; the entrance of the shop filled with wild-eyed outlaws. Georgi leveled the machine shotgun and cleared out the whole kit and caboodle of the crud, hurling and throwing and spreading parts of the outlaws halfway across the littered street as the magnum-pushed buckshot tore into and mangled and shredded flesh and bone.

"Oh, I like this!" Georgi said, inserting another drum into the belly of the machine gun shotgun.

"General!" his sergeant-major called.

"In here," Georgi yelled over the din of battle. "Come see what I found."

The sergeant-major stepped over and through all the gore on the floor and looked at the buckshot-throwing machine gun his general held. He shook his head in awe.

"Find me some more shotgun shells, Paul," Georgi said with a grin. "I *like* this weapon."

"Go!" Ike ordered his troops.

Before them, the city of Anchorage was smoky

from the fires started by the artillery rounds.

Ben had wanted to save as many artifacts and remnants of the past as possible from the two largest cities, and the other commanders agreed with him, so the artillery barrage had been cut short and the city would be taken by Rebels, working block by block.

The battalions split up as they hit Muldoon Road. Danjou's battalions raced south, following the lead tanks down to Tudor Road. All four battalions were stalled cold when they tried to push further west.

"We've got to take Parkway by nightfall," Ike radioed. "We've got to be firmly established by nightfall or we're in trouble. All units get their Big Thumpers up and start knocking holes in the enemy's defenses."

40mm grenade launchers were brought up, belts snapped in, and the Big Thumpers started chugging out M430 HEDP (High Explosive Dual Purpose) grenades. The automatic grenade launchers had an effective range of about 1,700 yards and could spit out grenades at about 40 rounds per minute. With every Big Thumper available chugging out rounds, the areas in front of the Rebels soon turned into a wall of destruction and fire. The outlaws, having never faced anything so destructive, began falling back. Within an hour, with main battle tanks adding their cannon to the howling Big Thumpers, the Rebels had advanced all the way up to Boniface Parkway, stretching out north to south from Oil Well Road down to Bicentennial Park.

Ike halted the advance and ordered the Rebels to dig in, with every available tank up close and looking over their shoulders. And the Rebels had taken a lot of prisoners. They didn't want to, but many of the men and women representing the outlaw faction simply threw their weapons aside and sat on the ground, their hands in the air. When the enemy offered no resistance and most of them were bawling and squalling with tears and snot dripping, the Rebels just could not shoot them.

"Shit!" Ike said, when informed of the surrender.

"What in the devil are we going to do with them?" Danjou radioed to Ike.

"Hell, I don't know," the commanding general of 1st Section radioed back. "Find some place over at Fort Richardson and guard them, I reckon. Damn!"

"I'm hungry!" a woman prisoner bellowed.

A female Rebel showed the woman the muzzle of her M-16, up close—against the woman's forehead, in fact. "You open that fly trap of yours one more time and you'll never have to worry about being hungry again, bitch!"

The prisoner peed her pants and shut her mouth.

"What are you going to do with us?" a prisoner asked Ike. Although Ike wore no insignia, the man knew from the way the other Rebels treated him that he was a part of high command.

"I don't know," Ike said honestly. He looked down at the man, who was sitting on the ground with his hands behind his head. Ike had left his command in the capable hands of his XO and driven over to Fort Richardson to personally eyeball the several hundred prisoners. They were a sorry-looking sight.

Ike walked away and found a Rebel doctor. "Pull every fifth one out, male and female, and run blood tests on them. Let's see what they've got that we don't want."

The reports soon came back.

"Every type of venereal disease you can name," the doctor told Ike. "We'd exhaust our readily available supply of antibiotics before we even made a dent in containing the diseases. That is, if the diseases would respond to treatment. And some of them won't."

Ike cussed, kicked at an aluminum can that some asshole had tossed on the ground years back and that would still be bright and shiny and kickable five hundred years down the road, and started considering options. There weren't very many of them.

He waved to a Rebel officer assigned to guarding the prisoners. "Keep this pack of crud isolated from the troops," he said with a sigh. "Feed them. We'll clean out the city and then decide what to do with this bunch."

After the first day's fighting, many outlaws began leaving the city. They had only one way to go: south, and they exited in that direction, carrying what food and weapons they could pack in their cars and trucks.

After questioning many prisoners—those co-herent enough to talk—and discovering that the outlaws did not have surface-to-air missile capabilities, Ike ordered his Apache, Cobra, and Huey gunships up, telling them to turn the road south into a graveyard. The pilots accomplished that mission in only a very few runs, leaving the highway south blocked with dozens of burning cars and trucks. The Rebels could easily push the vehicles aside when they made their move south, but for the outlaws in the city they formed an impassable barrier, leaving them trapped with no place to go and nothing to do but die.

By noon of the second day, the Rebel line had advanced up to within four blocks of the downtown area. Using long range artillery, Ike had disabled all the roads leading south out of the city except for one, the Seward Highway—and he had that blocked with tanks and troops at the intersection of O'Malley Road. He had then worked north from that point, lining both sides of the highway all the way up to Diamond Boulevard with Claymores. The outlaws in the city were trapped.

"How many got out before that goddamn ex-SEAL plugged the hole?" Lan Villar asked the question seated behind his desk in his CP south of the besieged city.

"Just under a thousand," he was told. "And they're still shaking in their boots."

"And McGowan is doing what with those trapped in the city?"

"He junked the original plan to save as much of the city as possible and is systematically destroying the city with artillery, block by block, working east to west toward the bay."

"What is the situation for the outlaws up in Fairbanks?" Lan asked, even though he knew perfectly well what the man's reply would be.

"Grim."

The three battalions of Rebels in Fairbanks had fought their way into the downtown area, stretching out north to south along Cushman Street from the river down to Twenty-first Avenue. Tanks and troops blocked intersections, playing a deadly game of wait-and-see with the outlaws trapped in the city.

One of the last three major bastions of lawlessness left on the North American continent was ready to fall. The outlaws had tried to run; they had retreated on the highways they thought were still open to them and were slaughtered by Rebel troops and Hind gunships. The roads leading out of the city were clogged with burned-out vehicles and bloated bodies.

"If I were trapped in that city," said Buddy at a meeting of commanders one afternoon, "knowing I was facing death anyway I chose to turn, I would try a suicide charge. A few would make it out."

"I concur," Dan said. "It's the last option open to them other than shooting themselves."

"Those that have staggered out tell us the food and water situation is getting very grim in the city," General Striganov said.

"Message from General Raines, sir," an aide

said, handing the Russian a slip of paper.

Striganov read it, then read it again, a smile playing on his lips. "Interesting," he whispered.

"What is it?" Buddy asked.

"Your father has ordered us to offer the outlaws surrender terms. If they surrender, they will stand trial with the survivors as the judges and the juries. Only those convicted of capital crimes will be given the death sentence. The others will be given prison terms. That will give the survivors jobs and those outlaws who wish to be rehabilitated a chance to do so. He has ordered Ike to offer the same terms down south."

"I've never heard of my father doing such a thing."

Dan smiled. "I can assure you, Buddy, there is no compassion in that anything-but-magnanimous gesture."

"I don't understand what you're saying," the young man said, shaking his head.

"Your father will do almost anything to save Rebel lives," Striganov said. "Correction: he will do *anything* to save Rebel lives. He knows that many outlaws will choose to surrender to a jail term rather than face death. He also knows that the harder outlaws will turn on them the instant they do. The outlaws themselves will kill probably twenty to thirty percent of their fellow partners-in-crime. That's a thousand that we won't have to fight."

Buddy walked away a few steps, his brow furrowed in thought. He turned to face the commanders. "Historians will not paint a very admirable portrait of my father, will they?"

"No," Georgi said. "They will not. Nor will they paint a very nice verbal painting of Ike, Cecil, Dan, Rebet, Danjou, Thermopolis, West, your sister, you, or me. They will sit in their paneled offices and studios and put cold impersonal words upon paper. They are not here. They have, in all probability, not even been born. They'll defile us, Buddy Raines. Just like many defiled Daniel Boone, Davy Crockett, Washington, Lincoln, in this country, at least half a hundred in my country, and others in countries all over the world. Warriors don't become historians, Buddy. Not in most cases. Timid little people who have never experienced the horror of battle, or seen the brutality that outlaws can do to innocent people will sniff in disfavor and say we could have done it differently; we did not have to be so callous, so unfeeling. But what the hell do they really know about it? The answer is nothing. And what will all the half-truths and sly innuendo mean to us?" He smiled. "Nothing. We shall be dust in some lonely grave here in America, or in England, or in Russia, or God help us all, Turkey or Libya. And in another five hundred years, some descendant of ours will have to do what we are doing, all over again, because of timid little people who don't know reality from a bowl of borscht."

Dan laughed at the expression on the Russian's face. "Do you miss borscht, Georgi?"

Georgi grimaced. "I *hate* borscht. I hate cabbage and I hate boiled potatoes." He laughed aloud. "I must have been a terrible Russian!"

15

The guns of the Rebels fell silent. In the cities under siege, the outlaws looked at each other, their eyes dull from fatigue, holding a vacant expression, their minds numb from the bombardment that had been a constant part of their lives for several days.

The silence was almost frightening to the gang leaders and their followers.

Many of the women urged their men to take the surrender terms and stand trial. Many of the men told their women to go right straight to hell.

"Jesus," one gang leader said. "How many survivors could there be? There can't be that many to testify against us. I say we got a better than even chance of walkin' away scot free."

"You're a fool," another said. "You think Ben Raines is just gonna sit back and let us go free? I wouldn't trust that bastard no further than I can see him. And I can't see him."

"It's a trick," another said. "What's that thing

191

that Geronimo or Daniel Boone or somebody said about divide and conquer? That's what Raines is doin'."

"I think he's sincere," yet another said. "I'm packin' it in."

He turned to walk away and a friend of his cursed and shot him in the back of the head.

"It's started," Georgi Striganov said to Dan and Buddy, as the number and intensity of firing picked up in the city.

The Rebels watched as outlaws and their women ran toward their lines, their hands in the air, some of them carrying sticks with dirty white handkerchiefs tied to them. The Rebels watched as the outlaws in the city shot their former comrades in the back.

"Don't fire a shot unless fired upon," Georgi gave the order to his troops. "Let those in the city do our work for us."

Ike issued the same orders to his people around Anchorage. Inside both cities, the carnage continued as friend turned on friend in savage and usually deadly disagreement over whether or not to take Ben Raines' surrender offer.

Groups formed in both cities and the fighting among the factions intensified. The Rebels sat back and relaxed.

Still confined to his bed, Ben lay back and smiled as the reports came in, knowing he was saving countless Rebel lives by this move.

"Pleased with yourself, aren't you?" Linda asked, sitting beside his bed.

"Shouldn't I be?"

"Did you ever have any intention of letting those people stand trial, Ben?"

"Oh, yes. I discussed it with a number of survivors before making the offer. But I told them not to rush in cleaning up the prisons and jails. I didn't think we'd have many coming out to stand trial."

"You knew, or guessed, that the outlaws would turn on each other?"

"Yes. It's a dirty, underhanded way to fight a war, Linda. But I'm saving Rebel lives. And to my way of thinking, that is the most important thing in war: saving the lives of your troops. Other commanders might put the taking of ground ahead of that. But I won't. Not if there is another way of doing it. History will probably not treat me very kindly."

"Does that worry you, Ben?"

"Not one damn bit."

She gave him his medication, waited to make sure he took it, then left the room, turning out the generator-powered lights and telling him to get some sleep.

"Hell, that's all I've been doing for days," Ben bitched.

"And you'll be doing it for many more days to come. Take a nap."

At the end of the third day following the notice of surrender terms from the Rebels, the cities lay quiet and stinking with death. Around the perimeters, bodies lay in bloated, swollen piles, shot in the back by fellow outlaws. From his hospital bed, Ben gave the orders: "Take the cities."

The Rebel push began toward the downtown areas of Fairbanks and Anchorage. If any Rebel thought the situation was grim on the former perimeters of outlaw territory, they changed their minds once the push got underway. Bodies of men and women and children were hanging from lamp posts and old power poles. Many had been tortured, mutilated, and sexually abused.

"Nice folks," Buddy muttered.

"We're fighting the true dregs now," Dan told him. "I cannot believe there is a single man or woman left in the city who is worth the effort of attempted rehabilitation."

Georgi settled that issue. "No prisoners," the Russian ordered. "No surrender. Shoot the enemy on sight."

The Rebels began taking the city.

Ike and his battalions pushed relentlessly in toward the center of Anchorage. Danjou and his battalion dropped down and did an end-around up the bay side, pushing with brutal efficiency toward the International Airport. Ike ordered his gunships up and at the end of the second day of renewed fighting, the old Anchorage airport was in Rebel hands and Danjou's people were being resupplied by air.

Everything south of the airport, all the way down to Rabbit Creek Road had been cleared. By the end of the third day, Ike's people had bulled their way to Gambel Street in the downtown area and his people to the south were in firm control of everything up to Northern Lights Boulevard.

Behind Ike's First Battalion, Therm's battalion had the unenviable job of mopping up, flushing out those outlaws who were still hiding in buildings in the hope the Rebels would not find them.

The Rebels found them, usually sealing them in their hidey-holes with explosives, bringing portions of the buildings down on them.

In Fairbanks, Georgi's three battalions had very nearly gained control of the much smaller city. They had put the outlaws in a box from which there was no escape. It was now down to fighting from building to building, house to house, flushing out the last of the lawless.

The remaining outlaws fought with an insane fury, carrying lighted bundles of dynamite and charging at tanks in a vain attempt to inflict some sort of damage against the seemingly invincible Rebels, screaming as they ran, only to be chopped down in the streets by the Rebels who advanced alongside and behind the main battle tanks.

It was bloody, awful work that none of the Rebels enjoyed. It was close-up, nose-to-nose, smelling the enemy's fear and body-stink, seeing the hopelessness in their eyes and sometimes, hearing them scream for mercy. But a Rebel, who asked to see a doctor or a chaplain—to provide solace or hear a confession—would be reminded by his or her platoon leader of the mass graves they'd found on the way up to the city, men and women and children and the family pet, tortured, raped, abused, and then lined up and shot.

The Rebels usually returned to duty, the steel in their backbones hardened and straightened out by nothing more than that memory.

Finally, on a day that dawned rainy and quite cool, the Rebels fanned out in the city and could find no outlaws alive.

"Nothing in our section," Buddy radioed in.

"We're clean," Dan radioed.

"That's it, then," Georgi spoke into his mike. "Let's scoop up the last of the bodies and get clear of this place."

Georgi asked his radio operator to hook him up to Ike.

"Shark here, Bear," Ike came on the horn.

"The city is ours," the Russian said.

"Take everything of value, past and present, then burn it," Ike ordered.

"That is affirmative," Georgi said. "How is your situation?"

"We're laying back now and holding. As soon as you get clear, come on down and we'll nail the lid on this coffin."

Georgi laughed. "I'll see you in a few days. Bear out."

They had been deliberately talking on an unscrambled frequency, wanting outlaws outside of the secure zones to hear them. And Lan Villar heard it all.

He sighed and walked out of the communications room to stand in the light mist. His breath steamed the early summer air. Already the nights were very short, with only about five and half

196

hours of darkness. He realized that Raines had planned this assault very well, to give his people the maximum of daylight; the longer to have to fight with less danger of night sneak attacks.

"You bastard," he cursed Ben Raines. "I could have conquered the United States if it had not been for you. I could have had ten million slaves, all answering to my every wish and whim. Instead, here I am in this cold, wet, miserable place, waiting for you to come kill me."

At that instant, the clouds started dumping a cold, driving rain on the Kenai Peninsula. That did nothing to improve the terrorist's mood. At this juncture in time, he doubted that anything would.

With the airport open Georgi had sent planes north to Prudhoe Bay to check on the pipeline. The planes carried two full companies of Rebels as well as a number of the best engineers in the Rebel Army. As had been expected, there were outlaws manning the equipment at Deadhorse and Prudhoe Bay. But they gave up without either side firing a shot. Other outlaws manning the pump stations along the way surrendered with no deaths or injuries on either side. They elected to take their chances with a trial and were flown back south and handed over to the survivors.

The Rebel engineers began the complicated job of shutting the operation down. The two companies of Rebels stayed with them, for it would be weeks before all the shutdown work could be completed. The nearly ten billion barrels of recoverable oil on Alaska's North Slope would stay in the ground.

Ben hoped it would never be needed.

Ike held his people where they were and let the trapped outlaws in the city stew for a time until Georgi and his battalions could join them for the push to retake Anchorage.

Ben was now ambulatory but was still a long way from being able to step back in as active field commander of the Rebels. He spent a lot of time reading, and that was something he'd missed doing in the field. He played cards with Lamar and gossiped with Linda, and the days moved by with a sameness that he never quite grew accustomed to.

On a reasonably warm summer's morning, Georgi and Dan and Buddy pulled their battalions in to Anchorage and linked up with Ike's battalions.

The men shook hands all the way around, Georgi saying, "We saw the smoke from a long way out."

"The city's burning all around those downtown," Ike said. "I don't see how they're standing it."

"They don't appear to have a great deal of choice," Buddy said dryly.

Ike grinned and said in his best Mississippi drawl, "Now that there's a puredee fact, boy. I talked to your father last night. He's gettin' better and better and chompin' at the bit to get back in action."

"What does Dr. Chase have to say about that?" Dan asked.

"He says Ben will see no action during this campaign. They're not taking any chances with him this time."

"Cecil?"

"Doin' great. I talked with him this morning. He says it's sure nice to be able to go home every evenin' and prop his feet up and have a martini and listen to recordin' or watch old movies on the VCR and all that homebody stuff."

"Of course, he's lying through his teeth," Georgi said with a laugh.

"Sure he is," Ike agreed. "He wants back out here so bad I could sense it over the air. But he also knows that will never be, so he's adjustin' the best he can." Ike got serious. "Let's ease on to my CP and go over the situation we got here. I think we can wrap this city up in a week."

In the CP, the commanders crowded around a wall map of downtown Anchorage.

"We're here," Ike pointed. "We're clean south of Northern Lights Boulevard and east from Gambel. That still leaves us about twenty-five blocks to clear over to the bay. We haven't found a damn thing worth salvagin' so far. The punks and crud destroyed every priceless bit of art they came up on. It's enough to make you vomit. They burned books, paintings, statues, scrimshaw, you name it, they fucked it up. And for no reason." He sighed in frustration and looked at Georgi. "Did you take prisoners toward the last up in Fairbanks?"

The Russian shook his head.

"That's the way we're gonna play here, too. What'd you find on Highway 3 comin' down here?"

"No outlaws. They fled weeks ago, running into the city or south to link up with Lan Villar and his trash. Survivors are reclaiming the few towns along the way. We listened to traffic coming from the west of us, out in the wilderness areas, but it was all friendly. They asked to be included in our outpost system; said they would conform with all the laws we advocate, but other than that, they wish to be left alone."

"That jibes with what our pilots and patrols have reported back. The crud and crap pretty much left those folks alone. Speakin' of prisoners, we were forced to take some prisoners earlier. Hell, you can't shoot a person who just sits down on the ground and sticks their hands into the air. They told us that any outlaws who ventured very far west just didn't come back."

"The ones who are left in the city, male and female?" Buddy asked, although he knew what the reply would be.

"Those left in there that know if they did surrender they'd be hanged by the survivors. Now, here's the way I see this operation: Ben's given the orders that we don't destroy the parks—we all share his feelin's about the environment and wildlife—so everything south of this city is gonna be hand-to-hand and tough goin'. There ain't nothin' left savin' in the city—human or otherwise. I don't see any point in sheddin' Rebel blood over the crap and crud facin' us in the city. I say we take it with tanks and artillery and mop up after they're done."

"That's fine with me," Therm said. "Just as long as you give the final mopping up to another battalion. My people are worn out and need a break from that kind of work."

"I'll do better than that. Since Buddy's battalion is two companies short after splitting up to go north with the engineers, you and Buddy take your battalions back to Ben's CP at Tok. I'll bump Tok and have Tina and West and their battalions ready to pull out as soon as you and Buddy arrive. How's that sound to you?"

"Great."

Ike nodded his head. "When do you want to leave?"

Therm smiled. "How about right now?"

I have never made but one prayer to God, a very short one: "O Lord, make my enemies ridiculous." And God granted it.

Voltaire

Book Two

1

While the battalions were being shifted around, Ike and his people took that time to resupply, the planes landing and taking off from Anchorage International. Those inside the smoky city could sense the growing urgency and knew their time was very short. South of the city, on the peninsula, Lan Villar and his troops grew accustomed to the drone of planes and the slap of helicopters on their patrols south of Kenai. No one tried to exit by boat or ship after the first few times—the planes and attack gunships blew them out of the water. Ben had sent troops by ship down to Kodiak, and after a very brief firefight, the planes and gunships were flying out of that city's airport.

"Bastard," Lan Villar cursed Ben Raines and the Rebels. "He never misses a bet."

Young Parr had grown increasingly morose as the days dragged on. He hardly spoke now, oftentimes not even when spoken to. Lan would wager that Parr would not wait around for the

Rebels to kill him; Lan had silently made a bet with himself that Young Parr would kill himself.

Khamsin prayed a lot, Lan noticed. The formerly much-feared Libyan terrorist spent more time on his knees, on his prayer rug, than he did on his boots.

Ashley was the only one who appeared to be taking his impending death philosophically. He spent a lot of time at a battered old portable typewriter, writing his memoirs, he told Lan. Bringing an end to an era, he added.

"The only thing that's comin' to an end is your smart-aleck ass," a big outlaw biker told him.

Ashley would only smile and continue his typing, occasionally laughing at some line or paragraph he found amusing.

"You know what Ben Raines is gonna do with that crap when he finds it?" the biker asked.

"Probably recognize the writings of a genius and save it for publication," Ashley replied.

"What he's gonna do is burn it," the biker said.

Meg, daughter of Matt Callahan, who had waged war against the Rebels in the western part of the United States, and had eluded the Rebels for months, had disappeared. Lan doubted she would resurface until the Rebels were long gone. But she'd survive, he was quite sure. Meg was a tough little bitch.

"Why don't we just go into the wilderness and hide 'til it's over?" Parr asked, a tremble of fear in his voice. "Ben Raines won't shell no timber. He's so goddamn concerned about animals and the environment and all that crap."

Lan smiled at the very frightened young man who once fancied himself a big, bad, tough outlaw. "He'd just wait us out, Parr. We couldn't take enough food with us to last through the first winter."

"Goddamnit!" the young man screamed. "I don't want to die."

"Well, you're going to die whether you want to or not," Ashley told him. He held out a plastic container. "Here. Take one of those every few hours. It'll help to calm you."

Parr grabbed the bottle out of his hand. "What is this stuff?"

"Tranquilizers. You're coming unglued, Parr. You're going to turn into a babbling idiot if you don't do something. Your hands are shaking so bad you couldn't aim a rifle if you tried. There are enough pills in that bottle to last you a couple of weeks." He shrugged his shoulders. "It'll be over by then."

Parr swallowed two of the pills and then went to his quarters and carefully hid his newly acquired stash.

"I'm tired of listening to his whining and complaining," Ashley responded to Villar's questioning look. "And we're going to need every person we have to make any sort of fight against the Rebels."

"You're very calm standing so close to your grave, Ashley. What have you got up your sleeve?"

Ashley laughed at the terrorist. "My God, Lan— I don't have anything devious planned. You don't think Ben Raines would let me live, do you?"

Lan smiled. "No. That is something I do not believe. I have heard how much he dislikes you." He laughed. "And also how he humiliated you years ago, in a fight, down in Louisiana."

Ashley's face showed some temper rising at that. He fought it back and joined the terrorist in a smile; but it was a forced curving of the lips. "Yes. He certainly did that. But he didn't fight fair."

Lan howled his laughter. "Fight fair?" he managed to choke the words off his tongue while wiping his eyes. "Do you still believe in fair fights, Ashley?"

"Certainly," Ashley said stiffly. "I might be a criminal—in the eyes of some—but I am still a gentleman."

Lan broke up again, the laughter bouncing around the room. When he calmed down, he walked over and patted Ashley on the shoulder. "We'll be sure to leave word that you want that on your tombstone, Ashley. Yes. We'll be sure to do that. 'Here lies Lance Ashley Lanier, a gentleman to the end.'" He walked away, laughing uproariously.

"Cretin," Ashley muttered. "I hope I stay alive long enough to see Dan Gray beat you to death with his fists."

Khamsin and a big outlaw biker called Bishop who had once ridden with Satan's bunch had sat at the table across the big room and listened to the exchange.

Bishop stood up, a sneer on his ugly face. "I was in prison once with a gentleman. He could suck a dick better than anyone in the block." He tugged at his crotch. "You wanna suck my dick, Gentleman?"

Ashley smiled thinly and pulled out a government-issue .45. "People of your ilk always confuse civility with homosexuality. It's a terrible mistake to make." He leveled the muzzle and shot Bishop twice in the belly.

The outlaw hit the floor, screaming as the hot pain hit him. Ashley stood up, leveled his .45, and shot the man in the head, stilling his screaming. He looked at Khamsin.

"Do you have any disparaging remarks you'd like to make about me, Hot Wind?"

"No," the Libyan said. "I rather like the time I have left me."

"That's good, Khamsin. Very wise move on your part." Ashley sat back down at the typewriter and began typing out more of his memoirs.

Khamsin motioned at a group of men who had gathered around the outside of the office. He pointed at Bishop. "Do something with him," he ordered. "And if you like, you can carve on his tombstone that you cannot judge a book by its cover."

The bombardment of downtown Anchorage began at midnight. Every artillery piece in Rebel hands—from 155mm SP to 81mm mortars—began tossing projectiles into the heart of the city. The incoming rounds tore the tops off the taller buildings and sent tons of concrete crashing to the streets below. Then Ike ordered white phosphorous rounds dropped in, and the city began burning. He stood the artillery down at dawn, after a thundering night of sheer terror and death for those in the heart of the city, and at his order helicopters came in dropping napalm.

Twelve hours later, at noon on a fine warm sunny day in Alaska, the heart of what had been the state's largest city was burning out of control.

"We'll let it burn itself out, and then go in and see what we've got," Ike said.

Lan Villar had traveled up close to the bay. He stood looking at the huge columns of smoke rising from the ruined city. "We're next," he said grimly.

Ike's battalions entered the city at dawn of the next day. They were equipped and ready to fight pockets of resistance, but very few were left alive in the city. The defending outlaws had simply not prepared for a sustained artillery attack. The Rebels knew there were certainly dozens of outlaws still alive, trapped under tons of rubble. They would stay there, entombed by their own stubbornness and savagery.

The Rebels spent that day and the next day in a search-and-destroy deployment. They searched a lot, but destroyed little, because most of the heart of the city had already been destroyed, and that included ninety-nine percent of those who had chosen to defend it. By dusk of the second day the Rebel platoon leaders declared the city dead.

*　　　*　　　*

Ben was up and walking around. He was doing more walking every day to keep his legs from atrophying, so he said.

"Raines," Chase said patiently, "you would have to lay up in bed for weeks, comotose, before anything like that would begin to occur."

"I know what I'm doing," Ben told him.

"A witch doctor knows more about medicine than you do," Chase fired back.

"Stuff it, Lamar."

"Stick it up your nose, Raines."

The two men argued and bitched and cursed each other as they walked the streets of the town. It was a welcome sight and sound to the Rebels. They knew that Ben Raines was going to be all right.

"You ready to start givin' 'em hell, General?" a Rebel called.

"You damn right, Shorty," Ben replied. "It won't be long now."

"What are we gonna find overseas, General?" a woman yelled.

"Trouble," Ben returned the yell.

"What else is new?" she told him.

Therm began joining the men on their daily walks. His wife had pointed out that he was getting a little tubby about the middle. Pissed him off mightily.

On this day, Ben was not using his cane. "You have amazing healing powers, Ben," Therm told him.

"Modern medicine," Lamar said with a smirk, knowing that would get a response out of Ben.

"Horseshit," Ben told him.

A runner came up and handed Ben a message. The man stopped while Ben read the note. He smiled. "Anchorage has fallen. Very few prisoners taken. The crud fought almost to the last person. Ike begins his move against Lan Villar in the morning."

Lamar pointed to a bench. "Sit," he told Ben. "You're overdoing it."

Smoot sat down on the sidewalk and looked up at Ben. Ben said, "Lamar . . ."

"Sit, goddamnit!" the doctor roared.

"All right, all right," Ben said.

"There is something I want to know, Ben," Lamar said. "Now is as good a time to ask it as any. The trip back east?"

"We're going to make one final sweep of it, Lamar. Lord knows, I've had enough time to work it out in my head. As it stands now, here it is: my battalion will take the top of the nation, leaving on Interstate 94. I'll deal with Sister Voleta in Michigan. Ike will be the next battalion south of me. He'll eventually link up with I-90 and take it to Chicago. Georgi will start out on I-80 and travel to the Atlantic. Danjou and West will be just south of him. Rebet below them. Then Tina's battalion. South of her will be Buddy, south of Buddy will be Dan's people along with Therm."

"Sweep it clean one more time before we head out, right?" Therm asked.

"That's it."

"Then it's Europe?" Chase asked. "I'd like to see it one more time, Ben. I'm an old man."

"Of course, you're coming, Lamar. But it's going to be a mean son of a bitch over there."

"I know, Ben. I've thought it over carefully. You realize, of course, the logistics involved in this move?"

"Yes. They're awesome. Once we're over there, until ships can resupply us, we're going to be on our own. It's a scary feeling, I'll admit."

The men were silent for a time, Therm finally saying, "No more getting on the horn and having supplies flown to us in three hours time. We've got to take it all with us when we go. How many ships, Ben?"

"I honestly don't know, Therm. All we can scrape up and get seaworthy. It's going to be a hell of an armada. We've got to transport all the tanks, artillery, trucks, everything that rolls or flies, and we'll have to have a tanker or two carrying raw gasoline, and that's going to be a lovely ride for those on board. I've got people on the East Coast working on it now. The last report I received stated that we—or they—have a dozen ships checked out and ready to sail from ports along the East Coast. I don't think I want to chance the North Sea during winter. So if all goes well, we'll sail next spring. It's about four thousand miles, give or take a couple of hundred. If my addition is correct, that is. And we'd all better pray that God is with us on this run, boys. 'Cause we just don't have many ex-ship's captains in our ranks."

"You have two," Therm said. "Sort of."

"Who?" Chase looked at him.

"Me, for one," Therm said.

215

"You really know how to drive one of those big bastards?" Ben asked.

"In a manner of speaking, yes."

"In a manner of speaking?" Lamar said, leaning forward to stare at him.

"Who's the other person?" Ben asked.

Thermopolis smiled. "Emil Hite."

"I feel ill, boys," Ben said. "Escort me back to the hospital. I need to lie down. Emil Hite! You've got to be kidding, Therm?"

"Nope. He worked in a shipyard as a kid and got to be friends with captains and harbormasters and so forth. I think he's on the level."

"God help us all," Ben said. "I can just see him now. Admiral Hite."

"War does make for strange bedfellows, Ben," Therm said with a smile.

"Strange is one thing. Emil is quite another."

2

Lan Villar and his troops braced for a frontal attack that did not come.

"What the hell?" Lan said.

Ike, meanwhile, was busy sending planes and helicopters far to the south, securing the towns of Seward and Homer. Those two towns and the towns of Ninilchik and Kachemak were in Rebel hands almost before Lan and his troops knew what was happening. The Rebels then began advancing toward Lan on three fronts: north, up Highways 1 and 9, on both sides of the peninsula, and pushing south out of Anchorage.

"Son of a bitch!" Lan cussed.

Ashley chuckled with dark humor.

Parr was eating tranquilizers like candy. One of the outlaw bikers had smiled and winked and given the young punk a very large bottle of amphetamines. Parr began mixing the uppers and downers, producing wild mood shifts. He was now totally unpredictable.

Ashley sat in his office in Kenai and continued work on his memoirs. He planned to be typing away when the Rebels entered the town and shot him dead.

Khamsin now spent most of his time praying to Allah. It is unclear whether Allah heard his pleas, or not. If he did, he chose to ignore the ranting and ravings of the terrorist.

The Rebels blocked Highway 1 south just a few miles outside of Kasilof. From the east, the Rebels secured the town of Sterling after a minor firefight and waited.

"Why are they stopping their advance?" Khamsin paused in his praying long enough to ask. "Why are they doing this to us? Why don't they come on and put an end to this game?"

Thousands of outlaws in and around the town of Kenai were asking the same questions.

"The Rebels are waiting for us to turn on each other," Bonny Jefferson said, finally guessing the Rebels' plan. "It's the same shit they pulled up north."

"We're running out of food," Moose added. "In a week we'll be eating each other."

"Then we'd be no better than them nasty Night People," Jake said.

"Who says we are?" Ashley asked.

The Rebels moved closer, tightening the noose around the town. The outlaws tensed.

"They're not going to risk a person," Lan put it together. "They're going to move artillery into place and blow us all straight to hell."

Khamsin started flogging himself with a piece

218

of rope, wailing out his prayers. He abruptly stopped as the sounds of big blades hammering the air reached the men.

"Gunships!" Lan yelled.

The words had just left his mouth when thirty helicopter gunships began raking the town with rockets, cannon and machine-gun fire. The gunships made one long pass at the town, then hammered away. Only the crackling of burning wood and the moaning of the wounded broke the deadly silence. The respite was very brief.

"Fire!" Ike gave the orders.

Every artillery piece at the Rebels' command began thundering from the east and the south. Outlaw Foley was running from one building to another when he disappeared in a smear of blood as an 81mm mortar round landed two feet in front of him. One of Foley's arms, neatly severed at the shoulder, landed on the windowsill directly in front of Young Parr's horrified eyes.

Ashley continued his typing.

"You son of a bitch!" an outlaw biker screamed over the thunder at Ashley. "Ain't you gonna fight?"

"Fight . . . with whom?" Ashley said, looking up. "The Rebels are two or three miles outside of town, you ninny. There is no one within our limited range."

"Well . . . we gotta do something!"

"Oh, we shall," Ashley assured him. "We're all going to die."

The outlaw biker cursed Ashley and ran out into the street. Shrapnel from a M731 antipersonnel round tore him into bloody chunks and scattered him all over the street.

The next round landed on the building in which Ashley was working, and the unrepentant gentleman outlaw was buried under several tons of brick and concrete and steel, his memoirs lost forever.

Outlaw Dixson tried to run from the burning and bloody streets of the town. A Rebel sniper, shooting a .50-caliber rifle from about 5,000 feet away, put a slug through the outlaw's chest. The impact lifted Dixson off his boots and knocked him flat on his back in the road. He died with his eyes wide open, staring up at the sun.

"Nice shooting, Rosie," her spotter said.

A group of bikers cranked their motorcycles and tried to make a run for it. They got as far as Beaver Loop Road before spotters zeroed in on them and called for artillery. The bikers were sent to hell in a burning howl of white phosphorous, their saddle tanks exploding.

Young Parr grabbed up his M-16 and went running and screaming toward the edge of town. With the luck of the stupid, he managed to avoid the incoming artillery. His system was so full of uppers and downers he didn't know where he was or really what he was doing. He ran cursing Ben Raines, cursing the Rebels, cursing Alaska, and cursing the fates that had brought him to this point in time.

Parr emptied the clip in his rifle, shooting into the air. He ran toward the Rebels' position, bullets zinging and popping all around him. His drug-overburdened heart suddenly quit and he fell to the street, his nose and lips smashed as his rifle went clattering on the road. The young outlaw's reign of terror was over.

Bonny Jefferson looked around him at what part of the town he could see through the smoke. Everything was on fire, blazing out of control. "It ain't right," he yelled. "It ain't fair. I got a right to a trial. My constitutional rights is bein' violated. I got . . ."

A 95-pound 155 M107 high-explosive round landed on the roof and Bonny Jefferson got several tons of building material on his head. The outlaw was crushed along with several of his men.

Jack Hayes and several of his men had been secretly planning a method of escape once the Rebels launched their attack. They had hidden a broad-beamed boat with a workable inboard motor just below the Beluga Whale Lookout. They managed to reach the spot without being blown to chunks and shoved off. They were all grinning and giddy with relief at their successful escape.

Their grins faded as they spotted a single Apache gunship slapping toward them, coming in low over the water. The gunner's aim was right on target as he fired the 30mm chain gun located in the nose of the chopper. What was left of Jack Hayes and those foolish enough to be in the boat with him twisted and turned slowly in the water as they sank to the bottom of the bay, and their blood left a momentary trail as they slowly slid deeper into the murky waters.

Art LeBarre was blown out of a building, his body cut in dozens of places by shards of concrete and splinters of glass. The outlaw staggered to his feet, looking wildly around him, just as an M692 round exploded directly in front of him. Seconds later, all that was left of Art LeBarre was one thumbless hand lying in the street.

Dickie Momford was blown off the top of a house. He landed on the handlebars of a motorcycle. One handlebar drove all the way through the outlaw. He dangled, jerked, kicked, and screamed for a long time.

Smithers was knocked down in the street by the concussion of an exploding round of HE. He crawled under the porch of a house and fought to regain his senses. Once his head stopped spinning, he began to dig frantically with his hands at the soft earth under the porch. He'd dig a hole, get in it, and pull as much of the dirt as he could over him. That way, the Rebels wouldn't find him and he'd be safe.

A 95-pound (94.6-pound, actually) M107 high explosive round landed directly on the house. Smithers had been right about one thing: the Rebels never would find him. No one else would either.

Pat Brown and Gil Brister—two so-called bad men who had outlawed, raped, robbed, assaulted, tortured, and in general made life miserable for anyone they came in contact with all over the lower forty-eight, Canada, and Alaska—left the cover of a building and ran for their lives, heading for the bay. Gil was running in a strange sort of jumping, loping way: during a barrage he had shit his underwear, and he was trying to shake his trousers and run at the same time.

The pair crossed Overland Avenue, and there their journey ended when an M629 round (called Area Denial Munition) dumped its cargo of 36 antipersonnel mines over the area and whizzed on. The antipersonnel rounds exploded all around the two outlaws, and, as the saying goes, that was the end of that.

Harris Orr and Peters had stuck pistols in their mouths and pulled the triggers.

Moose and his woman, Big Jean, made it to a pickup truck and were hauling ass out of town. The bed of the truck was filled to overflowing with scared outlaws, hanging on anyway they could. Moose fought the wheel, ducking and dodging the bodies and the burning cars and trucks and other blown-apart debris that littered the road.

Suddenly Big Jean started screaming, hitting Moose on the arm, and pointing out the window.

"What the hell's wrong with you, bitch?" he yelled. "Leave me alone, I'm tryin' to drive this damn thing."

Moose cut his eyes and saw what she'd been pointing at and screaming about. A main battle tank loomed in the distance, about five hundred yards off the road, the turret moving slowly, tracking the pickup truck with its 105mm cannon.

"Aw, shit!" Moose said. "Well, that's it, baby. See you in hell." He spoke just as the gunner fired. The pickup truck exploded, sending bodies and parts of bodies flying in all directions.

"Artillery cease firing," Ike ordered, looking at the ruined town through binoculars.

The sky stopped raining death, and the land grew quiet.

"Take the town," Ike said.

Tanks rumbled up. Ground troops followed them close in. Stunned, crying, wounded, and near dead men and women began staggering out of the burning rubble. The Rebels quickly tied their hands behind their backs with short lengths of rope already cut for this purpose, and the outlaws and their women were escorted to the rear of the column.

Dan Gray grabbed one man and jerked him close. "Lan Villar. Is the bastard still alive?"

"He was a few minutes ago," the outlaw said, the coldness in Dan's eyes frightening him. "I seen him down on Main Street."

Dan waved for his section and began walking toward the center of town. He kicked in the shattered door of the old post office and finally found Khamsin in a small room, on his knees on his prayer rug. Dan waited until the man had stopped ranting and raving and wailing.

Khamsin looked up at the Englishman, fear in his eyes, sweat on his face, and tears running down his cheeks.

"Are you finishing making peace with your god, you terrorist bastard?" Dan asked.

Khamsin replied in a language Dan did not understand. Dan cursed him and lowered the muzzle of his M-16. He pulled the trigger, put half a clip into the Libyan's guts, and left him to die on his bloody prayer rug.

Khamsin, the invincible Hot Wind, lay on the bloody floor and screamed as the pain tore through him.

Dan looked at him, scorn in his eyes. "I hope it takes you the rest of the day and all the night to die, you terrorist bastard."

Dan and his team walked out of the post office and began making their way toward Main Street. The streets were littered with bodies in every imaginable position of death. They came upon Jake and Buster, sitting in the middle of a street, their hands held as high over their heads as they could get them.

"Lan Villar," Dan said to Jake. "Where is the son of a bitch?"

"Last I seen him he was sittin' on the curb 'bout in the middle of Main Street. Said he was waitin' on a man. You're Dan Gray, ain't you? You look like how he described the man he was waitin' on."

"Yes. I am. Waiting for me, eh?"

"Yes, sir. He ain't armed neither."

"I find that difficult to believe."

"He ain't armed," Buster said. "And believe me, now would not be a good time for either of us to lie to you."

"You do have a point."

Rebels took the pair of no-goods back to the rear of the column.

The Rebel battalions quickly secured what was left of the town and those still alive in it. Ike had found and joined Dan by the time the Englishman

225

reached Peninsula Street and was walking toward Main Street.

"It's just about over, partner," Ike told him.

"Not quite," Dan replied.

"Seen Ashley or Parr or Khamsin?"

"I gut-shot the Libyan bastard in what appeared to be some sort of government building. I left him to die."

Ike grunted. "As much grief as he's caused around the world, I hope it takes him a long time to accomplish that."

"My feelings exactly. I was told that young Parr and Ashley are both dead. The building that Ashley was in took a direct hit from an HE round. He was working on his memoirs," Dan added. "Ashley and memoirs are buried under tons of debris."

"I'm sure Ben will be very disappointed when he learns that he won't be able to read them."

"I'm sure."

"You know where Lan Villar is?"

"Yes. Waiting for me, so I was told."

"Promises to be a good fight, I reckon."

"Good is purely up to one's own interpretation. My intention is to beat him to death with my fists."

Rebels had already found Villar, and hundreds were crowded around the street, sitting on piles of rubble and anything else they could find to sit on.

Ike disappeared into the crowd.

The Rebels parted to let Dan Gray through.

Lan looked up from the curb. "Well, it's been a long time, Colonel," he said.

"Yes, Villar. A very long time." Dan handed his

rifle to a Rebel and slipped out of his body armor. He unbuckled his web belt and dropped it to the street. His helmet followed the web belt. "Get up, Villar."

The men were about the same age, height, and weight. Both of them were in excellent physical condition.

Lan stood up slowly and stared at the Englishman. "I'm not armed."

"Neither am I."

"How's it going to be, Gray?"

"I'm going to beat you to death, Villar. That's exactly how it's going to be." Dan pulled out a pair of leather gloves and worked them onto his hands.

Lan smiled. "You always were an arrogant bastard, Gray. And your sister had some truly fine pussy."

Dan did not lose his cool. He knew the terrorist was trying to bait him, and he did not take the hook. "Are you going to talk the rest of the afternoon, or fight, Villar?"

Villar balled his fists and walked toward Dan. Dan waited.

"You won't be so pretty when I finish with you, Gray," Lan said.

Dan stepped forward and knocked the terrorist to the street with a crashing right fist to the jaw. He smiled down at the man. "That's just one of many, Villar. Now get up and fight!"

3

Villar rolled to his boots and came in swinging. Dan blocked the right and took a left to his head. The blow was hard and connected with Dan's skull, jarring him back. He recovered quickly and busted Villar in the mouth with a right fist that brought blood and momentarily glazed the terrorist's eyes.

Villar backed up and Dan pressed him. Dan connected to Villar's belly with a right and popped the man on the jaw with a left. Villar covered up, trying to catch his wind and shake the stars out of his head.

Dan back-heeled the terrorist and kicked him on the kidney. Villar screamed in pain and rolled away, trying to get to his boots. Dan gave him the toe of a boot right in the man's mouth. Villar lost some teeth and rolled further away, spitting out blood and busted pearlies.

Villar lunged and grabbed Dan around the knees, bringing him down to the street. He pounded Dan in the face with a left and a right. On their knees, the men fought silently, the only sounds their grunting with the effort of combat and the smack of fists against flesh.

The men fought to their boots and stood for half a minute, slugging it out. Dan's cheek was cut, and he had a growing mouse under one eye. Villar's lips were bloody and swollen, and blood sprayed from his mouth each time Dan connected.

Villar missed a wild swing. Dan set his boots and connected with a long right that knocked Villar flat on his butt. Dan stepped forward and kicked Villar in the balls. The terrorist screamed, fell over and puked and held up a hand.

"Enough," he gasped.

Dan reached down, grabbed the man's arm, and broke it with one smooth, practiced move.

Villar passed out from the pain.

"Give me your canteens," Dan said to a Rebel.

Dan poured the contents of one canteen over his own head, then stood over Villar and dumped the canteen empty on Villar's face. He held out his hand for another canteen and poured that on Villar. The man stirred on the littered street and tried to get up.

"Either get up and fight or I'll kick you to death," Dan told him.

"I have but one good arm," Lan protested, gritting his teeth against the pain.

"I'm sure my sister pleaded for her life, too," Dan spoke the words grimly.

"It was war!" Villar shouted.

Dan kicked the man on the side of his head.

Blood erupted from Villar's suddenly mangled ear.

The hundreds of Rebels stood and watched impassively. There was no pity in any of them for outlaws and terrorists. Most had spent their entire adult lives fighting the crud and crap of this earth, and all had seen what scum like Villar could do to innocent people. Villar was getting exactly what he had given to other people, and it was exactly what he deserved.

Dan stood while Villar crawled to his boots. The terrorist swayed for a moment, then lifted his right arm, the hand balled into a fist. His left arm hung broken and useless by his side.

With no emotion showing on his face, Dan then proceeded to beat the man to death. The Rebels heard Villar's ribs pop under Dan's big, hard, gloved fists. Dan backed Villar up against a wall of a building and killed the man with his fists.

Twice Dan had to stop for breath and to pour canteens of water over Villar's face, bringing the man out of unconsciousness. Villar begged for mercy.

"I'll show you the same mercy you offered my sister," the Englishman told the terrorist, and began working on Villar's belly, his fists hard hammers that smashed the man's insides to pulp.

When Villar could not be brought out of unconsciousness, Dan took a jump knife out of his boot and leaned over, grabbing Villar by the hair and jerking his head back.

Dan cut the man's throat, wiped his blade on

Villar's bloody shirt front, then spat in the terrorist's swollen and pain-contorted face.

The Rebels bulldozed the bodies of the dead outlaws into a huge pile, poured gasoline over the stinking heap and set the mound on fire. When the pile of inhumanity was burned to char, they pushed the remains into a huge hole they had scooped out with earth-moving equipment and covered it over with dirt.

One chaplain, chosen out of all of them by "low-card loses," said a very short prayer over the mound of earth, and the Rebels began the job of exiting Alaska.

"How's Dan?" Ben asked after Ike had informed him by radio that Alaska had been cleared of outlaws.

"He's all right. His hands are swollen but no bones are broken. The medics have him soaking them in some sort of solution."

"That's not exactly what I meant."

"I know. He's all right, Ben. He's finally got a lot of hate clear of his system. Villar has been a festerin' sore in him for a lot of years. How are you feelin'?"

"Chase admits that I'm about eighty percent now and gaining a percentage point every day. It's going to take us at least six weeks to clear the state. I'll be back in the saddle by that time. Our statisticians here at HQ tell me the Rebels killed nearly twelve thousand outlaws. We've taken a thousand prisoners. That still leaves two thousand unaccounted for."

"I don't think we'll ever hear from any of them again," Ike said. "I think they've gone hard underground and won't resurface as outlaws. The people we're setting up in outposts will never allow the criminal element to get the upper hand again. When those that got away do resurface, my guess is they'll be very law-abiding citizens for the rest of their lives. They know that one step out of line will leave them hanged or shot. Either way, they'll be dead."

"All right, Ike. Split your battalions and go over the taken ground again. Inspect every road you've covered and every road you didn't go down. Talk to the survivors and take down what they need in the way of supplies. We'll get it to them. Arm them. I'll see you in a couple of weeks."

"Ten-four, Eagle. Shark out."

The Rebels tried for days to contact Nome by radio. They never got any response. If there were survivors on the Seward Peninsula, they wanted to be left alone.

There were a hundred towns west of the last major highway in Alaska. The Rebels could only hope they were in kinder control than the towns and cities they had just liberated. They had no way of knowing and no way to find out. They had done flyovers in those areas where the planes and choppers could safely go and return without refueling. Anything beyond that margin of safety for the aircraft was charted as unknown.

Ben ordered Rebels to cross over into Canada, Yukon Territory, to take Highway 5 north as far as the last town shown on any map, and see what they might find. They radioed back that the town had been destroyed and there was no sign of survivors.

The Rebels would inspect all the other highways and side roads on their way back to the lower forty-eight.

Ben had looked like death the last time Ike had seen him. The man who met the columns this time was the old Ben. Ben Raines was now back in command, and Ike couldn't have been happier about that. Ben stood in the road at Tok and waved at the Rebels as they passed by.

"You are lookin' good, ol' hoss!" Ike said, grabbing Ben's hand and shaking it.

"I feel fine, Ike. I'm not a hundred percent yet, but I'm getting there. Let's get all the commanders together in my CP and have some coffee and conversation."

Coffee poured and honeyed, Ben said, "The only outlaws we couldn't account for this run are these: Satan, Meg, and Red Manlovich. All the others are either confirmed dead or prisoners waiting to stand trial. I agree with Ike that when those three I mentioned do surface they'll probably lead very quiet lives. The mood of the survivors is not likely to change anytime soon, and if any outlaws do show up bulling their way around again, they'll be dead meat before they can blink."

Ben walked to a large, laminated wall map of the United States. "Here is our routes back to the east coast. We're going to clean-sweep the lower forty-eight. Your battalion routes are clearly marked. Make a copy and study it."

"You're going to deal with Voleta, Father?" Buddy asked.

"That's correct, son. I won't leave for Europe until she and her followers have been neutralized."

"I'd feel better about this if our battalions were joined, Ben," Ike said. "Intelligence shows that Voleta has quite a following in Michigan. What about it?"

Ben slowly nodded his head. "All right, Ike. You link up with me. All the other battalions remain the same except for Georgi and Danjou. Georgi, you'll move north a notch as will Danjou. West, you'll stay where you are. Now then, I'm having a lot of supplies flown in for us to take out on way east. We'll be stopping at outposts and setting up new ones, so we'll need a lot of supplies; no telling how much we'll have to drop off along the way."

Ben sipped his coffee and looked over his commanders. He knew perfectly well they were also giving him a good eyeballing. They wanted to be certain that Ben was one hundred percent before shoving off.

Ben said, "Dan, you and Therm will be taking the southernmost route. You and Buddy will split up just inside Texas, with you taking I-10 all the way to the coast, with Buddy taking I-20. Son, that will put you right through Base Camp One. Stop and tell everybody hello, shake Cecil's hand, see how my dogs are doing, and then get back on the road."

Buddy grinned. "Yes, sir."

"Tina, you'll be taking I-40 all the way through. Rebet, you'll be wandering around on two-lanes most of the time, so you have fun, now, you hear?"

Rebet laughed. "I shall make a joyride out of it, General. But always keeping my ears and eyes open and my weapon at the ready."

"There you go," Ben said with a smile. "West, you're on I-70 to the Mississippi. Find a way across and get on I-64. Start angling south to Carolina once you cross over into Virginia. Danjou, you have a straight shot on I-80. Georgi will eventually link up with Ike and me in the Chicago area. All right, boys and girls. We'll get squared away here and then head out ASAP. Let's get to work."

Once the Rebels made up their mind to do something, they usually got down and did it very quickly. And packing up and pulling out was something they were experts at. On a late summer's day, hours before dawn, the Rebels pulled out of Alaska heading for the Canadian border, just a few hours drive away from Tok. They crossed the line early that morning, and late in the afternoon they linked up with the patrol that had been sent up Highway 5 in the Yukon to check on survivors. That patrol had angled on down to a tiny town called Haines Junction and was waiting for the main body of Rebels.

The Rebel columns, with Ben Raines once more riding at the head, stood down at the junction for the evening. They had traveled three hundred miles that first day out of Tok and had met absolutely no resistance.

The outlaw movement had been crushed and ground into the earth under the boots of Raines's Rebels.

Chase was waiting for Ben and sat him down and checked him over thoroughly. Finally, with a disgusted look on his face, the doctor said, "You're one hundred percent, Ben. Damn, I was hoping I could find just a little something to bitch at you about."

"Sorry about that, Lamar. But I'll confess that I am a little tired."

"Ah-hah!" Chase hollered. "Overdid it, didn't you? See that he continues his medication and that he eats properly and gets plenty of rest, Linda."

"It's my *ass* that's tired, Lamar!" Ben told him. "Jesus, we've been riding all day."

The Rebels made two hundred and eighty miles the next day, stopping for the night at a small town about a hundred miles west of Watson Lake. They dropped off supplies at Watson Lake, checked over the outpost and pushed on, with Ben sending West's battalion down Highway 37 and the rest of the column continuing on Highway 97 toward Fort Nelson. They would all link up at Prince George and push on toward the state of Washington, U.S.A.

The Rebels had not fired a shot since leaving Alaska. But they saw signs that the survivors were once more reclaiming territory. They saw a number of bodies that had been hanged from the nearest tree or pole, many with signs around their necks saying: OUTLAW OR MURDERER OR RAPIST.

At Prince George, Ben again split the column. Ike took half down Highways 16 and 5. Ben led the other half straight down 97. They would reconnect at Princeton, BC and a few hours later push over the line back into the United States.

Summer was now gradually giving way to early autumn. The leaves were changing colors and a hint of approaching winter was evident in the early-morning air. The Rebels had pushed off from northern California on March the fifteenth; they reentered the United States in the middle of September.

On their way back, the Rebels had checked out ten new outposts, resupplied those survivors, and had not fired one shot. Ben knew there were still outlaws in the brush and timber; only a fool would think otherwise. But those outlaws who had escaped the Rebels' purge would think long and hard before resuming their criminal careers. Some would, of course, but most would simply keep a very low profile and try to behave themselves. After a few years, they would resurface with a new name and work their way into the society of an outpost. They would be photographed and fingerprinted and become a part of the new order that was rising throughout the United States and Canada.

There would be those who would know what the ex-outlaws had once been. But as long as they remained EX-outlaws, their past could stay buried. Those who genuinely wanted it could start all over.

Inside the borders of the U.S.A., the commanders gathered for one more meeting before they split up and began their final eastward sweep of the States. They were waiting at a small town about a hundred and fifty miles south of the Canadian border to be resupplied by plane from Base Camp One.

"Anybody got any questions or suggestions?" Ben asked.

No one did.

"All right. Dan, you and Therm will be resupplied first and then shove off. Buddy, Tina, Rebet, West, Danjou, Georgi, Ike, and me—in that order. Once we're on the road and rolling, I want everybody stood down and in camp by 1700 hours every day. We'll make radio contact at 1800 hours, every day, until we've reached the East Coast and linked up.

"People, we're going to be gone a long time, so let's do this right and leave Cecil a nice, orderly country to govern in our absence. We're not going to push this time; we're going to take it nice and slow and check it all out. We're going to send patrols down every road and look around and talk to people. If something is wrong, we'll try to set it right. If communities don't want to be a part of our system, thank them, tell them goodbye, and don't call us for help. Ever.

"I want a complete remapping of the highway system this time around. If a bridge is out, chart it. If it needs repairs, log it and Cecil will send crews out to try to fix it. If you meet armed resistance, crush it.

"We're going to have planes and choppers in the sky, ranging ahead of us the entire trip. Another

239

squadron is ready to go out of the training school, so that will give each battalion at least four helicopter gunships, and by the time we reach the coast two more squadrons will be ready to go.

"That's it, people. Good luck. Godspeed, and take off."

4

The battalions began departing from the staging area in Washington state. No one would start eastward until Dan's command—the section the furthest south—was in place in El Paso.

The gangs of outlaws who still roamed the nation, and there were many, experienced a very sudden reduction in ranks when the news spread that the Rebels were sweeping the countryside. Life had already become very nearly intolerable for the outlaws still operating in the States. The law-abiding citizens living in and around the many Rebel outposts just did not have the patience nor the inclination to show very much compassion for those who chose to follow a life of lawlessness. One ex-outlaw summed it up this way: "Damn folks will shoot you for trying to steal a cow or a car or for just trying to take some pussy from a woman who chose not to give it up."

And the trials now were nothing like they were back in the good old days. They were very short.

The emphasis now was not on how the evidence was obtained, but whether or not the accused was innocent or guilty of the crime.

And to the criminal mind, or to the mind of those types of people who didn't care about the rights of others, the Rebel law was really odd. Start spreading untrue gossip about somebody, and that somebody would very likely come looking for you with a gun in his or her hand. It sure wasn't like the old days when anybody could say anything mean and cruel and malicious about anybody else and couldn't nobody do anything about it except argue and bicker in a so-called court of law.

Law was now very quick in Rebel country . . . and sometimes very final.

The criminal mind, and the minds of those who, before the Great War, had taken a perverse delight in bullying their way through life—physically or verbally—now found that old saw was double-toothed on both sides.

This new common-sense type of law was really hard for those types of people to comprehend. Like that fellow down there in Texas who asked that woman for some pussy and then slapped her around when she refused: woman's husband come around and shot him *dead*. What did the courts do about it? Nothing. Judge said the dead man should have kept his foul mouth shut and his hands to himself. Now, *shit*, boys! Who could live under such laws as that?

Obviously, a lot of people not only wanted to try the Rebel way, but after they tried it, they liked the concept, once they got used to how simple it was.

Criminals of all types, bullies, con artists, very arrogant folks, and those people who enjoy insulting, belittling, and browbeating others did not like the new system at all.

A lot of Rebels were amused and many were often baffled at the reluctance of some people to live in a society that had so few rules.

"It's too simple," Ben told them. "Too much responsibility is placed on the individual in our society as compared to what they were accustomed to when Big Brother was constantly looking over their shoulders. Now if someone screws up, they can't blame anyone but themselves. Many people don't want that responsibility; they'd rather blame someone else."

"Like a punk that goes out and kills somebody and then blames society for it?" Ben was asked.

"Exactly."

"And people really believed that crap back before the Great War?"

"Enough of them did—or said they did—until they had our judicial system so fouled up it was unworkable."

"Must have been a lot of stupid people back then."

"That's not exactly what those of us who were branded as conservatives called them," Ben said, very, very dryly.

It was going to take about a week for Dan to reach his location, so the Rebels busied themselves loading up the gear from the supply planes that landed every hour and transferring the fuel from the tankers that rolled in around the clock to their own tankers.

The tank commanders rolled their monsters out into empty fields and checked their guns. Drivers of the deuce and a halves and their mechanics went over the trucks, replacing one part or the other and sometimes rebuilding the engines.

The helicopter pilots and crews worked over their choppers. The medics restocked aid kits. The cooks cleaned and scrubbed and kept the Rebels fed. The nurses and doctors inventoried and kept their supplies up to date and full. The infantry people stayed sharp on rifle ranges and close combat courses. The clerks and office personnel kept ahead of the paperwork. Intelligence poured over maps and charts and reports. The engineers checked their Bailey bridges and road building and repairing equipment. Communications hummed around the clock. The commanders, from generals to sergeants, studied their routes and charted every road they would take in this final sweep of the lower forty-eight. Everybody had something to do, and they did it without being told. That also was the Rebel way.

"Everybody reporting in place, General," Corrie told him.

It was cold in central Washington for this time of year; the meteorologists were predicting an early and savage winter. No one knew why the Great War had produced such a change in the earth's climate, since few nuclear weapons had been used, but something had affected the weather:

summers were hotter and winters were colder. It made no sense to those who were supposed to be the experts in such things.

"Don't worry about it," Ben told them. "Someday we'll all get a chance to ask God."

On this cold fall morning, Ben drained his mug of coffee and put the mug on the seat of the big armor-plated wagon. "Mount up and roll, people."

Danjou and West had both asked Ben about crossing Utah. Those people who ruled Utah—and they ruled with an iron hand and a religious fervor that borderlined on fanaticism—had shown no interest in joining the Rebel movement.

"Proceed across the state," Ben told his people. "Don't bother anyone and be friendly. If you're attacked, strike back with everything you've got and make them understand the first time around that we're not going to take any shit off of anyone."

Both Danjou and West had grinned and returned to their battalions. Ben was going to let the religious community in that state run their own affairs. But he had also said that free travel would not be restricted and nobody was going to be hassled moving to and from and in and out of the state. And if he had to enforce that at the point of a gun, he would.

From border to border, the Rebels began their long slow sweep of the lower forty-eight. Before any battalion had covered fifty miles, they found communities sprouting up, small settlements, nearly all of whom welcomed the sight of the

Rebels. From lower Texas to Washington, the Rebels stopped and took pictures and fingerprints.

"So it's starting all over again, huh?" one man said, standing in line in a tiny town in eastern Washington.

"What's that?" Ben asked, leaning against a fender of a Jeep.

"Big Brother."

"No one is forcing you to take part in this."

"You're not going to make me get a mug shot and have my prints taken?"

"Not if you don't want to."

"What happens then?"

"You won't be a part of this group. Without an I.D. card with your picture on it, you can't get medical help or help of any kind from the Rebels or from any outpost. But that choice is strictly up to you."

The man stared at Ben. Ben stared back. The citizen had bright, hard, mean eyes, looked to be in good physical shape, and had a demeanor that irritated Ben. He came across as a man who wanted something for nothing—a type that had always brought out the worst in Ben.

"I don't think I'll go along with this," the man said.

"Your choice," Ben told him. "Step out of the line and carry your ass, then."

"What?"

"You heard me. Move on."

"I *live* here, Raines."

"Fine. But you're going to be a very lonesome man when it comes to health care, a job, food, and other necessities for staying alive. Not to mention that you won't be allowed to use the new money the government has printed."

The man stared at him. Ben sensed his words were finally getting through to him. Ben also could guess with a fair amount of accuracy what the man was going to say. He was right on the money.

"You think you're so high and mighty, don't you, Raines?"

Ben kept his temper. Barely. "Look, asshole," he said. "I'm going to say this once, and only once. Because I don't have the time or the patience to stand here debating how best to put this nation back on the right track with someone who is obviously suffering from a severe case of arrested development . . ."

"Hey, you can't talk to me like . . ."

"Shut your goddamn mouth!" Ben yelled at him. "And listen. You'll either follow the few rules the Rebels lay down or you can carry your ass outside this zone. That's it, and that's final. Now make up your mind and do it damn quick."

"Fine," the man said, his face flushing with anger and resentment. "I'll just get me a piece of ground outside this so-called zone and live the way I damn well please to live."

"Good. That's fine. I'm sure the people around here will be glad to see you go."

About two dozen men and women nodded their heads in agreement with that.

The surly citizen caught the nodding of heads and his angry flush deepened. He started cursing the men and women. Ben did not attempt to stop the cursing; let the man get it all out of his system. But when he started on the kids, Ben stopped it.

"That's all," he said quietly. "Knock it off, mister."

The citizen whirled around, fists clenched. "And if I don't?" he challenged.

Ben hit him. He drove the butt of his M-14 into the man's belly and the citizen hit the ground, choking and gasping for breath, both hands holding his bruised belly. Ben turned to the crowd.

"Exactly what is this jerk's problem?" he tossed the question out to anyone who could give him an answer.

"You just said it all, General," a woman told him. "He's a jerk. He's rude, he's loud, he's arrogant, he's a bully, and he always has been."

"He's not lazy," a man said. "He works hard. But . . . he won't pull with anyone else. What work he does is all for himself. I won't say he takes away from the group; but he sure doesn't contribute anything."

The citizen on the ground got to his knees, and with an effort, to his feet. He stared at the men and women of the tiny settlement. "I hate ever' damn one of you," he said, the words flowing like venom from his mouth. "I'm bigger and stronger than any of you and you're jealous of that . . ."

A man in the group sighed. "Jack, that's not true. Ever since we came together we've all shared what we had with each other. But not you. If you killed a deer, you ate the best and let the rest rot rather than share it as the rest of us do. You've

248

never been a part of this community. You know where the outlaws are in this area, you associate with them, and the general consensus is you run with them from time to time. Now it's time for you to choose what life-style you want."

"What outlaws?" Ben asked.

"Jack's cousin, Glenn Barlow," a woman said. "He's got a gang of about fifty men who operate out of a town just north of us."

"Glenn's all right," Jack said. "He just don't like to live under a bunch of rules, that's all. He ain't never bothered none of you people, has he?" He stared at the group, then smiled. "That's right, he hasn't. And he won't as long as I'm here. So think about that 'fore you link up with Raines here."

"What town?" Ike asked.

A man stepped out of the line, pulling a battered old map from his hip pocket. He pointed to a town. "There."

"Any women or kids with the group?" Ben asked.

"No kids. And the women are trash. Just as bad as Barlow and his men," a woman spoke up. "Maybe worse," she added.

"Prisoners, slaves?" Ben asked.

"No."

"Check it out," Ben ordered. "Let's start sweeping with a big broom."

Ike pointed to a company commander. "Go."

"I'll be leavin' now," Jack said.

"You'll stay here and enjoy our hospitality," Ben told him. "We wouldn't want your cousin to be tipped off, now, would we?"

Jack looked at the Rebels, looking at him. One of the Rebels smiled and lifted the muzzle of his M-16 ever so slightly. Jack got the message. He nodded his head. "Law and order and follow the rules, huh, Raines?"

"Those rules and regulations are helping to pull a nation back together, Jack," Ben said.

"How about those of us who like it the way it is?"

"If you like conditions as they are outside any secure zone, Jack, that makes you either a damn fool or a damn outlaw. I could excuse a fool, but I have nothing but contempt for the lawless."

"So where does that leave me, Raines?"

"Well, Jack, once we deal with your cousin . . ." He paused as half a dozen gunships hammered into the air, heading for the outlaw town. ". . . and his pack of crud, I'd suggest that you give some hard thought to what it's going to be like living outside of a secure zone. It isn't going to be pleasant."

"I think I'll take my chances on it, Raines."

"Your ass, Jack," Ben's words were void of emotion. He turned and walked away.

"That's a troublemaker, General," Jersey said, keeping pace with him. "We'd better deal with him before we leave."

"He hasn't done anything, Jersey."

"But it's a pretty good bet that he will."

"Yes. But I can't shoot him because I *think* he's going to turn bad. Dealing with him is going to be up to the people of this outpost. We can't hold their hands, Jersey. They've got to take control and enforce the rules. If they can't do that, the outpost will fall. It's just that simple."

Jersey turned and looked back at Jack, standing alone, outside the line of citizens being processed. "I don't like him. I think he's a creep."

Ben laughed at his little bodyguard. "Chill out, Jersey."

"Chill out, General? *Chill out?*"

"That's an expression that was popular about the time you were being born, I would imagine. Means calm down, cool it, take it easy."

"Chill out, huh? Chill out. I like it. Wait'll I spring that on Cooper. He'll . . ."

"Fuck you, Raines!" Jack screamed from behind them.

Ben was lifting the muzzle of his M-14 as he turned in a crouch to offer a smaller target.

Jersey beat him to the shot. She gave Jack a three round burst of M-16 5.56 lead into his chest. The man dropped his pistol to the ground and was only seconds behind following it. He was still alive when Ben and Jersey reached him, standing over the dying man.

"I'd have been famous," Jack managed to gasp. "I'd have been the man who killed Ben Raines."

"He's a hard man to kill, mister," a medic said, ripping open Jack's shirt, looking at the wounds, then looking up at Ben and shaking his head.

A chaplain pushed through the knot of Rebels and knelt down beside Jack. "Are you religious?" he asked.

"Shit!" Jack said, then closed his eyes, shuddered, and died.

Moments later, a woman yelled from the line, as she pointed north. "Look!"

Smoke was billowing into the sky.

"You won't have to worry about that bunch of outlaws anymore," Ike said. "Or the town," he added.

Jersey clicked her M-16 back on safety and looked up at Ben. "I told you I didn't like that damn Jack," she said.

5

The Rebels rolled on, the columns moving slowly. The unit commanders stopped at every crossroads and sent out patrols, checking every tiny dot of a town that showed on a map. And they were, to a person, amazed at the number of people who had surfaced after the Rebels' first sweep of the States.

Ben had left the interstate to bypass the ruins of Spokane and had stopped his columns at a settlement about fifty miles north of that city, on the Idaho line.

The survivors there looked as though they had just been through one hell of a firefight. Some of the buildings were still smoking and many others were pocked from bullets.

"Bunch of outlaws led by a man calls himself Burl hit us late yesterday afternoon," a spokesperson said. "We beat them back, but just barely. They outnumber us ten to one and getting stronger while we're getting weaker."

"Where are they operating out of?" Ben asked.

"Just across the old state line, about twenty-five miles east of here." She produced a map and pinpointed the town.

"Kids in there?" Ike asked.

"Yes, sir. They pick up every stray they can find knowing that we won't attack their town if it's full of kids. And it is filled with kids. It's disgraceful; they don't take care of the kids and many of them are abused. There are some people in this world who'd trade off anything they had for a young boy or girl . . . depending on their sexual preferences," she added, disgust in her voice.

"We'll take care of it," Ben said, patting the woman on her arm. "Right now, let's get you resupplied and settled in on a more permanent basis. Then I'll arrange to do something about the outlaws and get the kids out of there."

Later, over coffee in his big tent, Ben said, "Ike, send a company, tanks with them, and come in behind the town, using this road." He pointed to a map. "I'll send a company north and block the only other road out of town. We'll drop tear gas in on them at dawn. It'll be tough on the kids for a few minutes, but at least that way they'll be alive. We'll take the town hand to hand."

"I'll start moving Scouts into position now," Ike said. He stared at Ben. "Are you going in, Ben?"

Ben surprised him by shaking his head. "No. I'm not fully satisfied that I'm up to doing that just yet. I'll know when I am. Until that time, I'll just stay back and direct operations."

Ike grinned. "That will please Chase."

"He's still gloating about it."

The Scouts had worked in close to the town and were in position, wearing gas masks, before the other companies, with tank support, clanked up. The outlaws in the town were quick to respond.

"We'll kill the brats!" the voice pushed through a bullhorn informed the Rebels. "You attack this town and the brats go first. You better think about that."

"That tells you something about the caliber of people who control the town," Ben said. "Assault troops get into masks. Tell the choppers to drop the gas. Corrie, tell the assault troops to get ready to go in fast and hard."

The outlaws were expecting an attack from ground troops, but they were not suspecting the use of tear gas. The choking and blinding fumes caught them off-guard and ill-prepared. The Rebels were all over the outlaws before any child could be permanently harmed.

"Which one is Burl?" a company commander asked a man, his words slightly muffled by the gas mask.

"You go fuck yourself!" the outlaw snarled.

The company commander shot the outlaw between the eyes with a .45 autoloader and walked to another outlaw, pinned to the ground by the muzzle of a Rebel's M-16.

The young captain pointed the .45 at the man. "I'll ask you the same question."

"Over yonder!" the outlaw screamed, pointing frantically. Some of the dead outlaw's brains had splattered on him. "Jesus God Amighty. Ain't you people never heard of trials and lawyers and such as that?"

"Haven't you ever heard of common decency?"

The outlaw slobbered on himself in reply. He was trying hard not to look at his dead buddy lying only two feet away from him. Half his buddy's head was gone from the hollow-nosed .45 slug fired at nearly point-blank range.

"All the kids are out," a platoon leader told the captain.

The captain lifted a walkie-talkie. "The town is secure, General. What about the prisoners?"

"You know what to do with them," Ben's reply was very blunt.

Two of the outlaws in the town had escaped by running across a field into a stand of timber. They watched through binoculars as the members of the outlaw gang were lined up and shot.

"That's it for me," one of the two said, lowering his field glasses. "I'm done outlawin'."

"I'm with you," the only other outlaw to escape the wrath of the Rebels said. "You layin' next to a law-abidin' farmer from this moment on."

Both of them shuddered in horror as the bodies of the outlaws were buried in a mass grave, the hole scooped out with bulldozers from Rebel flat-bed trucks and covered over and smoothed out.

The pair slipped further into the timber and vanished. Outlawing held no more pleasure for either of them. They had seen firsthand what others had told them: you don't jack around with Ben Raines, 'cause he don't cut you no slack.

"You'll take care of the children?" Ben asked the people of the community, as the outlaw town across the line was being carefully picked over and then demolished.

"Oh, yes," the spokesperson said. "Half the children in this community have been taken in from off the road." She stuck out her hand and Ben shook it. "Thank you, General Raines."

The Rebels pulled out, moving westward. The outlaw gangs that lay in front of the mighty advance of Rebels also pulled out as news of the Rebels reached them, usually by shortwave radio.

"Just lined 'em up and shot 'em dead," the word came down the line.

"That damn Ben Raines ain't jackin' around, people," another transmission chilled the outlaws in front of the Rebels. "If you an outlaw, you dead. He's settin' up secure zones all over the country. I'm through, boys. I'm done with the outlawin' game. You ain't never gonna hear from me again."

"They could have won the war against drugs back before the Great War if Ben Raines had run the show," another said. "All the government would have had to do is put him in charge and it'd been the shortest damn war in history. This is it for me, boys and girls. This outlaw is a changed man. I done seen with my own eyes too many guys I knowed either shot or hanged. There ain't no stoppin' the Rebels. Get out while you can."

In Michigan, Sister Voleta, or what was left of the crazy woman, sat in her wheelchair and listened to the shortwave transmissions. She would pause only to curse Ben Raines and the child she had borne him, the child who had turned on her. Her wild hatred for Ben and Buddy Raines helped keep her alive. The once-beautiful woman now would turn the stomach of a buzzard. A tank had crushed her legs. Fire had taken her hair and nearly melted her face. Hatred had done the rest.

"We will make our stand here," she told a man standing nearby. "The Ninth Order will either emerge victorious, or we shall all die right here."

"Yes, Sister," the man said.

Voleta was trapped and knew it. She had no place left to run. Ben Raines and the Rebels had destroyed all her allies. Even Ashley was now dead. The Night People were so pitifully few in number they posed no threat to anyone. Citizens all over the United States were hunting them down and killing them.

Voleta could not go north. The damn Canadians were just waiting for her to show her ugly face there. She could not move east because of the lake. South were Rebel outposts. And Ben Raines was coming from the west.

Voleta turned in her motorized wheelchair. "Order all our followers to prepare for war," she told the robed and hooded man standing nearby.

"Yes, Sister," the man whispered, and then left the darkened room.

*　　*　　*

"Dan on the horn, General," Ben was told.

He walked to communication and took the mike. "Go, Dan."

"Everything is clean, Ben," the former British SAS man said. "We've had sporadic firefights with outlaws. But they're losing their steam. Word has gone out that the Rebels are advancing and many of the outlaws and their like are packing it in. We've got to talk about surrender terms."

"All right. I'll order all units to hold what they've got and we'll all fly into a central location for a meeting. My bunch has not been approached by any outlaws seeking amnesty."

"They're scared of you, Ben," Dan was blunt. "That's the bottom line."

"That's the way I like it," Ben was equally blunt.

Dan chuckled over the miles. "Looking at a map here, how about the outpost in western Nebraska?"

"Sounds good. I'll bump the others and we'll get together. See you soon, Dan." He handed the mike back and said, "Get all the other commanders on a linkup, please."

Ben lined up a meeting date then walked back to his tent. He found Ike waiting for him.

"What's up, Ben?"

"I just spoke with Dan. Seems a lot of outlaws have contacted our southern units seeking surrender terms. We're going to meet in Nebraska day after tomorrow."

Ike smiled. "We've done it, Ben. They're givin' it up."

"Yes. But how far can we trust the bastards? Anytime you have to put a gun to someone's head to make them straighten up and fly right, odds are as soon as you remove the muzzle, they're up to their old tricks again."

"That was true in the old days, Ben. But we—you, mostly—have changed all that. Back before the Great War, the laws didn't have any teeth to them, and the criminals knew it. They made a mockery out of our judicial system and the people who tried to enforce the laws. It's not that way now. We've buried too many punks and crud and slime on our back trail. They know we mean business and they know that when we set up an outpost, the people we leave there mean business."

"There will always be some crime, Ike. But you're right: we've shown the law-abiding people that they can have about a ninety-five percent crime-free society. Oh, well," he said with a sigh. "Pack your ditty bag, Ike. Let's get ready to put the cap on this campaign."

"Ben?"

Ben glanced at his friend.

"Sit down, Ben. Let's talk about Sister Voleta."

Ben poured a mug of coffee and sat down. "What about her, Ike?"

"I've been thinkin' on it, Ben. I want you to do me a favor."

"If I can, sure."

Ike pulled a map out of his map case and opened

it to the midwest. "When we get into Minnesota, Ben, I want you to take your battalion and cut south; link up with Georgi outside of Chicago."

"Now why would I want to do something like that?"

"You sent Buddy a thousand miles away from Michigan, Ben. And we both know why. Now I want you to stand clear and let me take out Voleta."

Ben sipped his coffee and studied his friend for a few seconds. "Tell me all of it, Ike."

"I realize that Buddy knows his mother is evil and has to be destroyed. He's told me that. But if you killed her, Ben, it would never be the same between you and your son. It might make only a small difference; but it would make a difference."

Ben nodded his agreement. "She's a tough bitch, Ike. And she's evil clear through. You know all that."

"Are you giving me the green light?"

"Yes. And I thank you for volunteering to do it." He smiled. "Now tell me the intelligence you have on her that you haven't shared with me."

Ike laughed and whacked Ben on the knee with his hand. "Same ol' Ben. Sharp, boy, sharp. OK. She's in a box, Ben. She made it thinkin' she was smart. But she was stupid. She's right here, Ben." He pointed to the map. "The Canadians have moved down this highway and are blocking this bridge. She can't go north. Some of the new outposts in southern Michigan moved forces north and are blocking her in that direction. She's trapped by the lakes east and west. She had a pretty good location a few months back; why she moved is anybody's guess. But she did. And now she trapped herself."

"How heavily dug in is she?"

"She's dug in tight. But I'll use gunships and artillery to loosen her up."

"All right. It's your show. Finish her, Ike, once and for all."

"I intend to, Ben. And you can bet the farm on that." He folded his map and replaced it in the case. "Now, let's talk about these outlaws who want to give it up."

"Let's have your feelings on it."

"Have you talked with Cecil about it? He's the one who is going to have to deal with them once we're gone."

Ben shook his head. "Not yet. Ike, where in the hell will we put them if we decide that prison is the answer?"

"Prison has never been the answer for anyone yet. Not without rehabilitation, and these are going to be hard cases. All prison is is a classroom for crime. Gang rape and perversion and despair. And these guys are going to be toughest of the lot. They've survived for over a decade. We've probably fought several of the gangs who are now offering to surrender."

"I know that only too well, Ike. That doesn't answer my question. But I agree with what you said."

"Ben . . . I don't know what to do with them.

How many are we talking about anyway?"

"Several thousand, at least." Ben was thoughtful for a moment, then he smiled, and soon the smile had turned into hard laughter.

"You find something funny about dealin' with these punks and thugs, Ben?"

"I just had a thought."

"Must have been a hell of a thought."

It was.

6

Striganov roared with laughter. Therm looked stunned at the thought that hard-assed, unforgiving and ruthless Ben Raines would even consider it. Dan chuckled. Danjou and Rebet shook their heads. West smiled. Tina and Buddy looked at their father in astonishment.

"Are you serious, Father?" Buddy was the first to speak.

"Can anybody come up with a better idea?" Ben challenged the group.

"What alternative are you going to give them, Dad?" Tina asked.

"Long prison terms, in some cases a rope or firing squad. The choice of the latter two can be theirs."

"Very magnanimous gesture on your part, I must say," the Russian said, wiping his eyes with a handkerchief. "Hell, I like it, Ben. The French had success with the same idea for years, albeit not on this grand a scale. Although they denied they ever used hardened criminals in the Legion."

"It would give us anywhere from three to five more battalions of troops," Dan said. "And we know these people can fight. I request to be their training officer."

"You can sure have the job, Dan," Ben told him.

"All right, people. I'm not going to force this issue on you. We have to take into consideration that these men, once trained and armed, might turn on us. They might reject the offer. They might all wash out during training. We're facing a lot of unknowns here."

"My vote is yes," Georgi said.

"And mine," Rebet said.

"You already know my vote, Ben," Ike said.

"I'm for it," Therm said.

"Count me in," Tina said.

"And me," Danjou spoke up.

"Go for it," West said. "Hell, half the men in my original battalion were criminals before they joined me."

"I'll vote yes," Buddy said.

"Chase agrees," Ben said. "All right. We're unanimous. Now let's find out how the outlaws feel about it."

The Rebels halted their advance to give the printers down at Base Camp One time to go to press, running off hundreds of thousands of copies of the Rebels' terms for surrender.

Copies were flown to Ben and he approved the final wording. "Start dropping them," he ordered.

"Blanket each state and let's see the reaction."

The Rebels on the ground relaxed while the pilots went to work distributing the leaflets from the air.

In Kansas, one outlaw leader read the message. "Be a fuckin' *soldier?*" he said, then laughed. "That damn Ben Raines. If this don't beat all I ever seen. That man don't miss a bet."

"What do you think?" a gang member asked.

"Well," the outlaw said with a philosophical shrug of his shoulders, "if you can't beat 'em, join 'em!"

In Indiana, members of a gang read the leaflets again and again.

"It's a trap," one said.

"No," another disagreed. "No, it ain't. If Ben Raines gives his word, that's firm. He's a man of honor."

"We ain't never gonna beat the Rebels," another said. "If we fight 'em, they're gonna kill us."

"We're gonna die if we join up with 'em, too," another voice was heard.

"How do you figure?"

"Hell, he'll use us for shock troopers. We'll be the ones who go in first."

"Maybe. Maybe not." He stood up and folded the leaflet, tucking it in a pocket. "The notice said to gather in Central Kansas. And to tie a white handkerchief on our upper left arm to show good faith."

"And we can come armed," a man said. "That's the part that spooks me. It might be a trap."

"It's no trap," the gang leader said. "If Ben

Raines says it's on the up and up, it's up and up. I'm goin' out there. There ain't no future in what we're doin'."

"Well," another said, getting up. "There ain't much future in joinin' the Rebels neither. But there's a chance we might come out alive. If we continue to fight them Rebels, we don't have any chance of stayin' alive for very long. I'm with you, Bob. Lemmie get my stuff packed."

In Minnesota, the leader of the largest outlaw gang left in the state read the leaflet for the umpteenth time. He sighed and put the leaflet in his pocket. "I'm tired of it, people. Tired of running all the damn time. Hell, I'm gonna pack it in and join up."

"And the rest of us?" a henchman asked.

"Do what you want to do. This is one job I can't order you to take. But I'll leave you with this: fightin' the Rebels means you're gonna die. That's hard fact. This leaflet says this is the only chance, the last chance that Ben Raines is gonna give us. After this deadline is up, he's gonna track us down and kill us. To the last person, people. No trial, no courts of law, no nothin' except a bullet or a rope or gettin' blown up by long range artillery or bein' chopped to bits by them damn gunships the Rebels is usin'. If we gotta die violent, let's do it with some honor for a change. Let's get on a winnin' side. God knows, we ain't done nothin' right for a decade."

A woman stood up and slung her AK-47. "Hell, Curt, let's go."

In Missouri, several small gangs came together

for a meeting. "What'd you think, Ned?" a woman asked the leader of a rival gang.

"I'm takin' the offer, Bette," he said without hesitation. "Look at it like this: we're facin' *thousands* of Rebels. They got tanks and artillery and helicopter gunships. We got a bunch of rifles and pistols and wore-out cars and trucks and that's all we got. Jesus, people," he said, turning to look for a second at everyone present. "Look at us. We're dirty, we're ragged, we smell bad. We're on the run from people in Rebel outposts. We're really something, aren't we? Big, tough outlaws. Is this what we started out to be?"

"The cops pushed me into this life," a man said. "They was always hasslin' me."

The others laughed at him.

Ned said, "Oh, fuck off, Pardham. Nobody pushed you into bein' what you are anymore than they did me or any of the rest of us here. We walked into it with our eyes wide open. If you got rousted by a cop—back when we had cops—you probably deserved it. I know I did . . . lookin' back. We thought the laws didn't apply to us. We thought we could just steal something and we shouldn't get punished for it.   Don't hand me any of that headshrink bullshit about society bein' at fault."

"I ain't goin' for this amnesty crap," Pardham said. "I'm stayin' right here and doin' what I been doin'."

"Then you're a fool," a woman told him. "Ben Raines has got this country put back together . . . at least he's got a good jump at doin' it. And the man that's gonna run this country while we're overseas—that's right, Pardham, *we*—Cecil Jefferys, is just as hard-assed as Ben Raines. Without a Rebel I.D. card, you're not goin' to get medical care, food, protection, money, nothing. The day of the criminal is over, and I think it's gonna stay over. You know what happened just a few miles from here when that guy got drunk last month and run over and killed that little boy. They tried him for murder and *hanged* him, Pardham. The laws in this country is all different, now. The old ways will never return, Pardham. Never. The people will never stand for that. Our day is over and done with. Times are closin' in on us. Not to mention the Rebels," she added softly. "And those people scare me, Pardham. They don't jack around with criminals. They just shoot you!"

Pardham shook his head in disgust. "What ever brought the country to this? And I don't necessarily mean the Great War, neither. How come ever'body started listenin' to Ben Raines?"

"'Cause the lawabidin' people of the country was tired of people like us," a man told him. He smiled. "Tell the truth, I'm tired of people like us." He picked up his rifle, stood up, and slung the weapon on one shoulder. "I'm headin' out to meet with the Rebels." He pulled a white handkerchief out of his pocket and tied it around his left arm. "I got room for four in my car if anybody wants to ride with me."

"It's an incredible sight, Father," Buddy radioed to his father. Ben was staying about ten miles from the rendezvous site. Buddy and Dan were seeing to the placement of tents at the site. Already, the outlaws were getting a taste of how the Englishman planned to run the camp.

At first, the outlaws pitched their tents and parked their raggedy-assed trailers every-which-way. When Dan walked onto the scene, all that quickly changed.

"Get those goddamned tents lined up and spaced properly!" he roared through a bullhorn, startling the hell out of the outlaws. "Good Heavens! I've never seen such a ragtag bunch of good-for-nothings in my life!"

Colonel West hit the area, yelling at the top of his lungs. He waded into the camp of heavily armed outlaws and jerked the rifle from the first man he spotted. He jerked the bolt back on the M-16, locked it in place and eyeballed down the barrel. "Disgraceful!" he yelled at the man. "This weapon is filthy." He threw it back at the man. "Clean it! I'll be back in fifteen minutes to check it." He stalked away.

The outlaw looked at his friends. "Are y'all just real sure you want to do this?"

"I don't know what you're gonna do, Pat," a friend told him. "But I'm a-fixin' to clean my rifle."

Ben ordered fully armed Hind, Cobra, Apache, and converted UH-1B Huey gunships to do a very slow flyby of the sprawling camp. The outlaws looked at the machines of war moving very slowly over their heads with all their weapons visible.

"Good God," an outlaw leader whispered.

"And we were gonna make a stand against that?"

"You might be interested in seeing this," the voice came from behind him.

The outlaw and his friends whirled around. The Russian General, Georgi Striganov and a dozen of his big Russian special forces (Spetsnaz) men faced the group. No one had heard them approach.

"Whatever you say, sir," a man in ragged and dirty jeans said.

"Follow me," Georgi told him. His men whirled around in perfect unison and marched away, following their commander.

The outlaws followed, gathering up others as they went. "Where are we goin'?" one asked.

"I don't know. I'm just doin' what I'm told to do."

"Them's the meanest lookin' bunch of guys with him I ever seen in my life. Who are they?"

"Russians, I think."

"*Russians!* Hell, I thought we was at war with Russia?"

"Naw. They're our friends now."

"Well, I'll just be damned."

Unbeknownst to the outlaws, Ben had massed all his troops within a forty-mile radius of the gathering place. There was no point in sweeping the nation; most of the outlaws were gathering here. Those that didn't would be taken care of by the people manning the outposts.

A dozen old cars and trucks had been dragged up into a field just over a rise. Half a hundred old mannequins—salvaged from stores, filled up with ketchup and then dressed in old uniforms—were standing around the vehicles.

"Tell the attack ships to give us a show," Striganov ordered. He faced the now several hundred outlaws standing on the ridge. "This is what you would have faced had you chosen to fight us. Watch."

Half a dozen Hind and Apache gunships came hammering in, firing everything they had at the cars and trucks and ketchup-filled dummies.

It was a sight that swayed any outlaw who might have been thinking the Rebels offer of joining them was not his or her cup of tea. Thick, red ketchup splattered all over the ground for fifty or more yards. The mannequins exploded under machine-gun and cannon fire. The vehicles went up with very loud explosions—since, unknown to the outlaws, the Rebels had planted boxes of old, unstable dynamite in each car or truck. Clouds of greasy smoke and bits and pieces of vehicles were blown hundreds of feet away.

The area was very silent for a time, after the last bit of metal, rubber, and glass had hit the earth. Striganov turned to look at a group of men and women who wore very shocked looks on their faces.

"Of course," the Russian said, "that was just for show and your entertainment. We become much more serious about war once it's for real."

He walked away, tapping his thigh with his swagger stick every few steps, his men right behind him.

"How much more goddamn serious can you get?" a woman asked.

"I got a hunch we're all about to find out."

"That suits me," she replied. "Just as long as I'm on the side that's giving and not receiving."

Buddy walked through the camp, a few members of his team with him. He wore what was by now his trademark—a bandana tied around his forehead—and his handsome face caused many an outlaw woman to get weak-kneed. Buddy's fatigue shirt strained against the muscles in his big arms.

"Ben Raines' kid," a man whispered. "Buddy Raines. When he ain't commandin' a full battalion, he runs a bunch of headhunters called the Rat Pack."

"He can pack my rat anytime he wants to," a woman said, and several other women giggled and agreed.

"What the hell is this?" a hard woman's voice jarred them out of their erotic fantasies. "A damn sewing circle?"

The women turned to stare at Tina Raines.

"I'm going to tell you pussies something," Tina said, fighting to keep a straight face. "You're going to find goddamn little to laugh about if you land under my command." She circled the women, a look of disgust on her tanned face.

"When's the last time you *ladies* took a bath or washed your hair? I shudder to even ask about other, more personal forms of female cleanliness . . ."

"You can't talk to us like that!" a woman yelled. "We . . ."

"Shut your fucking mouth!" Tina yelled at her. West, Buddy, and Dan stood off to one side, listening, all trying very hard to look grim and stern.

Tina got all up in the women's faces, after pulling them to attention. She traced their ancestry back to where they were mating with apes. She got all up in their faces and stayed there for several minutes. She left them with this: "I'll see you cunts at 0600 in the morning."

"That's my girl," West said with a smile.

7

The next morning, just after dawn, the camp of outlaws were rousted from their blankets by bullhorns and told to assemble south of the campsite. Like right now, damnit!

Then they were treated to hot coffee (which wasn't very good) and a hot meal (which was very good) served on mess-hall stack trays. The outlaws looked down at their trays. Hot cakes with real butter on them. Bacon and eggs and fried potatoes and biscuits and gravy and jam and jelly.

"I think I done died and gone to heaven," one outlaw said. "I think I found me a home, boys."

"Only if you can make the grade," the voice came from behind him.

The outlaw turned and looked into the face of Ben Raines, standing in line just like anybody else. The outlaw gulped a couple of times. Everybody knew the face of Ben Raines.

"You . . . ah, want to go on ahead of me, sir?" the outlaw said.

Ben shook his head. "That's not the way we do things around here. I may slip in the back and fill a tray. I may have one brought to me. But I'll never buck the line."

"Yes, sir. That's . . . ah, good, sir." The outlaw filled his tray and got gone.

The news that Ben Raines was in camp and having breakfast with them spread quickly, with outlaws craning their necks to get a glimpse of the man. Not everyone caught a glimpse of Ben, but it would have been difficult for anyone to not spot the two battalions of Rebels, all heavily armed and mixing in with the outlaws.

"Lord God Amighty," one man whispered. "Don't let nobody pull no gun on Ben Raines or we're all dead. Pass the word and pass it quick."

Ben was amused when Tina came jogging and jody-calling up with about fifty outlaw women in tow, the women staggering around and all looking like they were about to pass out from exhaustion.

"Fall out and get breakfast," she yelled at them. "Worst damn shape I've ever seen anybody in. Disgusting."

She got a tray and joined her father.

"How far did you run them, kid?" he asked.

"About a mile and a half. Easy jog. They're in pretty bad shape, pop. All of them, men and women."

"We'll get them in shape."

After breakfast, the outlaws were assembled in a huge field. Ben stepped up onto a flatbed and took the microphone. "I'll be very honest with you," he said, his voice booming over the flats. "None of you have shown me a damn thing yet. You're going to have to prove yourselves to me. Not just to me, but to your instructors—those of you who decide to stay, that is. And right here is where you'll be trained. My people will run you until you think you're going to die. And some of you will. When we're through with you and you can call yourselves Rebels, you'll be in the best physical and mental shape you've ever been in.

"There are about thirty-five hundred of you gathered here. I expect about a thousand of you to drop out. If you do, that's fine, just as long as you gave it your best shot. If you try and see that you can't make it, for whatever reason, you're free to go. Just as long as you don't return to outlawing. If you do that, we'll track you down and kill you on the spot. If you fail to make it here and you would like to join with a Rebel outpost, we'll do our best to get one to accept you. But I can't guarantee that. The survivors in those outposts have long memories. And they might decide to shoot some of you on sight.

"If you make it through the training, understand this: we are shipping out this coming spring. We are going to Europe. With you people neutralized—one way or the other . . ." He let that sink in. ". . . our work here will be finished. Some of you and some of us will not be coming back. That's the risk a soldier takes. I'm offering you people a chance to redeem yourselves and become a part of history . . ."

"Here we go," Therm whispered to Rosebud.

"Now he's going to wave the flag. There won't be a dry eye in the crowd when he's finished."

"Hush up," she told him. "I find it all . . . rather stirring."

"Good God!" Therm said.

"As far as I know," Ben said, "we are the largest standing army in the world whose sole reason for being is to restore democracy and law and order. We've done it on this continent, and south of us, in Mexico, an army much like ours, except much smaller, is clearing out the outlaws there. Canada is free, and, for all intents and purposes, a part of this nation. That was the decision of their leaders, not mine. But we welcome the Maple Leaf as part of us and we as part of them. Now it's time for us to look toward new horizons; to travel to new lands and free those who have been enslaved and beaten and have had their God-given rights and liberties taken from them."

"Pour it on, Ben," Therm said, as he looked at Emil Hite. The little con artist was standing with one hand over his heart, tears streaming down his cheeks. Therm rolled his eyes as Rosebud blew her nose and dabbed at her eyes. "Jesus, the man would have made millions as a TV preacher."

"Shut up," Rosebud said. "I don't buy all that he says, but if you didn't feel much the same way as Ben does we certainly wouldn't be a part of this movement, now would we?"

Thermopolis folded his arms across his chest and refused to answer except for a mumble.

"What'd you say?"

"Nothing, dear. Nothing."

"And you people can be a part of that," Ben said. "You can give your time and your sweat and your blood to a movement that is unparalleled in modern times. Or you can die fighting us or in a ditch or a road or in someone's living room with your guts blown out while attempting to rob some law-abiding citizen of possessions he or she gained through their own work. The choice is one only you can make. Thank you all."

Ben stepped off the flatbed and Dan took the mike. "We'll leave you people alone for the rest of the day and the evening. You can talk it over and decide. Lunch will be served to you as will dinner. We expect your decision by 0700 tomorrow."

The outlaws broke up into groups, sat down, and began talking it over. Really, as one woman put it, "We don't have much choice in the matter. But that sure was a pretty speech."

During the morning, probably two hundred and fifty outlaws pulled out. Another one hundred and fifty left that afternoon. During the night, another seventy-five quietly left the encampment. At 0700 hours the next morning, the rest stood in line for breakfast at the big mess tents.

"There it is, Ben," Ike said, looking at the long lines of men and women. "I'd guess close to three thousand. If we plan to sail by the middle of March, next year, we've got some work cut out for us."

"Six months," Ben said. "We can do it. We'll have to push them awfully hard; but it's something that has to be done. I damn sure don't want to leave them behind."

All the commanders knew that another reason Ben wanted the outlaws assembled under his command was to insure a minimum of trouble stateside when the bulk of the Rebels pulled out.

"When are you pulling out to wrap it all up, Ike?" Ben asked.

"Tomorrow morning. I figure a couple of weeks to get there and a couple of weeks to settle it once there. When I'm certain the Ninth Order is zero, I'll take the battalions over to the east coast and help getting the ships seaworthy. And by the way, Emil does know what he's talking about when it comes to ships."

"Incredible," Ben muttered.

Ike laughed at the expression on Ben's face and whacked him on the back. "I got to start getting my people moving, Ben. I'll see you before I pull out."

A head count was done just after breakfast and the outlaws—now ex-outlaws—numbered 2,775.

"Physicals first," Ben said to Chase.

"We're ready to start receiving," the doctor said.

"Tell Base Camp One to start humping it with uniforms and equipment," Ben told Corrie. "Get it up here. Tell the engineers to get busy working on that little town up the road. We'll house them there." He turned to Dan. "Have them turn in all their weapons and issue them M-16's and side-arms."

"Right, sir."

"You have instructors lined up, Dan?"

"Yes, sir."

"Start them off slow. We don't want to discourage them right off the bat."

"Right, sir. Easy does it for a couple of weeks."

"I've arranged for their kids to be transported to Base Camp One," Tina said. "The medics say the kids are in good shape considering the life they've led. Some of the women, understandably, don't want to leave their children. Those that want to stay with their kids will receive training down south and will be assigned to jobs with Cecil. He's ready to take them."

"Good enough."

"We've got quite a strange cross section, Ben," Georgi said. "Some of those outlaws were skilled workers before the Great War. Everything from EMTs to computer technicians." He consulted a clipboard. "We've got a dozen PhDs, four doctors, carpenters, truck drivers, two writers, one ex-editor from New York who knows you—he says your work was entirely too violent . . ."

Ben, and all those gathered around him, got a good laugh out of that.

". . . two reporters," Georgi continued, "a dozen salespeople, several cowboys. What is amazing to me is that very few of these people were criminals before the Great War."

"That shattered a lot of lives, Georgi. Many people just gave up and turned to lawlessness. Dan, what are your Scout patrols turning up?"

"Nothing, General. The nation is clean. Once Sister Voleta and her Ninth Order is neutralized, order will have been restored in the country."

Once the meeting had broken up, Ben took Buddy aside. "Get with Ike, Buddy. Tell him I said to offer Voleta amnesty."

"A noble gesture on your part, Father," Buddy replied. "But we both know she isn't to be trusted."

Ben sighed. "She is a crazed, crippled woman, Buddy. Tell Ike what I said. If she surrenders, which she won't, she can be institutionalized."

"Very well, Father. I request permission to accompany Ike to Michigan."

"Permission denied. I need you here."

Both knew that was a lie, but Buddy wasn't going to argue with his father. "Yes, sir."

Linda had been listening to the exchange. After Buddy had left the room, she came to Ben and took his hand in hers. "I keep seeing new sides to you, Ben. Little pockets of compassion that few people know you possess."

"I don't like to make war against the insane, Linda. And Voleta is about the nuttiest person I have ever encountered. She's dangerous, but she's insane. I've got to at least make this offer of amnesty."

"I understand." She kissed him and left the building, heading over to assist the medics with the new recruits.

Jersey walked through the new CP and into Ben's quarters. The little bodyguard never knocked. "Kinda gives me a funny feeling, General," she said. "We've been fighting here in the States for so long, and then suddenly, it's over. Now we're looking at another unknown. A whole ocean to

284

cross, and then we face only God knows what."

"I know, Jersey. And you're right when you call it the unknown. But we've got to hit them, over there, before they get it into their heads to strike at us, over here. They're not organized—yet. But give those dozens, perhaps hundreds of armies and warlords and criminals in Europe enough time, and they will get organized. Then they'll look toward the United States. That's why we've got to stop them."

"No way to figure how long it will take us, either, is there, General?"

"No. Because we don't know what we're facing. It will take years, Jersey. And many of us will never again set foot on U.S. soil. If you think about it very much, it gets to you, right in the belly."

"Damn sure does," the little bodyguard said. "It's a kind of an exciting-queasy-scared sensation." She laughed. "Sort of like your first sexual experience. And the letdown that followed it."

Ben joined her in the laughter. "Jersey, I couldn't have said it better!"

The training cycles began the next morning for those ex-outlaws who had completed their physicals. And the dispensaries stayed busy with sprains and cuts and contusions. A dozen of the new trainees dropped out after the first day. Ben had expected the number to be much higher, and he was pleased. But he knew as the training got tougher, dropouts would increase. If he could end the training cycle with 2,000 out of the 2,775 who stayed, that would give the Rebels three more battalions. And where they were heading those battalions would be desperately needed.

Ike had pulled out, taking Ben's battalion and his own, with plenty of tanks to back up the ground troops. Ike had reluctantly agreed to offer amnesty to Sister Voleta and her pack of nuts and screwballs.

Ben was sending out Scouts to the far corners of the lower forty-eight seeking out outlaw bands. They were reporting back that nothing even remotely resembling an outlaw could be found. But there sure were a lot of new farmers and chicken raisers and mighty friendly folks out in the country now.

Beth walked in the CP with a clipboard. She poured a cup of coffee, honeyed it, and pulled up a chair, laying the clipboard on the desk. "The final stats are in from Base Camp One, General. In the more than a decade the Rebels have been fighting to restore law, order, and democracy to North America—Ben Raines' interpretation of it, that is," she said with a smile, "the Rebel army has killed just under 750,000 punks, crud, crap, and human trash." Beth said it with about as much emotion in her voice as if requesting someone to pass the salt.

The numbers startled everyone in the room, including Ben. He stared at Beth. "Three quarters of a million people?"

"Yes, sir. And these figures are accurate to within five thousand, either way."

"Jesus!" Ben said. "I knew we'd knocked off a lot of crud, but three quarters of a million people?"

Even Dan was visible shaken. Stout-hearted fellow that he was, stiff upper lip and all that, he quickly regained his composure and said, "That explains the Scouts not finding any outlaw bands, Ben. There just aren't anymore to be found in America. We've done it, Ben. The nation is as crime-free as it has ever been in its entire history."

Chase walked in. "I just heard, Ben. Cecil bumped me from Base Camp One." He poured coffee and sat down, a smile on his face. "And it wasn't just force that accomplished it, Ben. We've had a decade of teaching morals and values in our outpost schools. Kids that were seven and eight when you started that controversial program are now young adults, and the lessons took, Ben. It stayed with them. You were right and your critics were *wrong!*"

Ben leaned back in the old swivel chair a Rebel had scrounged up for him—the Rebels were the most skilled scroungers in the world. "Maybe," he finally said. "But we're not taking into account those who live apart from the outposts. They're raising children, too."

"Sure, we raised kids, Ben," Linda said. "You're forgetting that I lived in that peaceful little valley where we were not a part of any Rebel outpost. But we still raised our kids to never violate any Rebel law. Not because we agreed with you—at the time—but because we were scared of you and your

287

followers. So your doctrine is working even in the communities who don't agree with your philosophy."

"And from these reports I've just read," Ben said, thumping the papers on his desk, "I was wrong about the caliber of outlaws still left in the States. Most of those who packed it in and came to us are in their twenties. At least sixty-five percent of them. We killed off the older, more hardened criminal—or they finally wised up and quit the business, which is what I think happened to a lot of them—and what was left were the young men and women who probably knew all along that what they were doing was wrong and were just looking for a reason to stop their lawlessness and put some purpose back into their lives."

"And you gave it to them," Dan said.

"*We* gave it to them, Dan. All of us," Ben corrected.

The Englishman shook his head. "No, General. *We* had nothing to do with it. It was your idea right down the line. Don't be modest about it."

"Well, it looks like it's going to work—so far— and that's what we all want."

"Emil Hite to see you, General," Jersey stepped into the room, unable to hide the big grin on her face.

"Why are you smiling, Jersey?" Ben asked.

She busted out laughing. She was laughing as she left the room.

Emil stepped in. He was wearing Navy whites, sparkling white, with an Admiral's braid and stripes. He had enough fruit salad on his chest for five admirals. Ben stared at the little man. Therm was right behind him, a don't-blame-me-I-didn't-have-anything-to-do-with-it look on his face.

"Do I salute, or what?" Chase, a former Navy Captain, asked.

"That won't be necessary, *Captain*," Emil said.

Chase muttered darkly under his breath.

"And we were just talking about things working out so well," Ben said, propping his elbows on the desk and putting his face in his hands.

8

Ben sent Emil to the east coast. But before he left, Emil gave a speech, assuring them all that when they arrived on the docks, the ships would be seaworthy and the forthcoming trip uneventful as they traveled over the bounding main toward their date with destiny in faraway savage lands, fighting Godless hordes of savages, crushing them under the boots of righteousness, and once more lighting the lamp of freedom for the oppressed of the world. And so forth and so on.

One Rebel grew so bored he fell asleep and when he hit the ground his M-16 went off. The slug hit the amplifier, bringing the speech to a halt.

The applause was thunderous. Of course, Emil thought it was for him. No one had the heart to correct the little con artist.

Reluctantly, very reluctantly, Therm went with him. He knew he had to check out the ships; but he really, really, really, didn't want to go with Emil, even though he genuinely liked the man.

Even the patient Thermopolis had his limits.

As the training continued, picking up in pace as each week rolled by, the number of dropouts continued to be low. By the end of the third week, the training was getting rough and the ex-outlaws were staying with it. And Ike reported that he was within striking distance of Sister Voleta.

"This is Ike McGowan," Ike radioed, once his communications people had found Voleta's radio frequency. "I have been empowered by General Ben Raines to offer you amnesty. What is your reply?"

"Tell him to go straight to hell!" Voleta screamed, the spit flying from her lips. Her eyes were wild with rage and hatred, and her burned face was mottled.

The message was sent, but it was not sent with much enthusiasm. The followers of Sister Voleta had seen the reports their patrols had sent from the field. They knew about the helicopter gunships, the massive tanks, long range artillery, and the two thousand Rebels poised to strike.

"Sister," a follower said. "I think that we . . ."

"Don't argue with me!" Voleta screamed. "Don't you know by now that we can't trust Ben Raines? He is not a man of his word. He has no honor."

Her personal team of bodyguards and subjects stared at the woman they had worshipped and served for years. But now there was doubt in their eyes. The world of fear and torture and perversion they had made was crumbling around them. They knew from radio transmissions that theirs was the last major holdout of enemies against Ben Raines and his Rebels. They also knew that they could not win this fight. They were surrounded.

"He is offering *me* amnesty," Voleta said, her voice calmer and her mind working frantically to save her little kingdom. "Me. Not any of you. You will all have to stand trial in a Rebel court and those of you who are not hanged or shot will spend the rest of your lives in prison. Think about that before you so willingly surrender to them."

"She is right," a man said. "I would rather die fighting than be led like a frightened lamb to the gallows."

The others in the darkened room nodded their heads in agreement. They were the leaders; the soldiers outside would do as they ordered.

"Are we in agreement?" Voleta asked.

"We are," the others said.

Voleta pressed a button on the arm of her wheelchair and moved to the communications center. She and the leaders were in a well-fortified basement of a mansion. Outside, on the hundreds of sprawling acres surrounding the mansion, were several thousand of the soldiers of the Ninth Order. Voleta pressed the mike button.

"We reject your offer of surrender, McGowan," she said.

"Voleta," Ike replied in his soft Mississippi drawl. "Listen to me. You and your people don't have a snowball's chance in a volcano of surviving this. And I'm not gonna lose a person takin' you out. I'll blow you all straight to hell. Tell your people to lay down their guns and walk out of there.''

"Never!" the woman screamed over the air.

Ike's communications officer had patched the transmissions through to Ben. Hundreds of miles away, Ben sat in his office, along with other commanders, and listened to the exchange. Ben's face was impassive.

"Go to loudspeakers," Ike ordered. "Try to talk her soldiers into surrendering.''

But the men and women of the Ninth Order would have no part of it. The words fell on unreceptive ears.

Ben sat behind his desk and listened.

"No go," Ben heard the reports come back in from the field. "They're not coming out, General Ike."

"Shit," Ike said. "Keep trying for a few more minutes. Maybe we can wear them down.''

The minutes ticked into a half an hour with no results. Not one soldier of Voleta's chose to give it up.

"Corrie," Ben broke his silence, "tell Communications to order Ike to open fire.''

"Yes, sir.''

That part of the peninsula of Michigan erupted in flame and smoke as Ike ordered his artillery to open fire. The gunners worked in preset patterns, laying the HE rounds in with the precision of a skilled surgeon. When the gunners had finished with their assigned sectors, nothing was left except pocked and scarred landscape, huge smoking craters, buildings on fire, and sprawled death. The gunners changed elevation and moved on to another sector.

The two battalions of Rebels who had gone north with Ike stayed back of the artillery and waited to go in. When the gunners were finished, they would begin the job of mopping up anything that might be left alive in the smoke and fire and rubble.

Ike pounded the Ninth Order relentlessly, using everything from 81mm mortars to 200-pound 203mm high explosive rounds, each round containing 104 M43A1 grenades.

"Goddamn you all to hell!" Voleta's voice screamed over the radio.

"The bitch is still alive," Ike muttered.

"I've got her location pinpointed," Ike was told. "She's in that old mansion in sector five." He handed Ike the coordinates.

Ike quickly marked his map and gave the orders. "All artillery, repeat: all artillery concentrate on sector five, map coordinate Charlie Charlie niner. Repeat sector five, Charlie Charlie niner. Let's finish it, people."

Voleta sat in the basement and listened to the Rebels' open transmission. She knew, then, that nothing would stop them. Not in America, not in the world. They were too powerful and still growing in strength. Through the madness that stained and rotted her brain, a moment of lucidity came to her. The Rebels would never be stopped. Never. Ben Raines' army would continue to grow, and he would conquer the world, stamping out lawlessness wherever he led his troops. It would take him years of brutal fighting in dozens of countries, but he would do it.

"I hate you, Ben Raines," Voleta whispered. "I loathe you and despise you. I hope you contract some horrible disease and you die slowly and painfully."

Artillery rounds began falling close to the mansion. The stone structure took a hit, and part of the second floor blew apart. The building shuddered as the rounds impacted. Tile and dust and dirt were knocked loose and fell from the ceiling of the basement rooms.

"Goddamn you to hell, Ben Raines," Voleta cursed the man she had once idolized, the man who had fathered their son.

Hundreds of miles south of the burning mansion, eyes studied Ben as he sat behind his desk and listened to the raging of war far to the north.

Men and women began screaming as a HE round collapsed part of the first floor, the debris falling into the basement, pinning members of the Ninth Order under beams and stone. The generator was knocked out, plunging the basement rooms into darkness.

"I'll see you in hell," Voleta screamed. "I'll make a pact with Satan and torment you for eternity. That's a promise, you son of a bitch . . ."

A round struck the mansion dead center, setting the mansion on fire as shards of Willie Peter were flung in all directions, burning into the dry wood.

". . . My son will lie in torment beside you, Ben Raines," Voleta squalled. "I'll have the devil's minions torture him for all eternity for betraying me. You and Buddy will suffer in agony for all eternity for this . . ."

The entire ground floor of the mansion took half a dozen 102-pound HE rounds. The mansion blew apart. The first floor collapsed into the basement, crushing everything in the basement rooms. Several tons of marble fell on Voleta; she became as one with the steel of her chair as the spokes of the wheels drove into her body and the imported marble smashed her as flat as the concrete floor on which she lay.

The barrage kept up for another ten minutes, until there was nothing left of the once huge and beautiful mansion except fire and smoke and rubble and ashes.

"Move in and secure the area," Ike ordered.

"Prisoners, sir?" a company commander asked.

"If they choose to surrender, take them alive. They're all certifiably nuts."

The Rebels moved onto the smoking grounds.

"Voleta must have really gone off her bean this time," a Rebel remarked. "She pulled everybody into about a five hundred area estate. What a stupid move."

They came upon a robed man, sitting on the edge of what had once been a very elaborate outdoor fountain. He was weeping openly and he had no weapon.

A medic ran over and began checking the man out. The man was babbling incoherently and it was obvious to all around him that he had soiled himself. The odor was foul.

The medic broke open a vial and waved it under the man's nose. The man fought the odor but his eyes began to clear. "She was in the basement of the mansion," he said, still weeping. "We wanted her to surrender. But she refused." He pointed to the house. "That will be her monument."

"Don't bet on it," a Rebel said. They had orders to find Voleta's body and cremate it.

Ike wasn't taking any chances this time. He wanted to personally eyeball the body.

Intelligence had estimated Voleta's strength at more than five thousand. But Rebels could not find anywhere near that many bodies. More like five hundred.

"They ran away," a very subdued member of the Ninth Order told them. "They deserted our glorious Sister Voleta and fled for their lives."

"Your glorious leader is squashed flat as a pancake over there in what's left of that mansion," a Rebel told him bluntly.

"No!" the man wailed.

"Yeah. We got prisoners who saw it happen. We'll be diggin' her out as soon as we get some heavy equipment in here."

"Then kill me!" the man screamed. "Put an end to my life. All is lost. Kill me now. I would rather die than live without my Voleta."

A Rebel said, "I surely do wish I could oblige you, nut-brain, but we got orders to get you people to an institution."

"Why?" the man questioned, looking from Rebel to Rebel. "What have we done wrong?"

The Rebels glanced at each other and shook

their heads. Voleta and her Ninth Order had tortured, mutilated, enslaved, and murdered thousands of people from one end of the nation to the other.

They tied his hands behind his back and he was led away, ranting and raving.

"How many left alive?" Ike asked, arriving after the grounds had been secured.

"Seventy. And some of them won't last the night."

"We'll start digging for Voleta at first light. I want this place sealed off so tight a flea couldn't get through. If that bitch is still alive—which is damned doubtful—" He paused and looked at the rubble that was once the mansion. "I want to see her body and have a positive I.D."

The Rebels worked for a week, using cranes and bulldozers and pure muscle and sweat. Ike paced up and down and walked the grounds countless times before the call came.

"We're about ready to lift the slab of marble floor out of the basement, General. I don't know that you'll be able to I.D. anything, though. Whatever is under that slab is mashed flat as a piece of paper."

"We'll try," Ike told her.

Ike stood on the edge of a huge hole, grim-faced and silent, watching as the cables were attached to the slab of marble flooring. The stench was horrible. Those working on the basement floor wore gas masks.

The slab was hoisted out and lowered to the ground outside the hole. Ike had already seen the flattened form of the wheelchair and the grotesqueness of the body that was embedded into the metal of the chair.

"A woman," a doctor called from the pit, as he stood over the body. "Both legs amputated and horrible burns all over her body."

Ike nodded and walked to the communications van. He bumped Ben and told him the news.

"Scrape her out and cremate the remains," Ben said. "This chapter is closed."

9

Ben drove to the edge of the huge training grounds and got out of the jeep. He was not alone—Ben was never really alone—but his bodyguards were giving him enough room so that he could at least have the experience of solitude.

He looked out over the quiet land just moments before dawn would be breaking. Since the news of the fall of the Ninth Order, Voleta's death, and her cremation, he had been alternating between jubilation and the strange sensation of discontent. Was that the right description for the feeling? He wasn't sure. But he knew what was causing it.

America was free of terrorism, free of outlaws, free of roaming gangs of punks and crud and other human flotsam. He and his Rebels had been fighting for over a decade. And it had ended with not a bang, but a mere whimper.

Now the Rebels faced, as Jersey had put it, the unknown. That was the problem. Ben knew that in Europe the Believers—the cannibalistic Night

People—ruled the cities and the war lords and their ilk roamed the countryside. The Rebels had faced that here in America; in Europe it was to be a thousand times larger than here in the States. But what else would the Rebels face in Europe? How many armies would they be forced to fight?

Could the Rebels pull it off?

Should they attempt to pull it off?

Ben's intelligence people said yes, they should. Hit them hard, hit them with everything Ben could, grind them down, before they could mass and strike here.

All his commanders agreed with that assessment. And Ben, in his heart, knew it had to be. But the cost in human life . . . ?

He shook his head. He could not dwell on that.

He walked back to his jeep and drove to the depot where the tanks were parked in neat rows, the little M-42 Dusters looking almost dainty parked next to the huge MBTs. They were about as dainty as a sledgehammer.

As dawn was breaking, Ben drove out to the airfield, gazing at the squadrons of helicopter gunships, silent but deadly-looking in the gray dawn.

He drove over to where the drivers had parked the monster self-propelled guns: the M109s, which fired the 155mm rounds, and the huge M110A2s, which could hurl a 203mm round, which weighed over two hundred pounds, many miles away and strike with amazing accuracy.

Ben sighed. He was the commander of the largest, most highly motivated, and best-equipped

302

army in all the world. And he knew that for a fact, having listened to hours of taped broadcasts from all over the world.

He looked up at the sky. "I know the age of miracles is long past, God," he whispered. "But if you could just stay with my people during this next campaign, it would certainly be appreciated."

The eastern sky broke open at that moment, the sun shooting golden rays all over the horizon, and it was the most beautiful dawning Ben had ever experienced.

"OK," Ben smiled and whispered. "Message received."

"They're looking good, Dad," Tina told her father. "We've leaned them down and they're walking tall and proud. The dropout rate has been surprisingly low."

"Much less than we anticipated," Buddy said. "We're going to come out of this with three very strong battalions."

Ben moved to an organizational chart on the wall of his CP and penciled in the three new battalions of infantry. That brought them up to just over ten thousand infantry personnel. The Rebels now had five more squadrons of helicopter gunships and two dozen more fully qualified tank crews. They would be leaving behind more than enough Rebels to defend Base Camp One and nearly anything—short of a large, full-scale invasion—that might pop anywhere else in the United States; and the States were once more united.

Rebel patrols were still wandering the country-side, finding and rooting out very small pockets of outlaws who refused to accept the surrender terms of the Rebels. They chose death instead, and the Rebels obliged them.

Christmas was three weeks behind them, the climate extremely cold, and training in Kansas had been cut back due to the inclement weather. In South Carolina, Ike and Therm and Emil reported amazing progress in the readying of the ships.

Ben turned around, looking at his commanders. "Start moving half the tanks toward the docks on the East Coast. Get them ready for loading. How about tankers?"

"Five are ready in Louisiana, Father," Buddy said. "We'll rendezvous with them at sea."

Ben nodded his head. "All right. Get half the gunships up as soon as weather permits and get them moving toward the East Coast for loading."

Ben looked at Beth. "Give us the latest on what we might expect to find in Ireland."

"Broadcasts indicate that Northern Ireland is pretty much a battleground between Catholic and Protestant factions . . ."

"Hell, that's been going on for centuries," Ben said. "I doubt those doing battle even know what they're fighting for after all these years. There must be nothing left of the towns and cities in that area."

"That's about right, sir," Beth said. "Not much left there except hate."

"It's been that way for as long as I can remember. All right. As it stands now, I have no plans to get involved in some damn so-called religious war . . . all the suffering and killing done in the name of God, of course. We'll see about the Republic of Ireland, see if they'd like to join in a program something like our outpost system, and then cross the Irish Sea to England. After that, we'll just have to play it by ear.

"We're not going in totally blind. Our intelligence sections have been in almost daily contact with people in Ireland and England—they need our help, they want our help, and they will assist us once we're there. We'll be facing pretty much the same type of crud over there that we faced here: warlords, outlaws, punk street gangs; the same type of human puke we had to contend with here."

"It's when we hit the continent that we'll really start having problems," Dan said.

"Right," Ben said. "The Irish and the English are overwhelmed with outlaws, punks, and Night People; but they really don't have the huge armies that we'll encounter in Europe. But we will get our bloody initiation on foreign soil there."

"What are their thoughts on saving the cities?" Striganov asked.

Ben grimaced. "They would like to save them if possible. Our people have told them that we will try to do that. However, if I have to make the choice between saving a building and saving a Rebel life, the building is going to go." He looked at Dan.

The Englishman stood up. "Of course there are pockets of armed resistance in Ireland and England. Secure zones filled with people who will help us in any way. I have informed them that we do not intend to be gentle; if they cannot accept the Rebel philosophy of warfare, there is no need in our coming." He smiled. "The people over there are so weary of crime and lawlessness the leader of one secure zone told me she would shake hands with the devil to get back to some degree of normalcy." He laughed out loud. "I told her that when we landed to slip on a pair of asbestos gloves." He waited until the laughter had subsided, then added, "She did not really see the humor in it."

Buddy raised his hand and Dan pointed at him.

"I don't know if this question can be answered," the young man said. "But I have to ask it: why has there not been someone like my father rising up from the ashes in all those countries overseas and forming an army such as the Rebels?"

Ben shook his head. "I can't answer that question, son. And nobody else can either. I'm sure there were men and women much more qualified that I to do just that. Perhaps the criminal element found them and killed them before any such movement could get started. I just don't know. But I do know this: gun laws were much more restrictive in Europe than in America. Of course the criminals never paid any attention to gun laws; only the law-abiding citizens did that. So the criminals always had access to guns. When the Great War came, the unarmed citizens were easily overpowered by the criminal element."

The young man had a confused look on his handsome face. "Why would anybody want to disarm law-abiding citizens? That doesn't make any sense to me."

West chuckled. "If you could have seen the ninnies and the yoyos the American people elected to high office, you would know the answer to that, Buddy."

"But why did the people *keep* electing them if they were so bad?" Buddy persisted. "I thought the old form of government was of the people, for the people."

"It looked good on paper, son," Ben said. "It read well. But it didn't work the way our forefathers meant it to work. I suspect that politics was always a dirty business; but toward the end of the last millennium it got worse. Very few citizens—elected or otherwise—were interested in what was good for the majority of the people. If a person spoke their mind, they might look out their windows the next morning and see a hundred other people boycotting their business. If a person went against the grain of the national press, the reporters could turn on them viciously and tear their lives apart."

"Then the people who reported the news and wrote the columns and hosted the information shows and so forth, they led exemplary lives—were role models for others?" Buddy asked.

That got a good laugh from the older members in attendance.

"I imagine many of them certainly thought they were," Ben said. "What is this? History 101? Come on, people. We've got troops to train and wars to fight."

"And history to write," Buddy said solemnly.

"No, son," Ben told him. "We won't write the history. But what we will do is shape it."

Ben and his personal team flew over to South Carolina, and for the first time, Ben walked the busy docks and was clearly in awe at what he saw.

Ben counted twenty huge ships tied up at the docks, with workers scrambling all over the vessels. Ike met him on the docks and shook his hand.

"They're beauties, aren't they, Ben?"

Ben was slightly less enthusiastic than Ike. "Yeah, great, Ike." He eyeballed one ship that appeared to be about the length of a dozen football fields. "What the hell is this monster?"

"Transport, Ben. It's called a ro-ro."

"Do you have something caught in your throat, Ike?" Ben asked.

Ike laughed and whacked him on the back. "No. That's short for 'Roll-on-Roll-off.' See the big ramp there?" He pointed. "We can just drive the trucks, tanks, whatever, right on and secure them. Then when we dock, we just drive them off."

"How ingenious. Who . . . ah, is the Captain of this . . . vessel?"

Ike smiled.

"Oh, no!" Ben said. "Don't tell me that."

"He's good, Ben," Ike said with a laugh. "The little con artist has already taken her out for sea trials. Therm is good at the helm, but Emil is better. And he doesn't clown at work. Brother, that little man is all business."

"What ship am I on?"

"Down here. Sorry we don't have any luxury liners. But the one you'll be on is a good solid ship that is just as seaworthy as anything afloat. Modern gyro. This one, Ben, is a LASH . . ."

"A what?"

"LASH: lighter aboard ship. A barge is called a lighter, Ben. The holds of these ships are specially designed to hold lighters. Less danger of cargo breaking loose. It's a real mess when that happens."

"These are warships, Ike," Ben said, stopping.

"Right. Two British ships were in port when everything went down the toilet. These are British Type 21 frigates."

"No activity on board."

"No need. We're not taking them. They won't carry enough personnel to make it worthwhile checking them out. They carried a crew of less than two hundred. They're warships, not transports."

"What if we come under attack while we're out there on the briny sailing merrily along?"

Ike glanced at him and smiled. "Oh, we've got that under control, Ben. You'll see."

"I just don't like boats, Ike," Ben said for the umpteenth time.

"Ships, Ben. Not boats."

"Whatever. Ship or boat. Same thing. Goddamn things sink."

"Not to worry, Ben. Thermopolis will be the captain on your ship."

"Only if he promises not to play that horrible music they all seem to have an endless supply of."

"Are you goin' to be a grouch on this trip, Ben?"

"Probably. I told you, I don't like boats!"

"Ships!"

"Boats, ships? What the hell's the difference? They float on water, don't they? And they sink into water."

"Planes fall out of the sky, Ben. You came in by plane."

"I had a parachute."

"So you'll have a life preserver on the ship."

"There are no sharks in the sky, Ike."

"Jesus, I'm glad I'm going to be on another ship for this run. Ben, we have the best lifeboats we could scrounge. Fully equipped. Damnit, the ship is not going to sink."

"That's what they said about the *Titanic*," Ben said sourly.

"We're not taking the same route, Ben."

"I don't like boats!"

"Ships, goddamnit, *ships!*"

Ben bumped his head a dozen times before he decided to stay the hell above decks. And even that was no delight. But anything that went on below decks could just damn well go on without his being there. Thermopolis and Emil and the other captains all got a kick out of Ben's antics. Being tactful, they kept their amusement to themselves.

On the third day, Ben waved Thermopolis over to him.

"Yes, Ben?" He discreetly avoided looking at the small bandage stuck on Ben's forehead, covering where he'd smacked his noggin on a low bulkhead.

"Get the lines cast off and take this barge out."

"Out . . . where?"

"In the damn ocean! Where else, on the freeway?"

"It's, ah, not quite that simple, Ben."

"Why not?"

"For one thing, Ben, the harbor is filled with all sorts of sunken and half-submerged boats . . ."

"Ah, hah! You said boats. Why can't I say boats?"

"Because there are no ships sunk out there. But lots of pleasure craft. It's tricky maneuvering out there. We've taken all the ships out several times, checked them out, and when we sail again, the next stop will be Ireland."

"Is that the only reason?"

"No. We're loading cargo, Ben, and I don't want to stop. We're also low on fuel and I'm not going to top the tanks until we get ready to set sail. Now if you'll excuse me, I have work to do."

Ike was standing close by. He smiled at Ben. "He's the captain, Ben. On this ship, on matters pertaining to the ship, he doesn't take orders from you. That's the way it is, and you'd better get used to it."

"Hell, all I wanted to do was go for a boat ride."

"Ship, goddamnit!" Ike yelled. "Not boats, *ships!*"

10

"What happens if we run out of gas out . . . there?" Jersey asked, standing on the docks and pointing toward the Atlantic.

"I'm assured that we won't. And they're diesel engines, Jersey."

"That sure is a big-assed boat, General."

"Ship," a Rebel said, walking by them.

"Stick it up your nose, pal," Jersey said. "It's a damn big boat to me."

Two weeks before sailing date, and the docks were filled to capacity with equipment of every description and size. The outlaw battalions—Devil's Battalions, they had elected to call themselves; Ten, Eleven, and Twelve Battalions were their official designation—had completed their training and were quartered nearby. Much of the equipment had been loaded, and much of the equipment still on the docks would be secured to the decks.

"What if it breaks loose?" Corrie asked.

"I have been assured that it will not," Ben said.

"Who assured you?" Cooper asked.

"Emil and Thermopolis."

"We're dead. Crushed by loose equipment in a friggin' hurricane and eaten by sharks," Jersey said mournfully.

"There will be no hurricanes on this voyage," Ben said.

"You've been assured of that, too, huh, sir?" Beth asked.

"That is correct."

"Who assured you?" Jersey asked.

"Those brainy people at meteorology."

"The same ones who said it wasn't going to rain today?"

"That's the ones."

They stood on the docks in foul weather gear, under an overhang which offered them some protection from the cold, driving rain.

"Then what is this stuff falling from the skies?" Jersey asked. "Greetings from friendly birds?"

"Everybody makes mistakes, Jersey," Ben said.

"That sure is a big-assed boat," Jersey said.

"It's a ship!" a Rebel said, walking by them carrying a coil of rope.

"And a toilet is a head, steps are ladders, the floor is a deck," Cooper said. "Tell you the truth, I'll be glad to get back into combat."

Ben fingered the new knot on his head. "I think we are," he muttered.

A runner found them under the overhang and handed Ben a message. Ben tore open the envelope and read it. He smiled and tucked the note into a pocket. "This is from Cecil down at Base Camp One." The Rebels now had two dozen Base Camps scattered around the nation. "The last Rebel patrol just wound it up, gang. They're coming back in from Maine. Not a single outlaw gang to be found. But plenty of thriving outposts. We can sail with a good feeling about America."

"I don't think I'll have a good feeling until I step off that tub in Ireland," Cooper said. "I'm seasick already."

"It's all in your mind, Coop," Ben told him.

"Beggin' the General's pardon," Cooper said. "But my mind ain't what's sick."

It was too good for Jersey to pass up. "You wanna put that to a vote, Coop?"

One week before sailing, everybody and everything that was going was ready.

The fuel tankers had sailed out of their ports in Louisiana heading for an eventual rendezvous at sea with the ships soon to sail from their docks in South Carolina. Once at sea, the tankers, loaded with millions of gallons of fuel, would maintain a five-mile distance from the troop and equipment transports.

A steady flow of communications between Ireland and the United States filled the airwaves. The outlaws, warlords, and Night People who had virtually taken over the island had learned that the Rebels were coming, and were fortifying their positions and intensifying their reign of terror against the law-abiding people. The emerald-green nation was torn and scarred by more than a decade of war.

"General Jack Hunt is the man we've got to put out of business," Ben said. "He's got an army that's damn near as large as ours and almost as well-equipped."

"I know him," West said. "And he's a professional. He was a soldier-for-hire back when the world was whole—more or less. It must really be rough in Africa for him to leave."

"What are we getting out of Africa?" Ben asked.

"Southern Africa—from Zimbabwe south—has been in a blood bath for years," Beth said, reading from the very latest reports compiled from intelligence. "Very little is known about events north of Zimbabwe. We haven't picked up a radio transmission from any country in that area in months."

"This Jack Hunt," Ike said, directing the question at West, "is he open to negotiation?"

"I doubt it," the former mercenary replied. "He's one of the most bloodthirsty bastards I've ever met. Totally ruthless. And his men will be highly trained and professional. It's going to be a slugfest for us, believe that."

"The latest communiqué says the people are desperate over there," Beth said. "They don't know how much longer they can hold out."

"Tell them to hold out for a few more weeks," Ben instructed. "We'll be there."

"We damn well better get there in a few weeks," Thermopolis said. "I just spoke with the leader of the group in Galway. That's the only port still open to us. He said Jack Hunt's people are knocking on the door and we'd better get there quickly. If Galway falls, we'll have to try for a landing in Londonderry and hope for the best."

"With external tanks, the Apache is capable of flying across the Atlantic," Striganov pointed out. "But I think that would be an exercise in futility, since once they discharge their weapons there would be no place for the birds to be resupplied."

Ben shook his head. "No. We can't risk losing a single one of them. This Jack Hunt, will he have SAMs?"

"I'm sure of it," West said.

"All the birds equipped with AAWWS?" Ben asked.

"All except the converted Hueys," Ike said. "All the rest are equipped with Longbow."

The Airborne Adverse Weather Weapon System—called Longbow—is a complex millimeter-wave radar that enables the chopper crew to detect and kill tanks, missiles, and aircraft, day or night, in smoke, fog, or adverse weather.

"What is the earliest we can sail?" Ben asked Ike.

"One week, Ben. We can't push any harder. Everything has got to be right. Got to be checked and checked and checked again. Once we're out there, we're alone."

"Jack Hunt," Ben said to Beth. "Does he have a Navy?"

"No. Not if you're talking about destroyers and battleships and things like that. He does have gunboats."

"We can deal with them," Ike said. "Don't sweat

317

that. The recoilless rifles alone that we've set up on the decks have a range of seven thousand yards. And we have much heavier guns than that ready to bark. Even if Hunt has missile capability to use against us at sea—and we have received nothing that would indicate he does—we could still deal with it. It's docking that has me worried."

"Jack knows nothing about Naval warfare," West said. "He's strictly a ground-pounder. But a damned good one."

"Then he and I have something in common," Ben said with a small smile.

"It ends there," West said, unusually grim-faced. "Jack Hunt is called 'the Beast,' Ben. And he makes Sam Hartline and Lan Villar look like angels."

Dan Gray arched an eyebrow. "I have never heard of this man. So I must deduce that Jack Hunt is not his real name."

"That's right. I don't know what his real name is, but he went under Bob French for years."

"Ahhh!" Dan said. "Now I know who you're talking about. Yes. A butcher."

"That's correct."

"He would have artillery," Ben said, bending over a map of Ireland.

"Yes. What are you thinking?"

"Galway Bay is twenty three miles wide at the entrance. It narrows down considerably. If he's got 155's, he'll be able to drop in on us. So the bay has to be secured before the ships enter. Dan, that will be a job for you and your Scouts." He thumped the map. "Damnit, I wish we had some aerial photographs of that bay. I hate going in blind like this."

"We tried all the local libraries, Father," Buddy said. "But they had all been looted years ago."

"Looted or vandalized?" Ben asked.

"Vandalized."

"Bastards," Ben muttered. "Goddamned illiterate punks."

Ben cussed for a moment, verbally sending anyone who would vandalize a library to the fires of hell and beyond.

"We'll have two gunships ready to fly on the decks of each ship, Father," Buddy said. "They could knock the guns out."

Ben shook his head. He met West's eyes, and the former mercenary smiled faintly and arched an eyebrow. Both men knew that Buddy was not nearly ready to step into Ben's boots yet. Not and make statements like that. "No, son. This Jack Hunt will know that we have the capability to attack from the air. So, considering how vicious the man is, he'll probably have men, women, and children he's taken prisoner scattered all around the gun emplacements. He knows me well by now. Believe that, son. He's studied me from every angle, knowing that someday he'd have to face the Rebels. And he knows that it would take something extreme for me to harm an innocent."

"You're right, Father," the young man said. "I apologize for being so stupid."

"You're anything but stupid," West told him, stepping in to get Ben off the hook. "You're the finest headhunter I have ever seen. And believe me,

I spent years in Africa; I've seen the genuine article. You're just young, Buddy, and that is not a crime or a sin. You're turning into a fine battalion commander. Just give yourself some time, Buddy. And don't be so critical of yourself."

"Thank you, sir," Buddy said with a smile.

"All right." Ben tapped the table with his fist. "Dan, you and your teams will probably have to go in by Huey and be dropped in the ocean. You'll be in wet suits . . ."

Ike cleared his throat. Ben looked at him.

"That's my field, Ben," the ex-SEAL said.

"Oh, damnit, Ike, you're a middle-aged man, just like me. You . . ."

"That's my field, Ben," Ike stood his ground, staring at Ben. "That's what I was trained for and did for years. You're forgetting the number of ex-SEALs in this army. They'd be awfully pissed off if they couldn't do this mission. No offense to you, Dan, or your ability to pull it off; I know you'd do a bang-up job of it. But I lead this one."

"Hard-headed, fat old bastard," Ben told Ike, but he was smiling. "Hell, there isn't a wet suit in the country you could get your big butt in!"

"Well, for your information, I have one, you silly-assed ground-pounder!"

"Who made it for you: Omar the tent maker?"

The others left the room and let the two old friends have at it. They'd work it out. Ben was going to cuss and stomp around and both men would insult each other. But all knew that Ike was going to lead the mission.

*   *   *

Ben was awakened by Linda's punching him on the shoulder. "Ben, wake up. There's a runner here to see you."

Ben rubbed the sleep from his eyes and swung his feet out of bed. He snubbed his bare toe on a trunk, banged his shin on a coffee table and almost stepped on Smoot. The Husky let him know real quick that would be a bad mistake. He managed to get dressed. Linda's laughing at him didn't add much to the moment.

He didn't know whether his cussing helped any, but Ben got his pants zipped up and his boots on and stepped out into the hall, leaving Linda's giggling behind him. He closed the door.

"Yes, Sergeant?" he said to the young man waiting.

The runner took a deep breath. The general didn't look to be in a real peachy mood. "Sir, there are several hundred punks waiting outside the post gate. They demand to see you."

Ben had glanced at the clock while Linda was abusing his shoulder. One o'clock in the morning. "In the middle of the damn night?"

"Yes, sir."

"Do you know what they want?"

"Yes, sir."

Ben waited. "Well, Sergeant?"

"They're all heavily armed, sir."

"What do they *want?*"

"Well, sir . . . the leader, a kid who calls himself Blotto, says they've come to declare war on us."

11

Ben blinked a couple of times. "I beg your pardon, Sergeant. Did you say they want to declare *war*? On us?"

"Yes, sir. It's gettin' sort of tense out there, sir. You better come quick."

Corrie had stepped out into the hall, along with the rest of Ben's team.

"This could be a trick, Corrie," Ben said. "Get the post on full alert."

Linda stepped out with Ben's body armor, M-14, and battle harness. He slipped it all on and picked up his old Thunder Lizard.

"Did you say this punk's name was Blotto, Sergeant?"

"Yes, sir."

"Why the hell would anybody want to call themselves Blotto?" Cooper asked.

"Let's all go find out," Ben said.

"That's all of them, Ben," West said, standing back about five hundred yards from the front gate of the old Navy base. "I've put teams out all around the gang. They're in place."

Floodlights had been turned on, the harsh lights illuminating the strange gathering outside the main gates.

"What are they?" Ben asked.

"They haven't said, yet. They say they declared this state to be free and neutral last year. They claim to have sent you a letter stating that."

"Sent me a letter? How in the hell did they send it? There's no mail service." Then he noticed that West was smiling. "Come on, West, give."

"They drove across the line into Alabama and dropped it in a mail slot at a post office in the first town they came to . . . according to Blotto."

Ben thought about that for a few seconds. Then he shook his head; this was getting confusing. "Why did they drive to Alabama to do that?"

West started laughing, doubling over holding his sides. He finally managed to gasp, "I . . . don't know, Ben!" He pulled out a handkerchief and wiped his eyes.

Ike had joined them, along with the other battalion commanders. Dan said, "You just stand pat, Ben. I'll find out what this ragtag bunch of misfits wants." He walked toward the gates.

"While you're at it," Ben called, "find out why they drove over to Alabama last year to mail me a letter."

That stopped Dan cold in the night. He turned around slowly and stared at Ben, a frown on his face. "I beg your pardon, Ben? They mailed you a letter?"

"Yes."

"This past year?"

"Yes."

"From Alabama?"

"Yes."

Dan took off his beret and scratched his head as he walked back to the group. "But there hasn't been any mail service in the States in over a decade."

"I know."

"Why don't we get Emil to talk with them?" Tina suggested. "He's sure the right man for the job."

"You're right, but no," Ben nixed that. "We don't want anything to happen to him. We need him to drive the boat."

"Ship," Ike corrected.

"You peoples is trespassin' on holy ground!" came the shout from within the group of punks.

"Holy ground?" Buddy questioned.

"This ground and all of what used to be the state of South Carolina has been claimed by the Church of the Holy Hoodoo." At that, they all started clapping their hands and rapping.

A black company commander raised his rifle.

Ben caught the movement just in time. "Hold it, Nick," he called. "I never liked it either, but you can't shoot someone for rapping."

"I did fifteen years ago," Nick said softly, lowering his rifle.

"Is he joking?" Buddy asked.

"I doubt it," Ben told him. "He loves classical music. We share tapes often. I know he shoved a

325

punk's head through the speaker of a boom box one time. Nick's from New York City. He was a stockbroker there before the Great War.''

"Shut that crap up, you goddamn heathens," Nick shouted.

"Let's see what Nick can do," Ben suggested.

The rapping and clapping stopped. The silence was wonderful. A big youth stepped from the gang.

"That's Blotto," West said.

"Is you a brother?" Blotto yelled.

"I'm no brother of yours, you idiot," Nick called.

"He an Oreo," another gang member said. "Black on the outside and white on the inside."

"How much of this crap am I supposed to tolerate, General?" Nick asked.

"What would you suggest we do, Nick?" Ben asked.

The Rebel officer shook his head and was silent.

"Come on," Ben said, and started walking toward the front gate.

He was immediately surrounded by Rebels.

Ben walked to the front gate and stood gazing at the crowd of young men; they were of all races. And they all shared the same vacant, slack facial expression.

"I'm Ben Raines. And you don't want to make war against me."

"We don't?" Blotto asked.

"No. That would be a very foolish thing to do. And you're not foolish, are you?"

"Hell, no, man!"

"We'll be gone from here in a few days. And then you can practice your religion and not be disturbed. During that time, we won't bother you if you don't bother us. That's fair, isn't it?"

"Seems like it. Yeah! You all right, man."

"Thank you. If there is nothing else, I'm going to go back to bed."

"We sleep all day," Blotto said, a big foolish grin on his face.

"We'll do our best not to disturb you," Ben assured him.

"Right on, man. Super cool. You boss, man. We gonna go chill out now."

The gang of young men and women faded back into the night, clapping and rapping.

"My God," Nick said. "They were mental defectives."

"Yes," Ben said, still standing by the gate. "Probably all of them. I would imagine they banded together for protection as well as for company, since no one else would have anything to do with them."

"They're still dangerous, Ben," Chase said, standing in his bathrobe. "Their guns were real."

Ben nodded his head. "Tomorrow . . . or rather, later on today, I'll have patrols check out where they live and see how they're staying alive. I suspect they grow gardens and hunt for food. I don't think we'll ever see them again. But stay on low alert just in case. I'm going back to bed."

"They live just outside of town," Buddy told his

father the following afternoon. "In a shanty town. Really, it's not as bad as it sounds. They have gardens and they raise chickens and hogs and have milk cows. There are people who live not too far from here who say the Hoodoos—that's what they call themselves—have caused no real trouble. They're more of a nuisance than a problem. The people I spoke with say none of the gang members have ever harmed anyone."

"Very well. Thank you, son. These people you spoke with, are they a part of our outpost system?"

"No, sir. And they don't choose to be. They're pacifists and vegetarians. A very nice group of people."

"All right." Ben looked up as Beth entered the office and placed a folder on his desk.

"All outposts from all forty-nine states have radioed in, sir," she said. "Not one incident of trouble was reported in any secure zone during the past two weeks."

Ben nodded his head. "One down and the world to go." He smiled at Beth. "We're gaining. How are the members of our newest battalions behaving?"

"No problems reported, sir. But everybody is getting a little restless with this waiting."

"Tell the battalion commanders to start limited exercise. An hour in the morning and an hour in the afternoon. That'll break the monotony. We don't have that much longer to wait."

"Yes, sir."

Buddy left with her. Ben unfolded several maps

of Ireland and spread them out on his desk. Ireland, he concluded, was going to be a real bitch to take, with its narrow, winding country roads and what looked to be hundreds of tiny villages. Many warlords and outlaws were sure to have taken over the castles that dotted the land—that would be their level of mentality. And Ben did not want to destroy those historical landmarks. Not if he could help it. Hell, even many of the cottages where good folks had lived and raised families were hundreds of years old.

But, Ben reminded himself, he and his Rebels had destroyed historical buildings all over the United States.

And what the hell was he going to do about Northern Ireland? Build a damn wall around the place?

He didn't know.

Ben heard a slight noise behind him. Some of Ike's SEALs were constantly playing their little games ever since Ike had told them they were going to spearhead the Irish invasion. The game was called: see if you can sneak up on the general and startle him by yelling: HOOYAH!

"How would you like a grenade stuck up your nose?" Ben said softly.

A few seconds passed. "Shit," a man said, disgusted at himself for getting caught. "Makes me feel like a tadpole."

Ben felt the floor record the sounds of the man's leaving and he smiled. He lifted his eyes to Jersey, sitting across the room in a chair, her M-16 laid across her legs. "You saw him, Jersey?"

"Right, sir. He wouldn't have made it much closer."

"Damn, Jersey. You wouldn't have shot him, would you?"

"Naw. That was O'Malley. I might shoot Plante. But only a flesh wound. They're pretty good guys. Full of shit, is all."

Ben laughed and returned to his studying of the maps.

Ike came in about an hour later and Ben was glad to ease up from the maps. He rubbed his eyes and watched as Ike poured a mug of coffee. Ike had been pushing himself to keep up with the younger members of the teams and had lost some weight.

"It's hell to hit middle age, isn't it, Ike?" he asked.

Ike turned and grinned. "You damn well got that right, Ben. Some of those younger guys are runnin' my old ass into the ground. These past few days have been like Hell Week back in Coronado."

"You could always turn it over to a younger member, Ike."

"Not a chance, pal. Only way I'd do that is if I sense that I can't pull my own weight. Then I'd do it in a flash. I won't endanger my teams." He stirred his coffee then sat down in front of the desk. "I nixed the choppers, Ben. As it stands now, we'll go in by Zodiac. At least part of the way."

"Fine with me, Ike. It's your show. Tell your boys to cool it with the sneaking up on me. Jersey's about ready to shoot one or two."

"I'll tell 'em to stop it." He twisted in his chair

and looked at Jersey. "You'd do it, too, wouldn't you, you little Apache?"

Jersey stared at him, a bleak look in her eyes. "Fuckin' A, I would."

On the day the mooring lines were to be cast off and the armada was only a couple of hours from getting underway, Ike sat with the other commanders in Ben's now-vacant CP. The maps were gone from the walls, the typewriters, filing cabinets, boxes, and bags all loaded on board ship.

"Well," Dan said, fiddling with a paper cup of lukewarm coffee, "you all remember what someone always said in the movies just before setting sail or hitting the beaches or the silk, don't you?"

"I guess this is it, boys," Ben mouthed the words that had become immortal on the silver screen.

The base would now be occupied by Rebels being shifted over from Louisiana. It would be the only shipping link to resupply the Rebel Army once they touched European soil.

"I have a funny feeling in my stomach," Tina said.

West gave her a sharp look.

"Not *that* kind of feeling!" Tina told him and the others burst out laughing, including Ben.

"It's sort of a . . . well, lonesome feeling," Tina said.

"I know it well," Ben said. He glanced at his watch. "About two and a half hours from now, when you can no longer see the shore, it will be much worse, I assure you."

"Thanks, Dad," she said. "I really needed that."

Smoot wriggled nervously around Ben's boots, while Chester was content to stay close to Dan. Both dogs knew something was up and they weren't sure they liked it.

Ben wadded up his paper cup and threw it in the garbage. He stood up. "If we hang around in here much longer, we'll all start singing dirges. The last one to leave please turn off the lights."

They stepped out into a cool, misty day. The docks were empty of equipment and containers and boxes and crates. The huge cranes were still; spider arms sticking blackly up into the air, cables dangling.

The captain of one transport—a man who had been a petty officer in the Navy—clicked on a bullhorn. "Start loading the troops," he called. "Third Battalion Pier Two. Third Battalion Pier Two."

"That's me," Dan said. He shook hands all the way around. "See you folks in Ireland," he said softly; then he turned and walked toward the ship.

"Second and Fourth Battalion load up now on Pier Five," came the electronically boosted voice. "Second and Fourth Battalion on Pier Five."

"That's us, lad," West said to Buddy. The handshakes were quick and firm and the two men were gone.

"Five and Six Battalions here on Pier Seven," the call drifted out.

Striganov and Rebet shook hands with the others and walked away.

Finally, Ben stood alone with his team. His

battalion and Therm's battalion were together on this run. Ben looked up at Thermopolis, standing on the bridge, by the railing. He motioned for Ben to come on.

Ben waved in reply. "Let's go, gang. Next stop, Ireland."

12

"What happens if we all go to one side and look?" Jersey asked.

"Damn tub will probably fall over and sink," Ben told her. Then he noticed her worried look and smiled. "Just kidding, Jersey."

"I'm sick already," Cooper said.

"Jesus, Cooper," Corrie said. "We haven't started moving yet!"

"It gets to me every time," Cooper moaned.

"What does?" Jersey said. "Cooper, you've never been on a ship in your life. Go below and lay down."

"There go the last of the lines," Ben said.

"Oohh, I don't feel good," Cooper said.

Jersey reached for her sidearm and Cooper beat a hasty retreat for the other side of the ship while the others laughed at him and at the expression on Jersey's face.

"Put him out of his misery," Jersey muttered. Just then the ship lurched and Jersey grabbed for the rail. "Oh, shit!" she shouted.

Laughing, Ben went to his quarters, laid down on his bunk (only banging his head once in the process) and went to sleep. He woke up about two hours later, raised up in the bunk and banged his head on the overhang.

"Goddamnit!" he said, then looked over at Linda, lying in her bunk, reading and trying to keep a straight face. Smoot was in bed with her.

"Watch your blood pressure, Ben," she said, doing her best to choke off laughter.

"My blood pressure is fine," he told her. "I'm not that sure about my head." He managed to get out of the bunk and into his low quarters without putting another knot on his noggin. "I'm going up to the bridge."

"I'm going to take a nap," Linda said, reaching up and clicking off the small lamp. Smoot yawned at Ben and conked out at Linda's feet.

Ben was momentarily startled to find himself completely surrounded by water. The shoreline was gone. He stood by the railing for a few minutes, letting the cold air blow the sleep from him. The other ships were maintaining a safe distance in the convoy. Ben enjoyed the sea breeze for a few more minutes, then headed toward the bridge.

"Enjoy your rest?" Therm asked from his chair.

"It was very nice. Where the hell are we?"

Thermopolis grinned. "Several thousand miles west of Ireland and proceeding smoothly."

"That's what I get for asking stupid questions," Ben said with a smile. "Any storm systems building anywhere near us?"

"That I can tell you straight out. No. It looks to be a very quiet crossing. And I hope to God it is."

"Ten days do it?"

"Oh, yeah."

"When do we rendezvous with the tankers?"

"They're off Bermuda now. They've been warned away and are taking no chances. They're steaming away from the islands now."

"Any hostile action taken against them?"

"No. The communiqué said go with God but leave those on the island alone."

"Suits the shit out of me," Ben muttered. "Where's the coffee pot?"

Ben sat with Therm on the bridge for a time, drinking strong coffee and chatting. "Has anybody seen Cooper?"

Therm smiled. "He's sure he's dying, last I heard."

"He better not let Jersey hear him say it. She'll offer to put him out of his misery."

Ben left the bridge and walked the bowels of the transport, checking on his people and being damn careful not to bang his head. There were only a few cases of seasickness, and they were not severe. Cooper, however, was another matter. It did not surprise Ben to find Jersey with him, putting cold, wet cloths on Coop's head. Jersey talked a good fight; but she liked Cooper and worried about him.

"He's been making out a verbal will, General," Jersey said, looking up at Ben. "Although I sure don't want any of the crap he's leaving people."

"You're sure as hell not included in my will, either," Cooper told her.

"You better be nice to me, Coop," she told him. "Or the next wet rag gets shoved in your mouth."

"OK. Fine. I'll leave you my collection of *Playboy* magazines, then."

"How thoughtful of you, Cooper."

Laughing, Ben left them arguing and walked back up to his quarters, wondering when they were going to eat and how the cooks were going to manage feeding all these people.

"The galley is working twenty-four hours a day, Ben," Linda told him. "The food is going to be simple, but plenty of it."

"I guess we'd better settle in for a boring run," Ben said.

On the third day out, Thermopolis called Ben to the bridge. "Radar has picked up a large object just ahead. Floating dead in the water. It's a ship. We're going to see a lot of them. I'm surprised we haven't spotted one before now."

"Tell Ike to get some of his SEALs ready. Board it and find out what happened, if they can."

Zodiacs were made ready. A SEAL team scrambled down ropes and headed for the seemingly dead ship. The convoy slowed and circled while the team checked out the ghost ship.

"It's a container ship," the leader of the SEAL team radioed back. "Looks like they had a hell of a fight on board. But it was a long time ago. Years back. Nothing but skeletons and a few scraps of skin and hair left here."

"Get the ship's log," Ben said. "And see what she was carrying."

After a few moments the SEAL team leader came back. "Scotch whiskey, among other things."

"What other things?" Ben asked.

"Women's drawers, bras, slips. Medical supplies that are way out of date. All kinds of other stuff that are either rusted or rotted to dust."

"Get some smaller craft over there to off-load the whiskey," Ben ordered. "And bring the women's undergarments. I'm getting dirty looks from the ladies." He looked at Therm. "Can you set an anchor?"

"It's about thirty-five hundred feet here, Ben."

"I guess that's out. Do the best you can."

Jersey told Cooper they were floating over thirty-five hundred feet of water. Cooper almost went into shock.

Additional personnel were sent over to help with the off-loading and soon the whiskey had been stored and the ladies' undergarments distributed among the women.

"You want us to scuttle the ship?" the SEAL team leader asked.

"You have limpets with you?"

"Yes, sir."

"Set the timers for an hour."

The convoy steamed on and Ben opened the log book. "We have no place to go," he read aloud the Captain's writings from years back. "The world has gone mad. Radio transmissions state the entire world is at war. Russia is bombing the United

States; the United States is hurling missiles at Russia. Germ warfare is rampant. Already, two of my crew have committed suicide. I feel that soon that will be the only option."

The next notation read: "We are being attacked by pirates. We are being boarded. My men are fighting gallantly. One of the pirates' vessels is burning and the other has been crippled."

The next notation was dated two days later. "My ship is dead in the water. Only four crewmen are left alive. The others died from wounds suffered during the attack. Has the entire world gone insane?"

The last entry in the log read: "I am alone. The other crewmen asked if they could take one of the lifeboats and try for land. I gave them permission to do so. I shall have a glass of wine and a meal, and then I shall put an end to my life. I am told that Paris is burning. This time, I fear it is true. To my darling wife, Daphne, I loved you to the end, and we shall soon be together in a better world. God forgive me for taking my own life."

Ben closed the log book.

"I wonder what happened to Daphne?" Beth asked.

The convoy passed a dozen dead ships. After inspecting three of them, Ben called for a halt; they were losing too much time. The Rebels sailed past the floating derelicts. The soldiers lining the rails watched in respectful silence until the rusting mausoleums were out of sight.

On the fifth day out, they found a United States warship of the destroyer class. Ben knew this ship had to be inspected and sent home. Ike would personally lead the team over to the destroyer to retrieve the log book and settle the old girl to the bottom.

"I served on that ship once," he said, lowering his binoculars. "I had buddies on her when the ballon went up. This is not going to be fun."

But the ship was barren. They found no bodies and no signs of any struggle. The log book was missing. Classified equipment had not been destroyed. The fuel tanks were nearly full. Obviously, the ship had just been refueled at sea.

"You people go on," Ike radioed from the destroyer. "This girl is soon going to be back in action."

"Ike, what the hell are you going to do?" Ben asked.

"Have some fun and provide a destroyer escort. Everything is intact. The guns have not been rendered useless. The ammo appears to be stable."

"That fuel is a decade old, Ike."

"So we can always pump it out and refuel from a tanker. The electrical system works. Hell, it looks like a new ship. Damnest thing I've ever seen. Don't worry, Ben. I can catch you very easily with this baby."

"If nothing else it will provide some thought on Jack Hunt's part," West radioed. "The sight of a destroyer sailing in might make for some fine psychological warfare."

"True," Ben agreed. "All right, Ike. We'll see you soon."

"We'd better not come up on anymore sailable warships," Emil radioed. "Ike is gonna be operating that one with a skeleton crew as it is. I got crewpersons over here that don't know port from starboard."

"Got one over here, too," Ben muttered. "Me."

"We can forget about this one," Ike radioed back before the convoy got underway. There was disgust in his voice. "The engines are locked up. I'm gonna scuttle her."

"That's ten-four, Ike," Ben told him. "It was a good try."

The Rebels pushed on. The weather was holding good and the convoy stayed on a southern route until it became necessary for them to cut north, and they didn't make that turn until they reached the Azores. They maintained radio silence as they drew close to the Azores. No one knew what the Azores held: hostiles or friendly, and the Rebels could not take the time to check it out.

Reports from Ireland were growing increasingly grim. Jack Hunt's army was knocking on the back door of Galway, and the defenders were running out of food, ammo, and medical supplies. They could hold for maybe a week. No more.

"Pour it on," Ben ordered. "Give it everything the engines will stand. If that port falls, we're going to be ankle-deep in shit."

"If those engines fail, we're gonna be eyeball-deep in water!" Cooper said.

"Idiot," Jersey told him. "If the engines quit

we'll just transfer to another ship. We won't sink! Go down below and get seasick."

"I'm too scared to be seasick."

"I wish I could believe that. Cooper, I've seen you wade into a crowd of creepies that had you outnumbered ten or twelve to one. How come you . . ." She never got to finish it. The ship shuddered as Therm called for more speed and Cooper grabbed at his stomach and bent over the railing and starting making all sorts of disgusting noises.

Jersey shook her head and went below.

The nights and days blended into the seemingly never-ending ocean. But there were no mishaps, no fatal accidents, and no one came down with appendicitis or anything else that required the use of the operating room.

The convoy was a few hundred miles off the Irish coast when the bridge speaker rattled out the words. "We've got company," the radar room reported to the bridge. "Two blips in the sky. Coming hard from the east. Too slow for jets."

Ben was on the bridge at the time. He grabbed the mike, flipped the switch for speaker, and said, "Man all guns. Man all guns. We have company."

"I believe the term usually spoken is battle stations," Therm said with a smile.

"They got the message," Ben said, watching as Rebels scrambled for heavy machine gun and quickly stripped the waterproof covers from them.

"Shark on the horn, General," Ben was told.

"Go, Shark."

"I've got people with surface-to-air missiles

343

ready to lock in, Eagle. Let's see if the birds make any hostile moves."

"That's ten-four, Shark. Do our friends in Ireland have any planes?"

"That's ten-fifty, Eagle. I just want to make sure."

It didn't take long. The twin-engine prop jobs came in low and fast and made a sweep of the convoy. Men on both sides of the planes fired what looked like M-60 machine guns, and the lead raked the ships. One of the pilots made the mistake of giving Ike the finger on the fast pass.

"Take those bastards out," Ike ordered.

The surface-to-air missiles fired and ran smooth and deadly. One hit dead center of a plane and blew it apart. The second missile blew the tail off of the other plane. Two figures left the plane and two parachutes popped over.

"Pick them up and bring them to me," Ben ordered. "And take them alive."

Boats were launched and the men were picked up. They were allowed to dry off and get into clean dry clothing before they were escorted under guard to a small conference room. Ben was seated behind a table. He had ordered the other chairs to be removed. Both men were acutely aware of the .45 laying on the polished tabletop near Ben's right hand.

"My name is Ben Raines. And I do not like to have my ships attacked for no reason."

"I'd like to say, sir," one of the men spoke, "that under the Geneva Convention we are accorded some rights. As prisoners of war, we . . ."

"Shut up," Ben said softly.

"Baggin' the General's pardon. But we had a reason for attackin' you. We were ordered to do so, sir."

"Ordered by whom?"

"I don't have to answer that, sir."

Ben picked up the .45 and jacked the hammer back. "Which of you wishes to be the first to die?"

"General Jack Hunt ordered us to attack the convoy," the second man spoke up very quickly. Unlike the first man, he did not speak with an Irish brogue. "We are flyers in his army. Were flyers in his army."

"You're not Irish," Ben said.

"No, sir. I'm not. He is." He jerked his head to the other man. "I'm from Oregon originally."

"You'll not get nothin' from me, General Raines," the other man said. "So tough boy that your reputation states you are, you can just go ahead and finish me with that pistol you're a-holdin'."

"All right," Ben said, then shot him. The report was enormous in the small, closed room. The .45 caliber hollow-nose slammed the man back and sent him bouncing off a closed door. He fell dead at the other man's feet.

Ben looked at the other man. His face was ashen and his hands were trembling. He clenched his hands into fists to still the violent jerking. "But you'll tell me what I want to know, won't you, man-from-Oregon?"

"Yes, sir, I sure will!"

And he did.

13

The mouthy one was sewn in canvas and buried at sea within the hour. The man from Oregon was given hot food and a comfortable chair in the conference room. A tape recorder was set up. He was very eager to talk to Ben.

"Galway is about to fall, General," he said. "They can't last another week. But you'll be there long before then. Watch out entering the harbor; Jack's got artillery on both sides. He's waiting for you."

"Range?" Ben asked.

"He can hit you anywhere in the harbor, sir."

Ben called for pen and paper and laid them in front of the man. "You show me where the gun emplacements are. As close as you can come to it."

The prisoner drew a very detailed map of the harbor, with a check mark at each gun emplacement. When he finished, he said, "Since I am your prisoner and have seen how ruthless you can be,

General, I'd be a damn fool to mark in false locations, now, wouldn't I?"

Ben smiled at the man. "I'm not ruthless, partner. I'm just a man who has a job to do and will do it in the most expidient manner possible."

The man from Oregon returned the smile. "However way you want to put it is fine with me, General."

He was led away and locked down.

Using a scrambled hook-up, Ben talked to Ike. "They're waiting for us, Ike."

"They can't see underwater, Ben. We've got thirty SDVs. We'll make it."

The MK-V11 MOD-6 SDV is a four-man, wet, submersible vehicle capable of withstanding sea-water pressure down to 500 feet. It has a fiberglass hull and uses nonfibrous materials for component construction; that useage mutes acoustic and magnetic signatures.

"That many SDVs will put over a hundred of us ashore. The battle will be over before dawn," Ike said with a chuckle. "We've be totin' enough C-4 to light up their asses, brother. Don't sweat it."

"Your humility is profound, Ike," Ben replied.

"Ain't it, though? I passed grovelin' with flyin' colors. But I'm a little rusty on fear and panic."

Ben called him a very ugly name and broke the connection. "Get us there," he said to Therm. "We launch SEALs tomorrow night."

The commanders gathered on Ben's ship—the flag ship, as Therm called it—for one final meeting before the Rebels, spearheaded by Ike and his SEAL teams, went ashore on foreign soil.

"Dan, you will take your teams and be in position to go in here," Ben thumped the map, "on the north side of the bay, at the village of Inveran, as soon as you receive the signal from Ike. West, you and your very best people will go in here, on the south side at Fanroe. Secure that village then force-march to this main highway and secure the towns of Ballyvaughan and Bealaclugga. Georgi, I want you and your people to secure the Aran Islands. We've got to have that airport at Kilronan to use as a base for our gunships. There isn't going to be any rest for the motor launch operators. Drop one team and get the hell back to the ships for another.

"Our friends on shore have spread the word for any civilians on the outskirts of Galway to head for the countryside. I've advised them that there will be civilian casualties and they have accepted that." Ben shrugged his shoulders. "I hate it, but it's almost impossible to avoid.

"We're going to take some losses, people. It's been a long time since we've been forced to fight from a defensive position, but that's what we'll be doing this time."

A runner entered the room and handed Ben a note. Ben read it and smiled. "Fishing boats are massing all along the free coast, people," he announced. "They'll set out at dark to help in ferrying troops to shore." He grinned. "I knew the Irish wouldn't sit back and miss out on a good fight." He waved the note. "This means we can get many more troops ashore than we originally planned and start shoving Jack Hunt and his bastards out of Galway." He looked at his watch. "Take off, Ike."

Chase's voice stopped Ike at the door. "Hey, fatso," the doctor called. "You be careful out there, you hear me?"

Ike grinned at him. "I got your best pecker-checkers goin' in with me, Lamar. Don't sweat it." Ike stepped out of the room and was gone. He didn't have very much time to get a hell of a lot of things done.

Ben looked at the gathering. "Get your people ready, gang. And be *damn* sure you stress that once ashore, it's going to be a while before they can be resupplied; for some of them, hours, for others, perhaps all day. The fighting is going to be heavy, so take enough ammo to do the job. Any questions?"

Silence greeted him.

"Take off."

The battalion commanders began returning to their ships just as dusk was settling over the ocean. Using binoculars, Ben watched the SEALs in their black wet suits lower the Zodiacs and the SDVs and then scramble down the rope ladders to the surface of the Atlantic. "You wish you were going with them, Father?" Buddy asked.

"I won't lie to you, son: Yes, I do. But they'll be plenty of fighting for us all very soon."

"It is the general consensus among the battalion commanders that you should stay on board ship, directing operations, until Galway is secure."

Father looked at son. "Do you know where the battalion commanders can put that consensus?"

"I have a pretty good idea, yes, sir."

"Fine. I will be leading One Battalion in just as soon as there is room for us on shore."

"Yes, sir."

"Get back to your command. You'll be going in directly behind me, as ordered. Once ashore, you will work your way up and stay on my right flank. We'll be going straight up the harbor and straight into the city."

"Right, sir."

Ben held his smile until Buddy was gone. Then he chuckled. "They think this ol' curly wolf is staying behind, they've got another think coming," he muttered. He stood for half an hour by the rail, looking at the still invisible shoreline. Using night glasses, Ben had watched the SEALs disappear under the water. The Zodiacs were a few minutes behind them. They would lay back silent until a toe-hold was established.

Chase appeared at his side. "Clear me space for a MASH unit, Ben," the doctor said. "And I mean do it first thing."

"It'll have to be on the harbor side, Lamar."

"I don't care if it's in the middle of a haunted castle. Just get me some room to care for the wounded."

"I'll do my best, Lamar."

"Do better than that, Ben. Just do it."

"A lot of blips appearing on the screen," the radar operator told Therm. "Still some distance away."

"Sails in the night," Therm told her. "Irish fishermen coming to help ferry troops."

"Sails, sir?" the helmsman asked.

"Sails, son," Therm told him. "The wind has shifted to their advantage and they're coming out silent."

"If Jack Hunt's gunboats find them, those fishermen won't stand a chance. They'll be chopped to pieces."

"They're Irishmen, son. And they don't bow their necks to anybody." Therm looked up as Ben walked onto the bridge. "Fishing boats coming, Ben."

Ben nodded and hit the intercom button. "One Battalion on top deck. Full battle gear and all the ammo you can stagger with. Let's go, people."

"I wish you would wait until at least part of the city is in Rebel hands, Ben," Therm said quietly.

"It'll be two-three hours before Ike is ready for us, Therm. I just want to be hard offshore when the call comes."

"You'll never give up the combat, will you, Ben?"

"When I can no longer pull my weight, yes. But only then. We'll secure the harbor, Therm." He smiled in the dim battle light of the bridge. "Think you can dock this tub, Therm?"

"I'll put her in there like fingers in a glove, Ben."

"I've got to get ready. So I'll see you in Ireland, friend."

"See you, friend."

Rosebud came to stand beside him on the

bridge. "See the faint glow of lights over there?" Therm said, pointing. "That's Ireland, honey."

She picked up binoculars and adjusted them. "Those are fires, I think."

"Yes. Part of the city is burning and the water is reflecting the light like a series of mirrors. This is going to be a tough one, baby. I won't kid you."

"There is a chance the Rebels won't secure a toehold?"

"Yes. And Ben and Ike know it, too. If Ike and his SEALs can't knock out those guns on either side of the harbor, allowing smaller craft to get in and resupply, Ben and the others will be trapped."

"It isn't a very big town," Rosebud said. "I looked it up in a travel guide. It's only about twenty-five thousand, before the Great War."

Communications said, "The Irish resistance fighters are fighting house-to-house with Jack Hunt's people now, sir. Hunt has really gone on the offensive."

"They know that the Rebels are knocking on the door." He looked at his watch. "Ike and his people should be very close to their objectives now. Striganov's Spetsnaz troopers have taken the west end of the big Island. They reported very light resistance. They have commandeered vehicles and are moving very rapidly toward the airport at Kilronan." He picked up the scramble mike and got Striganov's ship. "General, what do you think about getting the gunships we have on the decks ready to go toward the big island?"

"An excellent suggestion, my friend," the Russian said. "I was about to give the orders when

353

you came through. I had just been informed that my people have taken the small airport. I'll be going in on a Huey to have a look-see."

"That's ten-four, General. God speed and good luck."

"God speed and good luck to you, my friend."

The convoy was circling at dead slow a few miles off the big island. Therm felt helpless. There was nothing he could do except wait, hope, and pray a little.

Ike almost caused a woman to have a heart attack when he came out of the water just a few feet from shore. The woman and several kids were about fifty feet from a 155mm. The big gun was camouflaged and sandbagged.

Ike stripped his mask off and whispered, "Don't yell, ma'am. We're American SEALs with the Rebels."

"Thank the Lord," the woman whispered, holding a crying child close to her to still the sobs. "By the Lord, my boy, you've come just in the nick of time, I tell you."

Ike grinned at her as the rest of his personal team came out of the water like dark monsters, their wet suits glistening in the dim light. They stripped off tanks and fins and unpacked their equipment.

Ike pointed to the nearest gun emplacement and made a slashing motion across his throat. Two SEALs moved noiselessly in the night toward a silent kill.

"Jack Hunt's people tied us here, lad," the

woman told Ike. "Would you be so kind as to cut the bonds?"

Ike muttered some very uncomplimentary things about the caliber of men who would stake out old women and young kids to the ground in front of gun emplacements. He freed the woman and the kids and whispered, "Stay down and quiet. We'll get you out of this mess; but it's going to take a little while."

She nodded and smiled at him.

Ike felt a little chill run through him as one of the children, a girl of no more than five or six who obviously had not been eating much, put her thin arms around about his neck and kissed him on the cheek.

"God bless ye, Mr. Seal," she whispered.

Ike was afraid to respond due to the large lump in his throat. He looked up as the two men he'd sent to the gun emplacement came back, wiping the blood off their knife blades.

"That one's a zero," Ike was told in a whisper. "The next one's about a hundred yards west of here."

"Take it," Ike said, his voice hoarse. "Ma'am, are there prisoners there, too?"

"Oh, I should say. An old woman like me and two young people about the same age as Kathleen and Robert here."

"What kind of dirty motherf—" The SEAL bit off the words. "Would do something like this?"

"Scum of the earth," Ike said. "Take them out."

The men moved silently into the night. Ike went to the shore and retrieved a waterproof bag. He pulled out three packets of field rations and gave them to the woman. "Here. You people stay low and eat this. It isn't the tastiest stuff in the world but it's good food."

"What the hell's all that racket down there?" a man said, appearing on a rise above Ike.

Ike dropped to the ground and whispered. "Tell him the kid's sick."

"My grandchild's ill," the woman immediately called. "Please let us see a doctor."

"You'll get to see the pearly gates when the Rebels attack, you ugly old cow," the man said. "Now shut up. If that kid makes anymore noise I'll come down there and cut her goddamn throat."

Ike moaned.

"I warned you, old woman." The man clamored down the rocks. He never saw the black-suited figure who rose up behind him with a cold smile and cut his throat.

Ike lowered the body to the ground. He looked at the woman. "He isn't very good company; but at least he won't argue with you. Stay put. I'm gone."

Ike made the rocks and slipped on earphones. He tapped his mike twice and listened as answering taps came to him. All his people had made it and were in place. There was no need for him to speak. All his people knew what to do.

They were cutting throats, killing members of Jack Hunt's army with High Standard .22-caliber automatics with silencers, freeing prisoners, and setting blocks of C-4.

At that moment, Ben was stepping into a motor launch with his team. Bags of equipment were handed down and stacked. Ammo boxes were passed down and stored. On this run, Ben had left his old M-14 and was carrying a CAR-15 in 9mm caliber. He had laid aside his .45 and carried two 9mm model 92F Berettas. The motor launch, lowered from a transport filled quickly.

"Let's go," Ben said.

"Sir," a Rebel said. "The other teams aren't even loaded yet. We're going to be twenty or thirty minutes ahead of the others!"

"My momma always taught me it was better to be early than late. Get this damn boat moving!"

"Yes, sir!"

"Advise Therm we're shoving off," Ben said to Corrie, knowing full well what Therm would be doing seconds after being informed.

Therm received and immediately went to high-band scramble. "Shark, this is Hippie. Eagle has left the nest and will be a full thirty minutes ahead of the others."

"Son of a bitch!" Ike said, after acknowledging the transmission. He pushed a bloody body out of his way and walked to the entrance of the sand-bagged gun emplacement. He set his timer and lifted his walkie-talkie. "Set your timers and get your prisoners clear and then get your asses humpin', boys. The Eagle's done left the nest and you-all know where he's goin'."

"Holy shit!" a SEAL whispered over the scrambled frequency. "He's headin' straight for the heart of the matter, ain't he?"

"That's his style, boys. Let's go help the Eagle find the Blarney Stone."

14

The motor launch carrying Ben and his team entered Galway Bay on the north side of the Aran Islands, motoring stately past the waiting SEALs in their Zodiacs. The SEALs looked at each other in the darkness, astonishment in their eyes.

"That's the General!" one said. "What the hell's *he* doin' out here?"

"Team Five," Ike's voice blew out of the speaker. "Stay with the Eagle. Repeat: stay with the Eagle. We've got it covered in our sector. Acknowledge this."

"That's ten-four, Shark," Team Five's leader radioed. "He just sailed past us. Where the hell's he going?"

"Right up to the docks, probably. Stay with him and keep it puckered tight, boys. It's gonna be a hairy one."

The helicopter gunships were setting down on the small airfield at Kilronan.

Buddy was frantically yelling at his people to move faster. He was already twenty minutes behind his father.

"Gunship approaching, General," Ben was informed.

"Cut the engine," Ben ordered. "Everybody down low."

The gunship, actually a converted pleasure craft, would miss Ben's motor launch by a good hundred yards—if it stayed on its present heading.

"Corrie," Ben said. "Tell those in the Zodiacs to take out that gunboat. We can't let it reach the fishing boats."

"Oh, wonderful," a SEAL said, after acknowledging the order. "I guess we could take our little rubber boat and attack the damn thing." Then he grinned. "Hey, that's not a bad idea."

"Have you lost your fuckin' mind?" a buddy asked.

"No," the man handling the motor said. "I know what's on his brain. Besides pus, that is. Let's get some people on board. We can use that gunboat."

The SEALs looked at each other and grinned. "All right!" they said in unison.

Jack Hunt lost half his big guns on both sides of the harbor as the blocks of C-4 blew. The bay was now clear from the mouth down to Barna on the north side, and down to Corcomroe Abbey on the south side.

Ben was on his knees, studying a map with the

360

help of a tiny flashlight between his teeth. He pointed out an inlet close to the airport. Jersey nodded her head in understanding and passed the word back to the coxswain while Corrie radioed the change of plans back to those trying desperately to close the distance with Ben and his team.

"Goddamnit!" Therm roared. "He's going ashore with twenty people 'way to hell and gone south of the city."

"Buddy is asking whether he's still supposed to be on your right flank?" Corrie said.

"Tell him to come in directly behind me and try to catch us," Ben told her. "We'll be on Highway N18 heading for the airport. And tell him to quit jacking around and get here."

Corrie noticed Ben's smile and laughed softly. "Yes, sir. I'll do that, sir."

"Might I point out," Linda said, as the shoreline of the Irish coast became more distinctive, "that there are only twenty of us? We are lightly armed, and we don't know who is friendly and who isn't."

"If they shoot at us, we can consider them unfriendly," Ben said. "I've always found that to be a good barometer."

"You are an impossibly overoptimistic and arrogant jackass, Ben. Are you aware of that?"

"Does this mean our date for tomorrow night is off?" Ben asked.

"Jesus!" Linda whispered.

The bow of the launch crunched onto sand.

"Lovely ride," Ben said, stepping out of the boat. "Let's go, gang. We've got to liberate this island and return it to the good citizens of Ireland."

"All twenty of us," Jersey remarked. "Right." She stepped out into what was ankle-deep water for Ben and knee-deep water for her. "Shit!" she said.

When the team had assembled, all of them heavily loaded with equipment, Cooper said, "Now what?"

"We find a cottage, knock on the door, and ask where in the hell we are," Ben said.

"Rat to Eagle!" Buddy's voice sprang out of the speaker. "Where in the hell are you?"

"Tell him that as soon as I find out, he'll be the second one to know," Ben said to Corrie.

"It's dark, it's wet, it's sandy, and it's rocky," Corrie told Buddy.

Miles back, Buddy looked at his mike in astonishment.

"That's not exactly what I said," Ben told Corrie. "But close enough. Give me that mike. Rat, it's the deep inlet that runs almost to the highway. You'll find us. Eagle out. Let's go, people."

A SEAL caught onto the sheer line and pulled himself on board the gunboat while another SEAL was doing the same on the other side. A crewman walked from one side of the open cockpit to the other and knelt down to investigate a wet spot on the deck. He received a knife in his throat. The blade cut off any sounds as it ripped his windpipe and drove out the back side. The SEAL shook the blood off his knife, sheathed it, and took out a pistol from a waterproof pouch. The second Rebel on board had taken out the man behind an M-60 machine gun.

When the helmsman was lying dead on the deck with a small .22-caliber slug in the back of his head, the SEAL took the wheel while his buddy radioed the convoy.

"We are in command of a gunboat. It's a white Bertram with a flying bridge. We're at the mouth of Galway Bay, close in to the south shore. You need us to ferry troops?"

"That's ten-fifty. Stay in the bay to assist any Rebels who might come under attack and need to be fished out."

"That's ten-four."

Ike came face to face with a heavily armed man. The man's eyes widened in shock. Instinctively he brought up the muzzle of his Uzi. Ike shot him in the chest and stripped the man of weapons and ammo.

"Guy could have used a bath," another SEAL remarked as Ike handed the weapons and ammo pouch to a young man they'd found tied up in a shed.

"Yeah," Ike said. "These guys aren't too strong on personal hygiene. Bob," he told the young Irishman, "you go get your friends you told me about. Backtrack along where we blew the gun emplacements. You'll find lots of weapons and plenty of ammo. Join your friends along the waterfront. Tell them we're here and the password is 'Lucky.' You got that?"

"Branded in me brain," the young man said with a grin that split his freckled face, then took off down the road.

"Now where the hell are we?" Ike asked, opening a map pouch.

A SEAL trotted up in time to hear the question "One mile from Salthill," he panted.

They had taken time to change out of their wet suits and into cammies and tie bandanas around their heads. Helmets would have been too bulky to carry along.

"All right," Ike said. "Let's go raise a little hell in Salthill."

A woman peered out of the glass at Ben's knock. "I beg your pardon, madam," he said. "I'm General Ben Raines from America. We've come over to assist you in running the outlaws out of your country. Would you be so kind as to tell us how far it is to the airport in Galway?"

The woman grinned. She had no front teeth. "Just a few miles up this road. You going to do all that with this wee bunch, General?"

Ben smiled at her. "I do have a few more coming ashore, so don't be alarmed if you see a lot of soldiers passing by your house."

"Jack Hunt and his scalawags has taken all the vehicles from the people. They left us bicycles. If you see a vehicle a-comin' at you, it'll be driven by them bad ones."

"I thank you for that information."

"God go with you on your mission, General."

"Have a good evening, ma'am. Let's go, people."

As Ben and his team headed up the road, a man called out, "Who was them people, Mother?"

"Americans. General Ben Raines and his army has come to run Jack Hunt into the sea."

"My God, he did come. Get me my walkin' stick while I fetch that box of shells for my shotgun. They'll be needin' some assistance."

"Trucks coming at us," the point man called from the crest of a hill. "Three of them. Big ones. The canvas is off the top of the beds."

Ben waved his team to the side of the road and spread them out. He pulled a grenade from his battle harness and held it up. "Every third person. Toss them in the beds as they drive by. This ought to brighten up their evening."

The trucks rolled over the crest and past the hidden point man. They reached the flat, and Ben and his team chunked their mini-Claymores. The shrapnel-hurling grenades made a terrible mess in the beds of the trucks. What the grenades didn't finish, the Rebels did.

They left the burning trucks by the side of the road and in the ditches where the drivers had run off the highway—helped by automatic weapons' fire—and continued their advance toward Galway.

A woman leaned out of a window and shook her fist at the Rebels. "What's all that racket up the lane, you damned hooligans!" she yelled. "Ruffians and thieves and no-goods, the whole scummy lot of you!"

Ben chuckled. "Seems the Irish folks have had their belly full of Jack Hunt. We're Americans, ma'am," he yelled. "Just landed on your fair shore and it's a lovely land, to be sure. And it'll be a fairer place once we chase Jack Hunt and his thugs into the ocean."

"With that glib tongue of yours, you've a bit of the Irish in you, I'm thinkin'," she called.

"On my mother's side. She was a McHugh."

"Sure! From right here in County Galway. Although they's some McHugh's in Cavan, Donegal, and Longford. What's your name, lad?"

"Ben Raines."

"My stars and garters! Teddy, wake up, old man, it's him. He's come to free us. It's General Ben Raines, just a-walkin' up the road big as life, he is."

"Take five," Ben told his team, then walked over to the cottage. "Good evening, ma'am. Such a pleasant night for a stroll."

She laughed. "You got more of your mother in you than your father, General. And a fair eye for the lassies, too, I'd bet a pint. Where's the rest of your army, General?"

"I've got teams knocking out the gun emplacements in Galway Bay. That's the explosions you heard. Those same teams are now linking up with the Free Irish fighting along the harbor. I've got ten thousand more troops circling in ships out past the Iran Islands."

"God love you, boy! They'll be songs sung to

you for generations to come."

"Get my shotgun, old woman," the man said from inside the cottage. "I can't let the Yanks do all the work."

"Just sit back down in your chair, old man," she told him. "Let the young folks fight this one." She smiled at Ben. "Although you'll never see forty again, General."

"To be sure," Ben said with a laugh.

"My name's Flannery, ma'am," a Rebel called. "Was my folks from around here?"

"The damn Flannerys are everywhere, boy. But most of them come from Limerick and Mayo Counties. Limerick's a county north of here and Mayo's a county south."

"Tell me something," Ben said. "Who controls the cities?"

"Them horrid cannibals. Call themselves The Believers. Are you familiar with them, General?"

"We killed about a quarter of a million of them in the States."

"Then you know them well. Good huntin' over here."

"Northern Ireland?"

She grimaced. "Them folks been fightin' for centuries. Two world wars and the Great War couldn't break 'em up. They'll fight 'til the last son is gone and then the fathers will kill off one another. Only the women will end that one, General. Only the women."

"Can you gather up your neighbors?"

"Sure."

"We stacked the weapons and the ammo from the dead by the side of the road. They're yours. Pass them out. Don't ever let any government disarm you again, ma'am."

"We won't, General. We won't."

"My son will be coming up this road in about half an hour." Ben smiled. "He's the one who'll set the lassies' hearts to beating faster."

"Takes after his father, now, does he?"

Ben laughed and leaned into the open window and kissed the old woman on the cheek. A small fire was burning and a stew was bubbling in a blackened pot. It smelled like rabbit. "You get those weapons and then rest easy. We'll give your country back to you, and that's a promise."

"And you never break a promise, General?"

"Only the ones I make to the ladies."

She laughed and flapped her apron at him. "Get on with you, now!"

Ben and his Rebels walked on through the cool night. The sounds of heavy fighting began to touch their ears. Galway was about a mile away.

"We'll hold up here and wait for Buddy," Ben told his team. "Dig in, but not too deep. We might have to run like thieves in the night."

Linda lay by his side in the dewy dampness of a field and said, "It's finally sinking in, Ben. We're really in Ireland. We're really here!"

"What convinced you? Did you see a leprechaun?"

"If I did, I'd never tell. That's bad luck."

"Well, if you see another one, ask him to grant

us some good luck."

"We're going to need it, aren't we?"

"All we can get, Linda. Jack Hunt has tanks and mortars and artillery. Ours are still on board ship. We've got some tank-killing Dragons, but they're complicated bastards and they don't always stop the target. Why in the hell the U.S. didn't adopt the Milan is something I will never understand. I'm sure it was politics."

"Rat calling, sir," Corrie said, crawling to Ben's position.

Ben took the mike. "Go, Rat."

"I just talked to an old lady you laid the blarney on. I think we're about two miles behind you and I know we're coming hard. I've got two platoons with me and a full company is ten minutes behind me."

"That's ten-four. You have Dragons with you?"

"Affirmative, Eagle."

"We'll hold and wait for you. When you get here you can rest and we'll make some plans. Eagle out."

"Company on the way, General," the lookout called. "Tanks."

"Shit," Ben said. "Corrie, advise Buddy he's got tanks coming at him. We're going to lay low and hope we don't get spotted. Everybody get down."

"Lookout says he doesn't know what the hell these tanks are," Corrie said. "He's never seen anything like them. They're not big ones."

"Probably the British Scimitars. They carry a

30mm cannon. Thank God they're not Chieftains. I don't know if the Dragons could stop one of those."

"Passing by lookout," Ben was told. "The hatches are open."

"Hug the ground."

The tanks didn't slow down as they passed Ben's position. They rumbled on south.

"Scimitars," Ben said. He took the mike. "Eagle to Rat."

"Go, Eagle."

"They're British Scimitars. Five of them. You have antitank mines with you?"

"Negative."

"The Dragons will stop them."

"I have one Dragon."

"Damn!" Ben said. He keyed the mike. "They're rolling with open hatches. That tell you anything?"

"Indeed it does. Rat out."

"What will they do, Ben?" Linda asked.

"Buddy's got about a hundred troops with him. Those tanks were rolling bunched up. That is a very stupid thing to do. But Jack hasn't been fighting highly trained troops so that tells me he's gotten careless; or at least his men have. Those tanks are going to have about a hundred grenades raining down on them. Some of them will get inside the hatches. Then Buddy's only problem will be staying down when the ammo blows."

"I can imagine what that does to the people inside."

Ben looked at her. "No, dear. Believe me when I say, you cannot. Want me to describe it?"

"I think I'll pass."

"Good move. But I'm sure before the week is out you'll get to see it firsthand."

"I can hardly wait," she said dryly.

15

The Rebels could feel and hear the crumping sounds of the grenades that missed the open tank hatches. When the 30mm rounds and the smaller ammo stored inside the tanks blew, the ground trembled like the aftershock of an earthquake. Buddy's team had caught the tanks on the crest of a hill and the flames shooting out of the hatches were clearly visible.

Linda felt that a number of body parts also were blown through the open hatches.

The SEAL team that Ben had outdistanced and who had linked up with Buddy, were the first to reach Ben's position. "Fried 'em like chickens," one SEAL said.

Another said, "We got orders from General Ike to stay on your ass like a leech, General. You gonna give us a hard time about that?"

"Nope," Ben said easily. "I never give a man a hard time for following orders."

Buddy panted up; his load was nearly twice what the other Rebels were packing.

"You trying to prove something totin' all that, boy?" Ben asked, a smile on his lips.

"I will be the first to admit that I might have overloaded myself," Buddy said.

"Spread it around among the others. You need to stay just as light as the others."

Buddy looked at his father's CAR-15 in 9mm and the two 9mm pistols belted around his waist. "Retired the old Thunder Lizard?"

"For this operation. Have you been in contact with the company behind you?"

"Yes. They're just over the hill there."

"Corrie, tell them to hold up and take five. Then maintain a half mile distance between us. I don't want us all bunched up."

"Shark to Eagle."

"Go, Shark."

"We've linked up with the Free Irish. But brother, the harbor is only three blocks to our rear. It's like that comedian used to tell about that man up a tree fighting a bobcat. He told his buddy on the ground to just shoot up amongst us. One of us has got to have some relief."

"All right, Ike. We'll take some pressure off your west flank. Hang on." To Corrie: "Order Striganov's people to use everything that'll float to get to Galway by the sea. Attack the harbor head on." To Beth: "How many people do we still have on ship?"

"About seventy percent," she told him. "Those

374

being landed are scattered all over the place due to the winds picking up and the sea turning rough. Some of them were put ashore north of Kilkierran Bay. They're working their way toward Galway, some of them riding bicycles."

"Hell of a way to run a war," Ben said, standing up and adjusting his battle harness. "Let's go, people. Corrie, advise the ships' captains we are attacking Galway between the city and the airport."

Ben assigned Scouts to take the point. They had not advanced half a mile before hitting a road block, a blockade backed up by tanks and APCs.

"Leave it for those behind us to handle," Ben ordered. "We head cross-country from this point. Keep that rise to your left and then swing around. Move out in teams of five. Go."

The fires burning in Galway clearly pinpointed the Rebels' objective. Muzzle flashes and tracers briefly gave light to the pockets of darkness. The problem was, nobody knew who was the enemy and who was a friend.

"Corrie, tell the company behind us to take the airport. We're going into the city."

"People approaching from the east," Jersey pointed out.

"Rebels!" came the call from the darkness. "We're fighters from Kilkenny. Hold your fire, we're friendly."

"We'll see," Ben said. "Come on in, friends."

The leader's hair was as red as some of the flames in the city and his grin was infectious. "Pat O'Shea's the name. And I've seen your picture; you'd be General Ben Raines."

"I am." Ben stuck out his hand and the man shook it.

"They's some forty of us if the laggards ever catch up. We've set a fair pace this night. Left Ballyragget when lookouts radioed the ships was near the Arans. We're fighters and not a person among us will shirk no duty, General. What would you have us do?"

"Do you know the city?"

"Aye, sir, I know it well."

"Get us in there."

Pat grinned. "Right into the thick of things you want to go, hey, General?"

"That's where the action is."

Pat waved at two men. "Sutton, you and Murphy get with the General's point men—" He took a closer look at the way a Rebel's BDUs fit. "—Point *people*, and get us into the fracus, now, will you, lads?"

Murphy and Sutton moved out. Pat turned to Ben. "Them ladies can fight, hey, General?"

"You want to cross one and find out?"

Pat grinned. "My mother—bless her heart—raised one foolish child. My brother. I'll not insult no woman when she's totin' a tommy gun. Let's go."

They drew enemy fire moments after pulling out and hit the ditches.

"That's a .50," a SEAL said.

"Get that light mortar set up and start dropping

376

in on those bastards," Ben said. "Range two hundred fifty yards."

The light mortar began thunking out 66mm rounds, walking them up. The .50 caliber gun emplacement went up in a flash and a roar. The Rebels and the Irish Freedom Fighters surged forward.

"Where are we?" Ben asked Pat.

"In the city limits of Galway, sir. Just barely."

"My people have their backs to the bay, Pat. We've got to take some heat off them on the west flank. Get us there."

"Right you are, sir. Just follow me."

"Tanks!" a SEAL shouted. "Three of them. Rounding the corner at one o'clock. They're all buttoned up."

"Rocket launchers and recoilless rifles up," Ben called. "We can't penetrate that armor but we can knock a tread off. Cripple them. Do it."

Three Rebels ran forward, two of them with M67 90mm recoilless rifles which fired a HEAT warhead.

The tanks clanked forward, the machine guns spitting and flashing. Two Rebels went down, nearly chopped in two. The M67's fired, the HEATs struck home. The rocket launcher whooshed and flew true. The light tanks were disabled.

A medic quickly checked the Rebels. He looked at Ben and shook his head.

"Take their equipment and give it to the Irish," Ben ordered. "Slide satchel charges under those goddamn tanks. Corrie, radio that I want antitank mines up here and I want them like fucking yesterday.''

"Yes, sir.''

The satchel charges blew and made life awfully uncomfortable for those inside the light tanks. But the tanks didn't blow. Their bellies were heavily armored.

"Do it again," Ben ordered.

The tanks' main guns boomed. The 76mm cannon blew holes in the old brick building behind the Rebels and the Irish.

"You certainly do like to live dangerously, General," Pat remarked, after the dust had settled and the bits of brick had ceased falling all around them.

"Get the Dragon up here and knock that lead son of a bitch out," Ben ordered. "We're not going to leave here with those things operational.''

"My C Company is right behind us, Father," Buddy said, sliding on his belly across the road to reach Ben. "B Company is fighting at the airport.''

"Tell C Company to hold up until we neutralize these tanks. Where's that Dragon?''

"Set up and ready to go," Cooper called.

"Fire the goddamn thing!''

The light tank went up in a mass of exploding steel. The force of the explosion twisted another tank around, blocking the narrow passageway and preventing those in the third tank from utilizing their main gun. A SEAL ran forward, carrying a heavy satchel charge. He climbed over the rear of the twisted tank and laid the heavy charge in the narrow space between turret and the main body of the blocked tank. Then he got the hell out of there. The SEAL had just gotten clear when the charge blew and the main gun exploded, blowing the turret half off and twisting it around.

"Had to have been a round in that cannon," Ben said. "The charge bent the barrel and the round fired and stuck. That did it. Let's go."

The Rebels and the Irish were pulling out when the remaining 76mm rounds stored in the burning tank exploded. The force brought down a wall, covering the other tank.

Ben and those with him slipped further inside the war-ravaged town. Shadowy figures dressed in military uniforms darted out into the street about a hundred feet from Ben. Ben and the man in the lead spotted each other about a heartbeat apart. The man brought his weapon up and Ben gave him some 9mm hollow-noses in the gut. The man went down, kicking and screaming.

His team dropped to the street just as Buddy leveled an M-60 and began chopping up this bunch of Jack Hunt's army. The M-60 jumped and bucked in his strong hands as he sent the 7.62 slugs howling and whining and making a big bloody mess in the littered street.

"Pat, have your boys get their weapons and ammo," Ben told the Irishman.

"About half of Dan's people are on shore," Corrie told Ben.

"That's good," Ben said, squatting by the

corner of a building.

"They're scattered all to hell and gone, General," she added, light rain splattered on her helmet and splashing onto her face. The wind had picked up and was howling as the fingers of a large storm that had been building out at sea began touching land. "Therm says to throw out the original plan as to where each battalion was to land. They're all over the place. Scattered twenty miles in either direction. But he says there have been no reports of Rebels lost at sea."

"No. They're just lost on *land*," Ben said with a grimace. "All right, so big deal. We're on our own. Hell, what else is new? What's the word from the airport?"

"Fighting is heavy. But our people have knocked out Hunt's communication center and seized the building. They say it was very elaborate. He had links over in England and possibly on the continent. Intelligence is going over files and codes now."

Before Ben could reply, a dozen APCs rolled up and discharged their cargo of Hunt's fighting men. There was no more time for conversation for several minutes as the Rebels and the Free Irish fought a fierce firefight with Hunt's soldiers.

Ben crawled on his belly to the location of several SEALs and Scouts. "We need those APCs," Ben said, pulling the man's head down close to his mouth to be heard. "Take this bunch and work around and get on top of those buildings on their left flank. Take plenty of firepower with you including all the grenades you can stagger with. Go!"

A rifleman found Ben's range and started putting some lead around him. He rolled behind a stone fence and stayed low, working away from his team, following the progress of the SEALs and the Scouts until they disappeared from his view. Ben came to a gate and lay flat on the ground, listening to the sounds of war. The rifleman was still concentrating his fire on the place where he'd last seen Ben. Ben snaked across the shattered gate and wriggled through the shattered window of a stone home.

He lay with his back to the wall for a moment, catching his breath and assessing his situation. He concluded it was better than most of those coming under fire on the outside. He lifted his walkie-talkie and keyed the mike. "This is Eagle. I'm OK and in a secure position. Do not attempt to join me. That is an order. Acknowledge."

Corrie acknowledged and Ben clipped the little handy-talkie back on his harness. He froze, hearing the faint sounds of voices coming from the rear of the house. He rolled into a dark corner and behind a rat-chewed old sofa, his CAR-15 off safety and on full rock and roll. He lay on the rat-shit-covered floor and watched as four men crept into the living room area of the old home. Two of them carried bulky objects, the third man carried two huge haversacks bulging with something, and the fourth had an armload of what looked like tubes.

Ben smiled, hoping he had correctly guessed

what the men were about to do.

"That window right over there," the Germanic-accented voice came to him. "Gives us a good field of fire."

"Christ," the man who had carried in the haversacks said, setting his burdens on the floor and straightening up. "Goddamn things weigh a hundred pounds."

I hope so, Ben thought, for he was now positive what the men were planning.

"Yer gettin' old, Dave," another said. He stepped over to join the men who had set their burdens down and gathered in a knot by a wall.

Just as a mortar round exploded outside, Ben gave the men a full clip from his CAR and watched them fall like broken puppets. At this close range many of the slugs penetrated, and the back of the wall was gory.

Ben knelt down to avoid any stray slugs that might be coming through the windows and checked each man. One was still breathing. He wasn't after Ben stood up. Ben wiped his knife clean and sheathed it.

He inspected his new-found treasures and smiled. The men had been preparing to fire a rocket launcher called the Armbruster. The West Germans had perfected the launcher, and the old American Delta Force had used them with success, when there had been an America and the Delta Force was still around.

The knapsacks contained three dozen rounds. Dave hadn't been kidding about the weight. He'd been carrying about eighty pounds of 2.178 pound rockets. One great advantage of the Armbruster is that it can be safely fired within a closed space, unlike the American Dragon or the Russian RPG-7. The noise of the Armbruster firing is about like a pistol shot, and there is no flash, blast, or smoke.

The other man had carried spare launch tubes, for the tube had to be discarded after each firing. Ben inspected the two Armbrusters and found they were ready to fire. He moved to a window just as a tank clanked up and stopped, troops behind it.

Ben unclipped his handy-talkie and said, "This is Eagle. I just found some goodies, so I'm going to neutralize that tank that showed up and then knock out that .50 caliber in the building next to that church."

"Ten-four, General," Corrie said.

Ben uncapped the sights and smiled as he dead-centered the tank in the reflex sight. The 78mm Armbruster round has a muzzle velocity of 722 feet per second and is capable of penetrating a foot of armor.

Ben squeezed the trigger and the tank exploded in a massive ball of flame. He laid the launcher aside and loaded the second with an HE antipersonnel fragmentation round. He sighted in the open window where the .50 was spitting out death, then lowered the launcher to the jumping barrel of the heavy machine gun. The entire wall exploded, and the screaming of men filled the night.

Ben changed the tubes and loaded up with HE antipersonnel rounds just as the SEALs and the Scouts on top of the buildings began dropping Fire-Frag grenades on top of Jack Hunt's soldiers in the alley and street below them. Ben let another rocket fly and the alley was filled with dead and dying troops.

Ben smiled as the enemy troops tried to make the APCs and were cut down. Those that could still run did so, fleeing into the night.

Ben keyed his mike. "I'm in the house directly behind the stone fence. I got a sack full of goodies. Get some people over here pronto."

A SEAL was the first one in the building. Several Free Irish came right behind him. The Irish began stripping the dead of their weapons and ammo.

"All right!" The SEAL said, spotting the Armbruster.

A few more shots were fired outside as the Rebels finished off the drivers of the APCs.

"Hey," the shout reached Ben. "Most of these are American APCs. They're M113's."

"I don't know what this one is," another said. "But it's got a hell of a twin-mount machine gun on it."

Ben did not have to tell his people to collect all the weapons and ammo from the dead. But he did add, "Get all their field rations. It might be awhile before we get resupplied."

"How about their water jugs, General?" Ben was asked.

"Purify it."

"Prisoners, sir?"

Ben hesitated, conscious of Pat O'Shea's eyes on him as the Irishman knelt on the floor by a dead Hunt soldier. Then he smiled and cut his eyes to Pat. "It's your country, Pat. We're just here to help out."

"I'm a God-fearin' man, I am, General," Pat said. "But I've lived under the iron rule of these bastards for too many years to be merciful towards them. They've killed and raped and pillaged all over this land. They've turned this good green earth bloody. Kill them."

Ben lifted his handy-talkie. "No prisoners."

16

When the news that Ben Raines was not taking prisoners reached Jack Hunt, safely in his command post miles away from the small city of Galway, it came as no surprise. He had expected no better from General Ben Raines and his Rebels.

Jack had studied Ben Raines and his tactics for years. He had compiled hundreds of hours of taped broadcasts of Rebel transmissions and had listened to them again and again. And Ben Raines was by no means the first to sail the Atlantic after the Great War. Many of Jack's men were Americans who had faced thousands of miles of ocean to escape Ben Raines ruthless purge of gangs and criminals from America. Just the mention of Ben Raines' name was enough to bring out a fine sheen of sweat on those men's faces.

But, Jack thought with a smile, if Ben Raines thought this was going to be an easy fight, Ben Raines had another think due him.

Jack rose from his chair and walked to the

window. The storm was picking up, the winds howling and the rain hammering the earth. The terrible weather would slow the invasion forces leaving the ships. And Raines would not use those goddamned helicopter gunships of his. But it wouldn't slow up those Rebels and the fighting Free Irish already in Galway or proceeding toward the city.

Jack Hunt—he had used so many aliases over the long bloody years it was difficult for him to remember his real name—turned from the window to face his commanders in this sector. "How many men are in Galway?"

"Two battalions in the town proper and two battalions waiting just outside the city, between Galway and Tuam," he was told. "And those in the city are getting the shit kicked out of them," the man added.

Jack ran short battalions of five hundred men per battalion. He had plenty of light tanks, but nothing to compare with Ben Raines huge MBTs. He had artillery, but nothing like the monster guns that were at Ben Raines's command. But those were still on board ship. He had to strike now, within a matter of hours, and strike hard. But how? Jack had no navy, so sinking the transports was out of the question.

"Sink the damn ships," one commander said.

Jack shook his head. "Impossible in this weather. The sea is running high. You can bet that Raines has the best radar he could set up on those vessels. Any flotilla would be spotted immediately—providing we had a flotilla. Frogmen

388

couldn't get near the ships in this weather—if we had frogmen to send. No, we've got to contain Ben Raines inside Galway. Alert the two battalions outside the city to strike just before dawn. Raines and his people will have been up all day and fighting all night and they'll be weary and cold to the bone in this weather. They'll be running out of supplies and in this weather they can't be resupplied from ship. Hit them at dawn."

"Miserable goddamned weather," Striganov bitched from his airport command post on the big island of the Aran chain. "Twenty-four gunships ready to go and they're useless in this raging storm." He turned to his radio operator. "What is the status of the ships?"

"They've ceased all disembarking of troops, sir. The weather is just too foul and the risks are too high."

"And whose decision was that?"

"Thermopolis and Emil, sir. The winds are blowing the tiny fishing boats all over the place. Two were wrecked and sunk by the battering against the transports."

The Russian nodded his head in agreement. "The captains had no other choice in the matter. How many troops did we get ashore and where are they?"

"Less than a thousand, sir. And they're scattered all over the place."

"Merciful God," Georgi muttered. A small smile creased his lips. "Have the Free Irish turned

Dan Gray loose, yet?''

"Only after Colonel Gray gave them a tongue-lashing and a cussing that the leader of the resistance group said he'd never heard the like of. But Dan and the few Rebels with him are miles from Galway.''

"This weather won't stop that crazy Englishman,'' Georgi said.

A group of Irish resistance fighters had seized Dan and briefly held him prisoner, suspecting him of being a part of Jack Hunt's army. A few of Dan's troops had finally showed up and convinced the Free Irish that they were Raines' Rebels and that Dan was their commander. Dan, it was reported, was ready to kill the whole lot of his captors before he was calmed down. The former SAS man had a great many of very uncomplimentary things to say about the Irish and said them, including quite a few invectives concerning the Irish mentality, which, Dan concluded, was on a par with a hedgehog.

It was only after the leader of the Free Irish brought out a jug of whiskey that Dan began to mellow out.

Now the whole group of them were stomping through the rain and the storm, struggling to reach the Rebels trapped inside Galway.

Ben and his people now controlled several blocks of Galway, and Hunt's soldiers had been forced to move troops away from the harbor area to stop

390

their advance. That took some of the pressure off of Ike and his people.

"Shark to Eagle."

"Go, Shark."

"We got some breathin' room now, Eagle. I don't know how they managed it in this weather, but about a hundred more Rebels just docked. That's gonna be the end of it until the weather breaks. What do you hear from those who made shore in faraway places?"

"Dan and some of his people, including a group of Free Irish, are on the way, but they don't anticipate arriving at their objective until about an hour before dawn. I've assigned them to a crossroads north of the city. I have a hunch that Hunt is going to try a counterattack, and resistance leaders tell me he has a battalion or more somewhere between here and Tuan. Dan is carrying quite a bit of firepower. He might not be able to stop them, but he can put a hell of a dent in them."

"That's ten-four, Eagle. We're holdin' our own. You do the same. Shark out."

The heavy rain and high winds seemed to drive the cold deeper to the bone among the Rebel troops that were stretched along a very thin line some three blocks from the harbor and from the Rebels in Ben's command, many, many blocks away from Ike's position.

Ben waved his son and the SEAL Team leader to his side. "How many of your Rat Pack is with you?"

"Ten, that I know of, Father."

"How many in your team?" he asked the SEAL.

"Eight, including me."

Ben tapped the SEAL on the arm. "You take your people on the right side of this long street. Buddy, take your Rat Pack on the left side." The rain streaked his face, making his slow smile seem almost sinister. "Take along some mines and blocks of C-4. You don't have to bring back ears on this run, boys."

The Ike-trained SEAL and the Ben and Dan-trained Buddy were just about the same age. They looked at each other and grinned. Then they were gone silent into the storm.

Ben felt eyes on him. He turned his head. Linda was beside him, having moved up unheard in the hard-pounding rain. "I suppose there is no point in telling you to get into dry clothing, is there?"

Ben laughed softly. "Hell, Linda, none of us *have* any dry clothing."

She tugged at him until he moved. She led him under an overhang where at least the rain did not touch them. The cold wind was another matter.

"Open your mouth, Ben."

"You going to feed me?"

"In a manner of speaking." She popped two pills into his mouth and told him to swallow them.

He did. "What the hell was that?"

"A little preventive medicine." She tucked a small clear plastic bag in his pocket. "That's a twenty-four hour supply. Take two of those every

392

four hours. Every Rebel is getting the same dose. After twenty-four hours, if we're not resupplied, it isn't going to make any difference one way or the other, is it, Ben?"

"No." He was brutally honest with her, and he did not have to say more about their situation.

"This is pneumonia weather, Ben. And unlike some nurses and doctors, I always believed in preventive medicines doing at least some good."

She laid her head against his chest.

"Scared?" Ben asked her.

"You bet."

"Wanna find a dry place and play kissy-face?"

She laughed against his chest. "I know where one is."

A few yards away, in the darkness, Cooper and Jersey looked at each other and grinned.

There was no letting up of the rain. But by 0400 the main body of the storm had moved through, calming the winds, and the temperature had risen.

"How's the water look, Shark?" Ben asked.

"They're loading some of the bigger boats now, Eagle. I just talked with Dickerson on the *Virginia Lady*. Danjou and some of his people will be along shortly."

"I figure Hunt's people will try to hit us about dawn. That will put them at the crossroads in about one hour. You hard-pressed for anything?"

"A great big pot of hot coffee, a whole plateful of Momma's cat-head biscuits and a big bowl of milk gravy would be de-lightful right about now."

"Dream on, Ike," Ben said with a laugh. "Dream on. Eagle out."

Ben opened a packet of field rations, looked at the goop, sighed, wiped off his spoon and dug in. The cold rations were edible, but just barely.

"Stuff tastes like shit!" Ben heard Jersey say.

Buddy slipped through the darkness and sat down beside his father.

"When'd you get back?" Ben asked.

"About three hours ago. We all got some sleep."

"Do any good?"

Buddy smiled. "We planted enough Claymores to make Jack Hunt's people wish they'd never heard of Ireland. Some of them we just positioned on the little stoop in front of a door where Jack's men were sleeping . . ."

A very loud explosion split the rainy early morning. Screams of badly wounded men quickly followed the booming.

"I believe someone just opened a door," Ben said, chewing on a mouthful of rations.

"Wait until they try to crank some of their vehicles," Buddy said, rummaging around in his pack for something to eat and frowning at a field ration packet.

The words had just left his mouth when another explosion ripped the early morning. That one was followed by a huge fireball that lit up one end of the block.

"I see what you mean," Ben said. "How'd you rig that one, son?"

"Pressure sensitive," Buddy said, opening a

packet of rations. "With a wire running to a bundle of dynamite we stuck to the gas tank. The wire became hot as soon as the driver sat down."

"You certainly have a vicious streak in you," Ben said with a straight face. "Sure didn't get that from me."

Buddy choked and coughed on a mouthful of breakfast.

"Coming under heavy attack," Dan radioed to Galway. "We can hold for a while; but we can't expect to stop them. They're throwing at least a thousand ground troops at us and they're supported by tanks and heavy machine gun fire."

"Can you hold for thirty minutes?" Ben asked.

"No more than that, General."

"That's ten-four. When you're in danger of being overrun, split your forces and let the bastards come on through. But make damn sure they have to take the west fork of that crossroads."

"Can do."

Ben called his team leaders to him and told them what they were going to do. They nodded and returned to their teams. "Eagle to Shark."

"Go, Eagle."

"Charge!"

The Rebels took the fight to Jack Hunt's soldiers on two fronts in the small city of Galway, and the mercenary's troops were expecting anything but that.

"They're all over us!" Hunt's commander in Galway frantically radioed to his General's CP.

"We can't hold and have no place to fall back."

"Then stand and die!" Jack Hunt screamed into the mike. "Stand and die!" He threw the mike to the table then said the words that outlaws and scum and various types of human trash had been saying for over a decade: "Goddamn Ben Raines!"

Ben, followed by his personal team, charged into the open door in the rear of a building. Cooper was carrying a Stoner 63, a 5.56mm belt-fed machine gun with a 150-round magazine, and he stepped around Ben and cleared the ground floor of any and all living things.

Ben heard boots shuffling on the floor behind a closed door. He leveled his CAR-15 and gave the occupant a belly full of 9mm's at almost point-blank range. Jersey stepped to one side and jerked open the door. Jack Hunt's man had been sitting on the floor of the closet. The 9mm's had taken him in the face. He had practically no head left.

"Sorry about that," Jersey said, and closed the door.

Ben walked to the bullet-shattered front door. Pat had told him that the town had been evacuated and there were very few civilians left. Most of them had been used as sacrificial goats and were tied or chained to the gun emplacements along both sides of the harbor.

"Shark on the horn, General," Corrie said.

"Go, Shark."

"What's your position?"

"Ah . . ." Ben looked out the door. "About a block from a hotel. I can't make out the name."

"It ain't the Holiday Inn, is it?"

Ben laughed. "I haven't seen one of those, Ike."

"What the devil are we gonna do with the prisoners, Ben? They're surrenderin' like flies goin' to honey."

Ben smiled. "Bring them to me, Ike. I have an idea how we might use them."

17

Dan's Rebels and the Free Irish with him fell back and faded into the glens and brush on both sides of the road when it became apparent they were about to be overrun by Hunt's troops at the crossroads.

The commanders of the two battalions called their men back, refusing to allow them to pursue. "Too much danger of an ambush," they concluded.

"Try to raise those in Galway," a battalion commander ordered his radio operator.

In Galway, a very scared member of Hunt's army sat before a radio and waited for that to happen. The muzzle of an M-16 was pressed against the side of his head. "Screw up," a Rebel told him, "and you're dead one second later."

"Four Battalion calling Galway," the speaker spewed the words. "Come in, Galway."

"Answer him," the radio operator was told. The M-16 was very convincing.

"This is Galway command post. Go ahead."

"What is your situation, Galway?"

"We have the Rebels contained near the harbor. Fighting has been heavy and we have taken many casualties, but the Rebels appear to be running out of ammo and we have regained ground lost." He read from a prepared list of answers to possible questions.

"That's affirmative, Galway. Stand by. Four Battalion calling Galway Airport."

At the airport, another prisoner sat with a .45 pressed against his head. He keyed the mike. "This is Galway Airport."

"Have you been monitoring, Airport?"

"That's affirmative. The airport is secure." He didn't lie about that. It was secure.

"Say again, Airport."

"The airport is secure. Captain Kruger is dead. Lieutenant Monroe has taken command. We are too few to assist those in Galway. Could you assist them? Over."

"That's affirmative, Airport. We are on our way to assist troops in city. Four Battalion out."

At his CP, Jack Hunt, known as the Beast, smiled as he monitored the transmissions. "Beat the bastard!" he said. "Our people rallied and beat them. I knew that stand and die order would put steel in their backbones."

"It's a trick," one of his men said. "I fought Ben Raines in America for years. The bastard's got more moves than a snake. I'm tellin' you, Jack: this is a setup if I ever heard one."

"Nonsense!" Jack said, smiling and rubbing his

hands together. "Ben Raines just bit off more than he could chew, that's all."

"Galway to Four Battalion," the words silenced the room.

"This is Four Battalion."

"Rebel ships are leaving the harbor and taking a northerly heading. We have about two companies of Rebels cut off within the city."

"He'd never do it," the American mercenary said. "Ben Raines would never abandon his people. It's a trick, Jack."

Jack grabbed up the mike and consulted a clipboard. "This is General Hunt. Give me today's code, Galway."

"Dragonfire, sir."

"That's affirmative, Galway. Hunt out." He turned to the American. "Your great Ben Raines is nothing more than a fart in the wind. He's running with his tail tucked between his legs. Tell the lookouts at Clare Island to watch for those ships and report to me. I'm tired, gentlemen. I'm going to bed. Don't disturb me."

The American outlaw shook his head after Jack had left the room. "I'm tellin' you, boys: it's a trick. You don't know Ben Raines like I do."

"Ah, hell, Barton," an aide told him. "Relax. It's nearly over. Come have some breakfast and then we'll get some sleep. This afternoon we'll drive over to Boyle and check out those new cunts the patrols brought in. I was told they picked up some twelve and thirteen year old lassies that ain't never been cracked."

401

But Barton shook his head. "I'm not hungry. You go on. I'll stay by the radio."

"Suit yourself."

"Arrange some of the dead so they appear to be manning their posts," Ben ordered. "Dress others in civilian clothing and Rebel tiger stripe and scatter them around—face down so they can't be readily identified. Hang some of the bodies out of windows and so forth. Let's make it look good." He turned to Corrie. "What's the latest report on Dan?"

"He's coming in right behind the two battalions of Hunt's people on N17."

"Excellent. Have those prisoners we took ready to start waving the new battalions on through town toward the harbor area."

"They're going to cooperate," Ike told him. "They're so damn scared we'll turn them over to the Free Irish they'd eat wet concrete and shit blocks if we told them to."

"How many other Armbrusters did we find?"

"Six. That's enough to knock out the tanks these two battalions have with them. They've got a lot of old British APCs. FV 432's. We can handle them with what we brought with us."

"Get everybody into position. They'll be here in five minutes. Start popping some caps and tossing a few grenades. Let's make this academy award time, people."

The storm had reversed itself and the winds had

once more picked up, the rain continuing to drench the land. Ben had decided not to use the helicopter gunships grounded on the big island in the Aran chain.

Those prisoners selected to meet the convoy of Hunt's soldiers and wave them on through were in place, each knowing that a Rebel sniper had them in the crosshairs and would blow a hole in them if they screwed up in any manner.

"About three blocks from the waterfront," the driver of the lead tank was told. "Hear the fighting?"

"Yeah. But not much of it going on."

"We just about got them. It's a cakewalk from here to the harbor. You can ride easy."

"Bet you'll be glad to get out of this weather," the tank commander said with a grin, as the rain lashed his own face.

"You got that right. So hurry up, will up?"

"Keep your pants on."

The convoy rumbled on through the body-littered and ravaged streets of the beautiful old town.

"Bump the commander of Four Battalion," Barton said, back at Hunt's CP. "It's too damn quiet."

"Jesus, Barton," the radio operator said.

"Just do it!"

"All right, all right, goddamnit. Four Battalion, Four Battalion, this is CP One. Give me a status report."

"Rebel and Free Irish bodies all over the

403

goddamn place," the words came through the speaker. "We're almost to the harbor and have encountered no resistance. Some firing can be heard near the waterfront. Our people . . ."

The speaker went silent.

"What the hell?" the radio operator said.

Barton's face was grim. He had a pretty good idea what had happened. That bastard Ben Raines had pulled another of his vicious little ambushes. "I warned you not to underestimate this man, Jack," he muttered. "But you just wouldn't listen."

"Jesus God in Heaven!" the words screamed out of the speaker. "It's an ambush. They're all over us. Captain Lloyd's APC just exploded right in front of me. I can't . . ."

The speaker fell silent.

The lead tank turned into a ball of flames as the Armbruster rocket tore through the armor and seared those inside.

Rebels manning heavy machine guns captured from Hunt's troops turned the streets into a flesh-mangling, bloody slaughter house. Rebels hurled HE grenades from the top of buildings. Rebels fired rocket launchers at almost point-blank range. Rebels and Free Irish with weapons on full auto cut down any of Hunt's troops who managed to escape the initial killing fire.

Dan's people had pedaled bicycles and ridden horses and reached the city just in time to block the highway leading out of Galway and chopped down those few scared troops who fled the city, thinking they had escaped the horror of the deadly ambush.

"Mop it up," Ben ordered.

"This is Command Post One!" Barton had taken over the radio. "Come in, Galway Airport."

"What'd you want, prick?" a Rebel replied.

"Who is this?"

"Lieutenant Alverez of the Rebel Army. Tricked your ass, didn't we?"

Barton chose not to reply. "Four Battalion, Five Battalion. Come in. Over."

"Sorry, partner," Corrie told him. "But you might want to come down for the funeral. It's going to be a mass burying."

"Go get Hunt," Barton said to the radio operator. "Now, goddamnit. Move." He keyed the mike. "Monroe, if you can hear me, reply."

"Monroe's been dead," a bored voice touched his ears. "We cut his throat last night."

"Captain Dalley, Captain Hayden," Barton radioed. "Come in, please."

Jack Hunt walked into the radio room, his face pale with shock and anger.

In Galway, Ben shoved a very frightened soldier into a chair and pointed to the mike. "Talk to him, soldier. Tell him what happened."

The man keyed the mike. "This is Sergeant Harrison, of Five Battalion, Company C, First Platoon. I'm just about the only one left, sir." He was shaking so violently he could hardly hold the mike. He started crying, the tears dripping from his face. "They killed us all, sir. And they're gonna

405

turn me over to the Free Irish. They're gonna hang me, sir."

Ben took the mike. The weeping soldier was led away to face the people he had helped brutalize and terrorize over the long, bloody years. "This is General Ben Raines. To whom am I speaking?"

Barton handed the mike to a very shaken Jack Hunt. "This is General Hunt."

"General Hunt, listen to me. We have established a firm beachhead in Galway. The town is ours. I have thousands of troops and hundreds of thousands of tons of equipment being off-loaded this moment." That was only a small lie. "I have squadrons of helicopter gunships. Soon the country will be restored to the Free Irish. I would rather not have to chase you all over Ireland. So I am offering you surrender terms."

Jack Hunt held the mike away from him and looked at it, astonishment on his face. "Do you hear this asshole?" Jack finally found his voice. "This . . . *bastard* is offering me surrender terms. I have twenty-seven battalions of troops, tanks, APCs, artillery, and this jerk is telling me I better surrender. Who does this son of a bitch think he is?"

"Twenty-three battalions, Jack," Barton reminded him. "Raines just slaughtered four battalions, remember?"

That got Barton a very dirty look. But that was all; Barton was right.

"Are you there, Hunt?" Ben asked.

"Yeah, yeah. I'm here, you asshole! Now you

listen to me, Raines. You got lucky, hotshot. That's all. Just lucky. But now you're on *my* turf."

"Sounds like a street punk, doesn't he?" Dan said, sipping on a mug of hot tea.

"Probably reverting back to his childhood," Ben said. "I'm sure he was denied the right to play on the first team, or the most beautiful girl in the class wouldn't date him, or his father spanked him, or some such shit as that."

The Rebels gathered around the radio room all laughed at a few of the excuses that used to be accepted as to why a person turned to a life of crime. Excuses that only those who walked around with his or her head up their ass really believed.

"Are you there, Raines?" Jack screamed.

"Sounds quite irritable," Dan said. "I'm beginning to dislike this fellow."

"Yes, Hunt, I'm here. Are you willing to surrender?"

"Fuck you, Raines!"

"And quite profane, too," Dan added. "My word, and all that going out over the air where little kiddies can hear it. Tsk, tsk."

Ben laughed at Dan. He keyed the mike. "Is that your reply, General Hunt?"

"You goddamn right it is, Raines."

"Then I suppose we have nothing left to say to one another. And I'm sorry about that, Jack. For unlike you, I don't particularly care for war." Buddy almost choked on his chewing gum and Dan arched an eyebrow in disbelief at that remark. "But you won't win this one, Jack. The Rebels

407

have left over three quarters of a million dead behind them. Think about that."

That statement brought all of Jack Hunt's men to attention. And Jack with them. "I don't believe that, Raines," he finally said, but his voice was shaky.

"I have no reason to exaggerate the numbers, Jack."

There was no reply. Jack had tossed the mike down on the table and walked back to his quarters in a fine old home.

Ike and his people got some old tugs running and the first captain to bring his ship in for unloading was Thermopolis. Emil followed him as another area was cleared off along the old docks.

Many Rebels of Irish ancestry got down on their knees and wept when they touched Irish soil. Other Rebels thanked the Lord for safe passage. Still others simply thanked the Lord for getting them off those damn ships. The storm had tossed them around quite a bit.

"Mother of God," Pat O'Shea breathed when he saw all the troops wandering around, getting their land-legs again, and all the equipment being off-loaded. "Did you ever see anythin' so beautiful in all your life, Bobby Flynn?"

Bobby was speechless. And for an Irishman to be struck dumb—even for a few seconds—was quite a feat. "And that's just two ships," Bobby finally said. "There's a dozen or more still out yonder in the bay."

People had gathered from all over the county to watch the American troops disembark. For the first time in years, the people had reason to celebrate, and celebrate they did. The Rebels feasted on fresh-baked bread and real home butter. They ate cakes and pies and then danced and sang songs into the night with the Irish people.

"No more," Ben gave the orders to his commanders the next morning after the street festival. "The food we ate was probably all these good people had. Just remember that and share what you have with them.

"Now, then. The first thing we do is remember this: this is not our country. Many of these people are going to be appalled at the harshness of Rebel law. But I've hashed that all out with the Irish leaders I've met. They've had a decade of lawlessness and they're ready to try Rebel justice. Once we've done our work here, whether they continue to maintain our system of justice is up to them and none of our business.

"First we help them to clean up this town. While that's going on, some of us will be meeting with county leaders to find out what they need in the way of grain for farming and so forth. Fortunately, there are a lot of unemployed ship captains in this area. They'll be taking the ships back to America for resupplying and freeing us to fight. That's what we came here to do.

"All right. Galway County is clean. Jack has taken his men and moved over to Dublin, Cork,

Wexford, and up into County Donegal. You all know what that means."

"He's linked up with the damn Night People," Tina said.

"You got it. And that's all the firm intelligence we have on him at this moment."

"So when we do get lined out and ready to go," Georgi said, "we're going to be fighting on at least four fronts."

"That is correct. Probably more than that. Jack is an experienced soldier. We'll never be as lucky again as we were here in Galway."

"When we do shove off?" Rebet asked.

"One week from today."

18

Ben stood on the dock and watched as the last ship left for the return voyage to America. The sight filled him with a myriad of emotions, ranging from joy at one mission accomplished and another just beginning, to a feeling of being orphaned.

He recalled an old song, something about a stranger on the shore. The lyrics escaped him.

"The people are in surprisingly good shape, Ben," Doctor Chase broke into his thoughts.

Ben turned. "What?"

"I said the people are in surprisingly good shape," the chief of medicine said. "Considering how they've been forced to live for the past decade."

"No serious illnesses?"

"None have turned up yet. We're starting vaccination programs for everybody, especially the children. What's wrong, Ben? You looked troubled when I walked up."

"Nothing, really. I was just lost in thoughts, that's all. Thinking about all that we've done and what lies ahead of us, among other things."

"Not worried about us being outnumbered by Jack Hunt's army, are you?"

Ben smiled. "Hell, Lamar, when *haven't* we been outnumbered? No, no. We lost some people this time, and that always bothers me. But you know something? Every Rebel we lost taking this town was of Irish descent. Every one of them. And that gives me an odd feeling."

"Eerie."

"Yes."

"How do you feel, physically?"

"I feel great, Lamar. Even after being soaking wet for twenty-four hours, I didn't even catch a cold."

"Soaking wet has nothing to do with it, and there is no such thing as a cold, it's a virus."

"Right, Lamar."

The two old friends stood in silence, watching as the last ship began to fade from view. Behind them, in the old town—and it was very old, having first been incorporated by Richard the Second— were the sounds of hammering and sawing and nailing as the townspeople began attempting the first stages of repairing their own lives and that of the town.

Scouts had cleaned out County Galway. They had found pockets of Night People—the hated creepies—and dealt with them in typical Rebel fashion. The Free Irish had pointed out the collaborators among them and Ben had told them to deal with them as they saw fit. It was their country.

The most serious offenders were tried in a court of law and hanged.

Every citizen of the town was armed. And heavily armed, with weapons taken from the dead troops of Jack Hunt's army, and a civilian militia was formed.

"Don't ever let anyone take your weapons from you," Ben had told them. "No man, no law, no government." And from the looks on their faces, Ben knew that would never again happen.

And as Ben had seen so many times in the past, his Rebels were getting restless. His people were highly trained, staying almost on the razor's edge, highly motivated, and they were not accustomed to inactivity. It was time to strike before they started fighting among themselves. And highly trained people will sometimes do that just to relieve and release the tension.

Ben huddled with his intelligence people for several hours, going over intercepted radio broadcasts and maps.

On a very pleasant late spring morning, with the land all around him green with new life, Ben walked the sprawling encampment of Rebels around the airport. Smoot was right beside him. The husky greeted in its own fashion the Rebels they encountered during the stroll.

"Ready to go, Nicky?" Ben called to a tank commander.

413

"Let's go give 'em hell, General!" she returned the shout.

"How about it, Sergeant-Major?" Ben called to Adamson.

"Standing tall and tough, General."

Ben's son and daughter fell into step with him. Two generations of Raines walked the encampment.

"This campaign is not going to be an easy one, is it, Father?" Buddy asked.

Ben smiled. "It never is, son. But freeing a people is right and just, and that's all that matters."